Sandra Beck

Sandra Beck

JOHN LAVERY

ANANSI

This edition published in 2010 by
House of Anansi Press Inc.
110 Spadina Avenue, Suite 801
Toronto, ON, M5V 2K4
Tel. 416-363-4343
Fax 416-363-1017
www.anansi.ca

Distributed in Canada by
HarperCollins Canada Ltd.
1995 Markham Road
Scarborough, ON, M1B 5M8
Toll free tel. 1-800-387-0117

House of Anansi Press is committed to protecting our natural environment. As part of our efforts, this book is printed on paper that contains 100% post-consumer recycled fibres, is acid-free, and is processed chlorine-free.

14 13 12 11 10   1 2 3 4 5

Library and Archives Canada Cataloguing in Publication

Lavery, John, 1949–
Sandra Beck / John Lavery.

ISBN 978-0-88784-256-6

I. Title.

PS8573.A845S36 2010   C813'.6   C2010-902471-0

Cover design: Daniel Cullen
Text design: Daniel Cullen
Typesetting: Sari Naworynski

 Canada Council   Conseil des Arts
for the Arts   du Canada    ONTARIO ARTS COUNCIL
                                       CONSEIL DES ARTS DE L'ONTARIO

We acknowledge for their financial support of our publishing program the Canada Council for the Arts, the Ontario Arts Council, and the Government of Canada through the Canada Book Fund.

Printed and bound in Canada

for Claire

Ce n'est pas pour devenir écrivain qu'on écrit. C'est pour rejoindre en silence cet amour qui manque à tout amour.

— Christian Bobin

CUNNKITAY

I WOKE IN MY SALTWATER ROOM, a bed-dweller, bottom-feeding in the warm sheets.

Shhh.

I heard my mother's footsteps on the frozen beach outside my room. The hallway, I mean. My girl's-gills filled up with happiness, a happiness indistinguishable from my mother herself.

The game was on, a complex and difficult game. I must not move now, not until she reached my bed. If I so much as blinked or twitched a shoulder, my happiness would congeal, become dry and white. My mother would turn into a statue of salt.

The door opened, brushing over the carpet with a sound like a wave receding.

I must not move. Not yet, not yet. She was coming, she was. I must not move!

She stood above me, my happiness, radiating cold.

Ahhh. Weak with victory I was. A dangerous game, not to be played often.

The jury of my dolls was silent, unimpressed. The lamp-boy, carved in wood, leaned brazenly against his streetlight. His lips were plumped into a horrid kiss, his cheeks ballooned. He whistled when his light was turned on, his white, imbecilic eyes clicked from side to side. The lamp-boy was my mother's darling, my blackest enemy.

She stood above me, immense, weightless. I, a puny, dense lump.

Later she would exhale her daily perfume of relentless competence. But for now she smelled faintly of urine and lassitude.

She bent over and pulled at my covers, still radiating cold. Her hands explored me under the prim sheets, searched the big pyjama buttons that never stayed done up. I cringed with delight, yearning for the inevitable moment when the icy needles of her fingers would pierce the bare skin of my hot spine and inject me with sky.

So my day began.

—

"J'ai mal au cœur," I said to the babysitter. Literally, my heart hurts. Meaning I felt bloated, nauseated. Sick to my stomach.

It was strictly forbidden for me to speak in French to the babysitter, who, although she spoke only English, understood French to an irritatingly mysterious degree. Her forehead was a meadow of pimples, her thick glasses seemed to prevent her porcine eyes from ever closing, her polo shirt, with its blue-and-black stripes, strained over the seams of her bra.

"You have to have a crap, that's all."

"*Non! J'ai mal au cœur, je dis. Je vais vomir!*"

"You're not going to ralph. You just have to have a crap."

She hoisted me onto her shoulder, carried me upstairs. I pressed my knee into the side of her spongy breast, took advantage of her occupied hands to read the Braille of her forehead with my fingertips.

The winter sun crashed into the plastic curtain that covered the bathroom window, filling the room with a froth of pink light. She undressed me completely, to be certain I wouldn't soil any of my clothes, knelt to pull down my *bobettes*, tugged listlessly while I barely lifted my regal feet, my infanta's hand on her shoulder. I could see, crouching behind her glasses, her true eyes, more naked than me.

The pressure of the toilet seat numbed my legs, my feet hung like pieces of stone. I pressed my chest onto my thighs, felt the inner surfaces of my body touch, my spine expand.

The babysitter sat on her hands, opposite me, on the bathtub. She lowered her head. The long grass of her hair drooped. The jaggedness of her part made her skull appear misshapen.

I reached down, squeezed my bloodless feet as hard as I could, forced my chin up.

"*Maman!*" I screamed.

The pinkness of the bathroom rushed into my mouth.

"*Maman! J'ai mal au cœur!*"

The babysitter did not look up.

"*Maa-man!*"

Downstairs my happiness was on the telephone, as always. She was in her office, which was crammed with tottering stalagmites of books, folders, and music scores. The walls were covered with concert posters, autographed studio portraits of violinists, snapshots of musicians wearing convivial scarves in foreign cities. Vines of cigarette smoke were climbing the trellis of light that entered through the slats of the tall window's broken Venetian blind, the desk was buried under a snowdrift of paper. My happiness, that is, was managing the symphony orchestra.

"Mamaaan!"

I heard the dry click of her crutches as she climbed the stairs. She entered the bathroom, impatient but not harried, ignored the babysitter, bent down in front of me, played with my hair. I breathed in her pungent, accomplished odour of cigarette ash and Oscar de la Renta, observed the mole under her eye like a permanent, brown tear. Come upstairs she would, but speak to me in French she would not.

After a time she stood up to leave, pausing in the doorway to say, "You can call me when you're done," a magic formula whose laxative powers unfailingly melted the knots in my seven-year-old digestive system.

To this day, no matter how imperious the need, I stamp and jiggle as I remove every article of clothing, undo every button, snap, and zipper with my fluttering, thumbling fingers. I have my crap. Without recourse to magic formulas. And then I press my chest onto my thighs, I feel the inner surfaces of my body touch, my spine expand. I rid myself, not only of all clothing, but of the entire corporeal bailiwick to which clothing belongs. I relive, that is, the precarious joy I learned from the babysitter, who did not look up. But who knew me best of all.

—

MY HAPPINESS UNDID the two wooden bullets that closed her handbag, fished out a warm banana.

My head sang, I was starving, drained after the oratory, l'Oratoire Saint-Joseph, so huge and oppressive, so swollen with air and the humid odour of stone as to seem like the outdoors indoors, its disparagingly high band of windows the source not of light but of a thin, grey haze.

It was a relief to be in the crowded foyer. I ate the pudgy banana as though it were a small prey, devoured its sticky flesh, discarded its bruised hide in the hand of my mother, who wrapped it in a shroud of Kleenex and replaced it in the temporary grave of her handbag.

There was, in the middle of the foyer, a display case containing a model of the oratory. A group of men were circling the display case, arguing among themselves. My happiness watched them with an absorption that irritated me.

I pulled on her sleeve as though it were attached to a bell. "What are they doing, Maman, what?"

She ignored me.

The men were very tall, stiff-kneed, loose-hipped, wearing winter boots that required, but were not equipped with, laces. They had tangerine toques like upside-down flower pots on their heads. Their skin was as black and dull as cooking chocolate.

"What language are they speaking?" I said anthropologically, changing tactics, mimicking my mother's absorption. The men bickered noisily, their incomprehensible talk bubbled and spurted, as though their voices were hot in their throats.

"English," she said sternly, turning away slightly, as though to protect herself from a draft.

I, the draft, fumed, the warm banana leapt into my throat. My happiness watched intently as the men moved from the model to a window and back to the model, gesticulating, pointing.

"As far as I can make out," she said, prepared at last to divulge the results of her observations, her eyes never leaving the men, "they are trying to determine just where in the model is located the model of the model. And where, therefore, they are located themselves."

She sighed warmly, emitted a wistful smile meant to celebrate the naïve inquisitiveness common to all humankind despite variations in cultural heritage, skin colour, and choice of footwear. She allowed her gaze to fade, drifted poetically on her crutches over the foyer floor and through the door, expecting me to follow.

Outside the wind was up, the sky was sagging with black cloud, trees were spinning on their trunks, throwing off leaves like sparks. I stood on the first of the hundreds of steps that led down to the parking lot far below. My happiness was descending without me, like a ghost, into the living world of buses and cars. My legs trembled, I was sure the wind would sweep me away. She turned, looked up at me, her face hidden by her flailing hair, and signalled for me to advance. I did not do so, my attention was taken up by a spider venturing out of its crack, a weather-proof spider apparently, rubbery, fake-looking. I let it trundle for a while and then I stepped on its daylights, dragged its body under my shoe. My mother seized me by the wrist, the first gelatinous drops of rain were sputting, umbrellas were blooming below us like underwater flowers. She shook me as though I were a jointed doll, dragged me down the steps behind her, crushing my hand between her own and the handle of her crutch, my hard soles slid on the wet stone, I was sure I would fall to my doom, I closed my eyes, catching the rhythm of the stairs as they rolled under my feet like teeth in a wheel.

How we whirled, my mother and I. Until we hit bottom and raced to the car. She hurled her crutches into the back, hopped in, and slammed the door. The car rattled under the rain, the windows were opaque with steam. I was drenched, breathless, my chest was heaving, my stomach lurched, I dug out the Kleenex from my pocket and regurgitated the liquid banana into it.

After which I looked up timidly at my happiness.

"Peuken like a champ," she said, breathless too.

—

THE DOORBELL RANG. "Daneeelo!"

Uncle Danilo was not my uncle. He was a clarinetist who played in the symphony orchestra. He called the clarinet his licorice shtick.

"How do you know it's Danilo?" My mother's voice trailed after me, losing ground as I ran headlong down the corridor.

I knew because the doorbell had sounded with the unmistakable vividness, the clarion authority of, and only of, Uncle Danilo.

I looked through the peephole at his distorted face. His bloated nose leapt out from under his retreating forehead like the glabrous snout of a pig-dog. He twitched his gruesome nostrils, knowing I was there.

I opened. He stood up straight, his nose having snapped back to its rectilinear trimness, and sustained my inspection. His navy blue trench coat was buttoned up to the icy white collar of his shirt, his pagan hair was combed with black honey. He bent towards me, turning his face so I could run my finger over the surface of the magenta continent whose jagged shoreline contradicted the smoothness of his left cheek.

A birthmark, a port wine stain, a *nevus flammeus*.

I kissed him there. I only kissed him there.

"Why there?" he murmured. We had been left alone at the dinner table, while the floating island was being prepared in mysterious, agitated silence on the other side of the swinging kitchen doors. "Why do you want to kiss me there?"

He looked down at me, tranquil, derogatory, his eyes coated with aristocratic dew, the ardent redness of his birthmark barely attenuated by the masking cream he used.

"Because."

"Because why?"

"Because it looks like it hurts."

"Oh, but it doesn't. Not in the slightest."

"I don't mean it hurts you. I mean it hurts *it*."

I said this. But do I remember saying it? Or do I simply remember Danilo remembering, later on, talking to me, leaning against his kitchen table?

He was bearing one of the gifts that only he could find. It might have been a tin of chestnut icing, a gritty, Scottish cheese, a pineapple as big as a head and so fresh it made the lining of my mouth wither. Whatever it was, he deposited it on the kitchen table with little enthusiasm. And while the women present — for there were always women present: my mother, one at the very least of her friends or associates, I never knew which was which, a visiting harpist perhaps, the Hungarian cleaning lady who spent more time making pastry than dusting the piano — while the women present bobbed Danilo's treasure away on a tide of effusive conversation, he sipped his coffee in silence, standing up, his left cheek facing the window, his jaw set in stern self-sufficiency.

I climbed up onto the counter where I could see the freshly shaved blueness of the cheek that didn't hurt. He had the habit of rolling his lower lip under his teeth after each sip of coffee to be sure none dribbled down his chin. Every time he did so, I did so. Every time. After a while, he turned a dark eye towards me.

"How old are you, Josée?"

"Twelve."

"Would you like to be thirteen one day?"

"Ooo, tough guy! Danilo goana kill me. Are your carburetors holding their tune, tough guy?"

Uncle Danilo had a red MG, an MGA to be precise, with twin carburetors that he tuned while I stomped on the accelerator.

The first time I rode in his MG, he drove me to the Douglas Hospital. I had his licorice shtick in my lap. The top was down, the breeze buffeted the back of my head, blowing turbulent streamers of hair forward, incongruously as it seemed to me, into my face.

We parked in the sun and waited, the June air shimmering over the MG's long hood. The hospital was sober and withdrawn. I imagined the varnished floors, the striding doctors with their metal clipboards, the starched, white wings of the nurses' hats. I closed my eyes, listened to Danilo whistle in his vague, breathy way while he rubbed his forehead.

After a time my mother arrived with the other musicians.

She squatted solemnly in front of me, her sunglasses so big and round as to seem edible. She adjusted my sleeves.

"Écoute, Josée,*"* French being reserved for communications of especial earnestness, *"ici, c'est un hôpital pour des gens. . .exceptionnels."* The sun lit up her fillings, revealed the powdered duvet along her jaw. *"Ils sont malades, oui, mais pas du cœur, pas des poumons. Du cerveau. Tu comprends, ma puce?"**

They weren't *ill* ill, they were mentally ill. Certainly I understood — in the privileged, holiday sun of the parking lot. But inside, under the lidless rows of fluorescent lights, I did not understand.

Inside, there were no benevolent nurses. No doctors. There was only a woman with a scoured doll's face under a nest of golden crinkles, a body bobbing with fat, her elephantine hips wrapped in brown slacks the colour of plum sauce. To this woman my well-turned mother talked with an outrageous affinity, the two of them, as the musicians prepared their instruments, unfolding metal chairs and grating them into place, discussing the duration of the concert and the need for

---

*"Listen, Josée, this is a hospital for. . . exceptional people. They're sick, yes, but it's not their hearts or their lungs that's the problem. It's their brains, do you understand?"

pauses, the woman pointing out hesitantly that the audience might not always applaud at appropriate moments, my mother gushing reassurance, my mother worrying that the audience might not really care for the music, might prefer something with electric guitars and drums, the woman gushing reassurance, the two exclaiming over the flowers, so generously donated and so tastefully arranged, as they straight-armed the snapdragons and moved them around.

I pressed myself against the wall during the entire concert. I stared only at Danilo's fingers, listened only to his clarinet. My mother and Plumsauce sat glued together, eyes forward, radiant with placidity, as around them the audience fidgeted and gooed incessantly, interrupted its whispered quarrelling only to cheer with idiotic uproariousness.

And oh, they were horrible to look at, the members of the audience, beady-eyed, slack-jawed. They held their faces in their hands and looked at me through their fingers. They were giant, fleshy beetles, dressed in pyjamas, their torsos appallingly thick, their heads appallingly small. Their heads were no bigger than pineapples.

And after the concert, they came at me, the three of them: my mother, Plumsauce, and a member of the audience. Plumsauce was holding a daffodil. A tear had leaned too far out over her lower lid and fallen off, leaving a shiny rill that trickled down her cheek to her lips. She gave the daffodil to the member of the audience to give to me.

My mother took Plumsauce by the arm, scolded her, said it was unprofessional to cry, she must bear in mind the extreme sensitivity of the members of the audience. The woman nodded vigorously, shook her golden crinkles, snuffled her self-possession up her nose.

Arm in arm they left me, the three of them, with my wall, alone, unable to comprehend how the daffodil had found its way into my hand.

I remember the ride home, the late afternoon sun and Danilo's MG. His MGA. But I do not remember falling asleep, or waking up, screaming, screaming. I may remember Danilo stopping the car, getting out, and taking me in his arms. I do remember his voice, yes, definitely. My head was under his jaw, in the crook of his neck, and the soothing, guttural vibrations of his larynx made my forehead tingle.

"My carburetors are just fine," said Uncle Danilo, placing his hand between my shoulder blades, exploring my spine through my middy-blouse.

He stopped playing in the orchestra once. Before I knew him. For over a year. He was living with a viola player then. She wanted to get married. Danilo wanted to get married too, but first he needed to be sure he was who he was, a musician, a true musician. So he set off with his clarinet, travelled to countries where discouraging words in English, or French, or Serbo-Croatian, were seldom heard. He spoke very little, panhandled, played his clarinet all day every day, in streets, under bridges, in markets and washrooms and temples.

And how did it go?

Some days were incredible, he was joined by other musicians, taken into homes. He even took part in a recording session in Bombay.

And other days?

Other days were unendurable, he was infected with foreignness, the sound of his clarinet ate into his brain, he would have hurled it into the bay had he not kept on playing, playing.

And most days?

Most days were most days.

And was he sure now he was a true musician?

No. But at least he was sure he would never be sure.

And was he ready to get married?

Oh yes, yes, he wanted to talk now, to have someone to talk with, all day every day, in streets, under bridges, in markets and washrooms and temples.

"Although *your* twin carbs," murmured Uncle Danilo, "are nicely tuned. Very." To underscore his meaning, he pulled lightly on the back strap of what may have been my second bra. I leaned into him, grateful not to be on the side of his birthmark, my forearms locked together in front of me, and drummed my outrage with the heels of my hands on his flat, resilient chest.

And were they happy, he and the viola player?

No, just the viola player, who'd been happy for quite a while, having long since lost interest in Danilo.

Lost interest in Danilo! But that was impossible, incomprehensible.

He laughed, put his arm around my shoulder, pressed me against himself so that my fists were pinned between us. My exasperation mounted, I squirmed and twitched, furious with myself for allowing his effortless, mechanical strength to separate us.

"Josée!" called out my mother. "How many times have I told you not to climb up on the counter. Don't cling so. Let Uncle Danilo be."

I slithered down from the counter. We looked at each other under our lids, Danilo and I, reunited by my mother's sense of territorial decorum.

No, you could not lose interest in Danilo. I was the spirit of his birthmark, the kelpie of his cheek. I did not permit such things.

It was I who dismissed the viola player, retroactively, condemned her to her paltry happiness.

—

MY MOTHER, AT TIMES, could be seen hunched over her sewing machine, her reading glasses perched on her nose at such a distance from her eyes that it seemed as though the glasses themselves were observing the whirring needle and broadcasting the images directly to her brain, while her eyes looked on like two crew chiefs, self-important but largely unnecessary.

She was tense and irritable as she worked, her pulse fluttered in her neck. She gasped suddenly, froze with horror, slumped, ripped out her stitches, started again. The results disappointed her. Always.

She might hold up her latest production as though on the point of throwing it back in the water and say, "How could I have not seen that the waist would be too high for me? It makes me look like a salt shaker with a screw-on top. Your mother is no good at this, Josée." To which I responded, a child throwing feed to a grown fish, "Oh, not at all, Maman! It's lovely, it makes you taller."

When utterly defeated, she swayed in front of the mirror, her arm around the freshly sewn garment, beamed brightly, and did not ask my opinion at all.

It was fabric my mother loved. Flowing bolts of printed cotton, rich with colour and possibility. Her linen closet was stuffed with tablecloths made of kitchen gingham, with percaline-lined cretonne curtains, floral and heavy, with organdy sheers, serviettes in milky, stiff brocade. Not actualized mind you, no, but in a fine state of dollhouse potentiality. Only the fabric itself existed. It had been examined, crumpled, bitten into, paid for and folded away with proprietary jealousy. The closet shelves sagged under the weight of my mother's hoard, variegated and very expensive, making her dream of sky-washed sheets on the grass of Champagne, of Irish dingles and smoky Flemish streets.

Her work table was a lake of gold lamé. She had volunteered to make hangings to decorate the summer stage in Joliette. She was festive, enthusiastic, for once, I was helping her cut out the long strips, we were up to our waists in the lake.

The doorbell rang. "Daneeelo!"

"It's open!" hollered my mother, drowning my eardrums. "She's busy!" Reducing me to a pronoun, making my cheeks burn with importance. "She's helping me!"

Uncle Danilo was in the entry, scraping his shoes.

I held the material taut with an application as great as my desire to ditch my mother who, determined not to make a slip, continued to cut with a self-chiding deliberateness.

He was in the kitchen.

She held her breath and squeezed the scissor blades, *sschllt, sschllt, sschllt,* let out her breath in a rush, muttered encouragement to herself.

He was depositing his gift on the table with little enthusiasm.

She made three more cuts, stopped again to regroup.

Danilo entered the room, nonchalant, his birthmark like a vinyl iron-on, the edges making my fingers tingle with wanting to pick at them.

"Hi," he said. "Lovely material," lifting the free end up off the floor.

My mother flushed with pleasure, squeezed the hefty scissors, the material yielded suddenly, the scissors surged forward like an intent reptile and bit hard into the palm of Danilo's startled hand.

My mother gasped, froze with horror.

"Gack," said Danilo, as though to minimize a fault perceived as being somehow his own. "I'm supposed to play the clarinet with that hand."

His blood flowed with the unhurried persistence peculiar to blood. And to Danilo himself. It dribbled in tributaries between his fingers.

I was shocked by their stunned, adult helplessness. I grabbed Danilo's wrist, wiped off his palm with the golden lamé, and wrapped his hand as tightly as I could.

"You have to have pressure!"

"Do you," said Danilo, woozy, amused.

"Not with that!" screeched my happiness, reviving suddenly, shouldering me out of the way and tearing away the material, holding it as though it had betrayed her by so humanly absorbing Danilo's blood. "Ruined. Ruined. What is it with you two? Do you ever think about anybody but yourselves? Do you?"

There followed the litany of her dissatisfactions, pointed comments regarding Danilo's indecisiveness, his inability either to live up to the promise of his own gifts or to recognize those that life dropped in his lap, his lack of endurance or tenacity, his simply leaving the orchestra under the assumption that the manager would make all the necessary arrangements for him to take up his old position on his return, his penchant for driving young girls in his sports car, usurping the place of their fathers in their lives, and so on and so forth, with the result that Danilo, squeezing the wrist of his wounded hand and holding it aloft, left a trail of blood spatters all the way to the front door through which he exited, decisively.

And through which he never re-entered.

After that, Uncle Danilo referred to my happiness as La Beetch, as in: "Of course, everything she said about me, La Beetch I mean, was perfectly true."

———

"YOU MUST BE AN ADULT NOW, JOSÉE," said my mother. "You're getting mail from *Reader's Digest*. Where did they get hold of your name, I wonder." She held up the plump, eupeptic envelope. "Nothing but commercial rant. Shall I just chuck it?"

"No! It may be rant, but it's rant addressed to me. Give."

I opened the envelope in the loo, where it was cool. It contained a long letter with the important words printed in green. A picture of a Japanese man wearing rubber boots and sleeping with geese. A thin, plastic phonograph record that could actually be played, although I never did, and that was entitled "Wordsong."

It also contained a key. The colour of old honey. The key was wrapped in a small piece of paper and on the paper was written, "If you ever need to get out of la beetchhouse, you've got a roof. Danilo."

I cannot say I was displeased. It was so like Danilo. So like the horsey sounds he could make on his clarinet, the whinnying and plooping. So subterfugal.

I cannot say I was pleased. Because, although it certainly seemed that Danilo was dealing to me behind my mother's back, I could not rid myself of the feeling that he was dealing to my mother behind my back. A key? For me? All I knew about keys, apart from how to lose them, was that they were a necessary adjunct to locked doors. And locked doors, whether or not they made adults feel hot-eyed and rosy, filled me with foreboding. I didn't even dare click my lock shut at school. Not because I was afraid of forgetting the combination, not at all, numbers slid into my memory like tiny lights that lit up instantly at the first bidding. But because a shudder might, it might, at any moment, ripple down the school corridors, a spectral, mischievous thrill, and render my lock unopenable, my lock and my lock only, absolutely and forever.

Besides, why should I want to get out of my happiness's house? Unless to live in a black, flapping tent on the Russian steppes, or in a firelit cottage behind a Norwegian fjord.

So I stashed away Danilo's key in my room somewhere, amid all the crud that I could not throw away for fear of unliving something I had lived, and that, as I slept, orbited my bed in a state of fitful, neglected uselessness.

That is to say, I forgot all about it.

Not that the key forgot about me.

This was at a time when every one of my sudden sneezes, every ache in my eyebrows, every whim and glitch in my mood, was attributed to the fact that I was growing.

But I was not growing.

Granted, there was the oily sheen on my danger-keep-out sign of a forehead, lit up with flashing, red pimples.

Granted, I wounded my happiness by starting to menstruate. "Look, Maman," I mewed, indicating vaguely the toilet I had not flushed.

"Josée! Did you cut yourself? Did you dis . . ." She looked at me, saw me greenish, foreign, a little pathetic and proud. ". . . oh."

She barely talked to me the next day. Her chest seemed to have collapsed around her deflated heart, her cheeks clung to her colourless face.

But the day after that, she took me out to the air-conditioned Bel-Air restaurant, which was in Canada's very first shopping centre, in the Town of Mount Royal. It was one of her favourite restaurants, partly because she could slide her crutches easily under the table, but mostly because the pancakes arrived spread out on the plate, requiring her to perform the Rite of Heaping and Embutterment, followed by the Pouring-on Syruptitious. "Don't worry," she said, tilting to the point of strangulation the jar of maple cello varnish, "I'm not going to embarrass us by attempting to tell you the facts of life. You'd just keep correcting me, in any case." The sacramental Ingestion of the First, Dripping Wedge. "I would have liked to have had lots of children. Well, not lots. But more." She paused, looked at me bravely and straight. "And now I haven't any anymore, have I?"

That's okay, I thought, crap out on me when I need you the most.

She touched the back of my hand. "Which of course isn't true at all, is it?"

No. It's not true. That now is when I need you the most.

She leafed through the moldy-oldies pages of our booth's juke-box, her left cheek a-bulge with pancake. "'Mellow Yellow!' Donovan." She swallowed the contents of her cheek. "'Mellow Yellow' was when I was going out with Kevin McDonnaugh. His eyes were two straight slits, his mouth was a straight slit, everything *about* him was straight, except his straight tie which was so crooked it made him look from a distance like he had a crack in his chest. I broke it off after seventeen hours. Kevin the boy was stupefyingly full of himself, I loved deriding his fatuous tales of his own prowess. But Kevin the boyfriend was such a silent little horse. I did all the clucking, and he did all the straining. What else? 'Uptown!' The Crystals!" She inserted a quarter, pressed the sagging red buttons. The song emerged distantly, as though from an outdoor speaker at the beach, my happiness went through her moves, her hand-rolls and shoulder-jerks, she sang the back-up vocals.

"What are the lyrics?" I said, when the song was over. "Uptown what?"

"Uptown eecheemee doomai Tiananmen. You didn't pick up on that?"

I scowled, inserted my own quarter. "Shh!" I hissed. My happiness gagged herself with both hands, sang with her eyes.

"'Uptown,'" I said deliberately, when the song was over again, "'each evening to my tenement.'"

She continued to hold her palms over her mouth, grieving with her eyes.

And then she hoisted high the jar of cello varnish. "God, you're great, Josée, you really are. Here's to you. To Josée, and the Right Words." She chugged the syrup straight from the jar, wiped her mouth beerily with the back of her hand. "Aaaaa."

And so we celebrated. My acceding to womanhood. By my mother's receding into girlhood.

So granted I was getting older. But I was not growing. My life was simply leaking time, shrinking around me.

I was ever more rigidly myself, unable to suspend my disbelief in my immediate surroundings. At Christmas, I dreamt of the droning summer sun, of fat bees working the blooming clover. In July, I shrieked at the most innocuous of insects, ran indoors, longed for the crispness of snow.

Until.

A marvellous thing happened: I woke up. Literally, I mean. I woke up. My eyelids opened with a soundless pop.

It was twenty past two in the morning. Never in living memory had I woken up in the middle of the night. Never. I had always been too deathly afraid.

But behold, there were no flitting, nameless terrors skimming the walls of my bedroom. No moonbegotten, giggling creatures suspended in the hideous black, waiting to leap at me. No, my room was suffused with silence, awash in calm.

I was fascinated. It was so much, for example, easier to see, seeing as my eyes were not overwhelmed with light-borne data, not cowed with the relentless need to observe with precision. They were free to explore, to speculate, to ply the variations in density of the dark.

Fascinated. The patterns of light and dark had become inverted. What, during the day, was strongly illuminated, the mass of objects, was densely black now. What, during the day, was in shadow, the edges and undersides, was brushed with luminescence.

My air-tight skin slackened, became permeable, casual, allowing the tight tangles of sensation trapped in my nerves to dissipate into the night, and the tangles of night to creep slowly over me, to seep into my every pore.

My little heart raced with recognition, and I was sore afraid.

—

le samedi, 28 mai / Saturday, May 28
09h30: me lever / get up
09h32: faire pipi / point Petunia at the porcelain
09h33: retourner au lit, attendre que Maman me crie après / go
    back to bed, wait for Mamooshka to yell me at
10h12: Maman me crie après / Mamooshka yells me at
10h15: déjeuner / breakslow / gaufres belges / Belgian gophers
10h45: débouffage des broches / defooding of braces

12h00: travailler / please! you've had three (3) weeks, merde / pour
  ton projet sur Charlemagne

List: The last of the Mérovingiens, the fainéants, the do-nothing
kings
  Childébert III, 695–711
  Dagobert III, 711–715
  Chilpéric II, 715–721
  Clothaire IV, 718–719
  Thierry IV, 721–737
  Childéric III, 743–751

12h08: assez travaillé / phone Marie-Noëlle
  "Marie-Noëlle, want to go play mini-golf?"
  "Charlemagne, Josée, Charlemagne. I haven't even started yet.
  Unlike you who've had it done for a week already."
12h30: L'Île de Gilligan. Sacred.
13h00: manger / eat
13h30: débouffage des broches / defooding of braces
14h30: mini-golf with *some*body, *any*body
17h00: s'il te plaît, Josée, s'il te plaît, work on your Charlemagne
  project
17h01: anything good on?
18h30: manger / eat
19h00: débouffage des braces
20h00: s'il te *plaît*, Josée / yokay, yokay

List: The first Carolingiens
  Pépin de Herstal
  Charles Martel

Pépin le Bref, maire du palais, palace mayor, 741–751, roi des
   Francs, king of the Francs, 751–768
followed by his two sons, Carloman, and . . .

List within a list: Carloman's brother's names
   In French: Charles le Grand, roi
   In Teuton: Karl der Grosse, König
   In Latin: Carolus Magnus, Rex
   In Freutin (English): CHARLEMAGNE, King. Also Emperor,
      800–814. Charlie the Tall. "Charlemagne was of an ample
      and robust body, of an elevated stature, but that exceeded not
      the just proportion, since he measured seven times the length
      of his tool. *Sorry!* Foot, foot. Since he measured seven times
      the length of his foot." But how long was his foot? My foot
      is, let's see, 21.5 cm. Times 7 equals 150.5 cm. Although I
      am, in fact, 158 cm tall. Therefore: either Charlemagne had,
      like his mother, Berthe au Grand Pied, very grands pieds, or
      else he wasn't tall's all that. Unless people were shorter then,
      relative to their feet, which they very likely were, seeing as
      chocolate hadn't been discovered yet.

      List within a list within a list: The ten (ahem) wives of Char-
      lemagne
         Himiltrude
         Désirée (Desiderata)
         Rolhaide (Aunt Acid)
         Hildegarde
         Fastrade
         Liutgarde
         Madelgarde

Gervinde
Régine
Adelinde

22h00: Il est quelle heure?
22h02: dodo / bedtime

—

THE JURY OF MY DOLLS was comatose. The lamp-boy asleep, out like
a light. My feet touched down. The links in my spine stiffened, my
pneumatic thighs engaged, lifting my tailbone off the mattress. I
stood, uneasily, my inner ears reconfiguring for night balance, my
fingers probing the air like stubby antennae. I took my first steps in
my new, noctambulant life.

A prowler I was, a nightfoal, my leathery nostrils twitching and
wet. I picked my way through the housebound labyrinth, the walls
crowding my shoulders, the ceilings grazing my hair. The darkness
hummed with a rhythmic murmur that infiltrated every room
except the one I could not enter, the one from which it emanated,
where my happiness lay snoring by her beau.

Such pleasure. The ten-watt bulbs in my nipples glowed, searching,
searching dead ahead, I was flimsy, thick, my ancient, ratty pyjamas
were the surface of the night against my breathing skin. I lolled on
the living room sofa, my flowery *bobettes* low down on my hips,
and let the amorous light that leeched through the watching drapes
bleed over me.

Such pleasure. Though not nightly, no, far from it. When I was
tired, when my nerves were frayed and I needed sleep, I was certain
to wake with a lurch, my brain buzzing and weird. I would get up

then, the dark house soothing me, like rainwater on a gash. But when I went to bed early, eager to prowl, the alarm set for two and stuffed under my pillow, I slept through like a stone.

Such pleasure.

———

8:45 P.M., ROSEMONT:

The boy gets into the taxi. He is coming from one party and going to another. He has never been in a taxi before, has never been invited to two parties on the same evening either. It is an exceptional day for him. He holds out a paper on which his mother has written the address. The driver takes the paper. He is sullen, hairy, he does not look at the boy, does not speak. They drive off. The boy listens to the edgy ticking of the meter, he is thrilled, circumspect, his eyes watchful, his head very still. He notices the muddy floor mats, the torn upholstery, observes at length the driver's ID card on the pillar between the front and rear doors. The driver's name is Robert Lanteigne. His number is composed of six digits of which only one is odd, the other five are even. The number itself is odd. Therefore the digit in the number that is odd is the last. Obviously. The driver is not as hairy in the picture, not as sullen, although he does look taut, apprehensive. As though he were afraid of the flash.

8:58 P.M., ROSEMONT:

The boy gets out of the taxi. He has been instructed to ask the driver to wait until he is inside the house. He does so, addressing the driver as Monsieur Lanteigne. The driver does not look at him, does not speak. He waits. The boy can feel in his pocket, against his thigh, the coins Mr. Lanteigne has given him as change. He can still feel the spot on his hand that came in contact with Mr. Lanteigne's hand. He understands, admires even, the uncommunicativeness of the driver.

10:37 P.M., POINTE-AUX-TREMBLES:

The woman opens her front door. She is wearing a sweatshirt that is much too large for her, that almost touches her knees. Her former husband is standing on the doorstep, slightly below her. She crosses her arms under her breasts, grips her elbows, leans against the doorframe in a pose of fragile authority. The man does not ask to be invited in. He speaks softly, rapidly, she has difficulty understanding what he is saying, although she gathers that he has been driving aimlessly for some time. It is not healthy, she thinks, for a man to be alone in his taxi, to brood, when he should be working. Her impatience grows. She must say something, must be sure that she is seconded by her voice. She interrupts, asks him to speak more clearly. The man is caught short, remains silent. The woman is taut, apprehensive, as though she, too, were afraid of the flash. She notices that a piece of the door decoration, a metal flower, has fallen to the ground. She looks forward to picking up the flower, when her former husband will be gone. The former husband says, distinctly, that he wants to see his son. Not now. At Thanksgiving. He would like to have his son over Thanksgiving. The woman sees the endless rows of ceiling lights in the store where she bought the door decoration. She refuses, suggests Christmas. Perhaps at Christmas. The man remains calm. He does not speak, does not look at her.

2:43 A.M., RIVIÈRE-DES-PRAIRIES:

The elderly woman does not at first realize that it is not her knee that has woken her. She has never spoken about her knee to a doctor, has never limped in public. And yet she wakes at night frequently, perspiring, breathless, her knee as though blossoming with every heartbeat, the pain iridescent, dreamlike. She hears the sound of glass breaking, realizes in the same instant that it is this and not her knee that has woken her. An electrocution of alarm pierces the small of her skull. She throws off the covers, hobbles to the window, sees a man across the street throwing rocks at the church. For years, years, she has been looking out her window at Notre-Dame des Saints-Martyrs. She has never been inside. The man is screaming that he wants to speak to a priest, that church doors should never be locked, never. *Jamais! Jamais! Jamais!* He continues to throw rocks. A drunk, she thinks, a madman. She dials 911, speaks with an assurance that astonishes her, as though one of God's officious bureaucrats had usurped her voice. She returns to the window, standing back somewhat, absurdly wary of being seen by the man.

2:56 A.M., RIVIÈRE-DES-PRAIRIES:

The police car arrives. The woman is relieved, pleased with herself. Until it strikes her that someone else had, perhaps, dialled 911 before she did, and that person is the one responsible for the arrival of the police. The thought nettles her. She frowns, watches the officers get out of their car and approach the man with caution. Words are exchanged. One of the officers takes the man by the arm and walks him towards the police car, while the second officer cleans the broken glass off the church steps with his foot. The man suddenly breaks free from the first officer. His arms flail wildly, savagely. The officer's head snaps back. He falls in a heap that appears unnatural, impossible physically. The man runs to his car, a taxi, he is a taxi-driver. He reaches it almost at the same moment the second officer reaches the police car. The two tear off with a squealing of tires that the woman considers to be unnecessary, excessive. She observes the first officer, who is still lying on the ground and has still not moved. Her hand is over her mouth. Never before had she heard the sound of a bare fist striking a human head. It had reached her ears slightly after the moment of impact, as the head snapped back, giving it an abstract quality therefore, disassociated from reality — percussive certainly, but musical, hauntingly resonant. She has the impression the sound has stained her hearing forever. The officer does not move, the woman's dread intensifies, she stands back further from the window, as though she were afraid the window might explode, shatter over her. At last, at last, the officer stirs. He gets to his knees, squeezing his head between his palms as though to deaden its vibrations, and it is only now that the woman begins to tremble. She limps to her bed, slumps on the edge of the mattress, nauseated, her head back, her jaw slack. She receives, as it were, the familiar, taunting pain of her deteriorating knee. Receives it gratefully.

3:21 A.M., LAVAL:

There is nothing but mute obscenity in the mouth of André Lanteigne. He is looking through the curtains of his living room window. His brother's taxi is parked in his driveway. His brother, Robert Lanteigne, is standing beside it. Two police cars are blocking the end of the driveway. A police officer is crouched behind one of the cars, his revolver trained on the brother. It is a .32 Colt PPS. André knows it is a .32 Colt PPS because he has one himself. He too is a policeman. But he will not intervene, he will not.

List: Characteristics that, according to André Lanteigne, he shares with his older brother, Robert

His last name

André can hear the hysteria in his brother's voice, although he cannot make out what he is saying. He does hear his brother scream,

"*Tirez-moi! Tuez-moi!* Shoot me! Kill me!" He considers this a good sign, it being rarely necessary to shoot an individual who desires to be shot. It is his opinion that his brother, unable to gain attention by doing things properly, is attempting to gain attention by fucking things up. Again. A childhood memory infiltrates his thinking: he catches his brother stealing money from their mother's purse. A trivial memory, and yet insistent, obsessive, exasperating. His brother, instead of simply putting the money back, bolts, spends what he has stolen, and then insists upon confessing, burbling and weeping, to their mother, who is burbling and weeping as well. André feels his throat tighten, he leaves the curtains, he is going to intervene. No sooner does he place his hand on the knob of the front door, however, than he hears a sudden change in the quality of his brother's voice. It is more muted and yet more intense. He returns quickly to the window. His brother has been overpowered, he is being carried by the arms and legs down the driveway, he is squirming, kicking. André goes to the door again. His hand is on the knob, but he cannot make it turn. He cannot make his hand turn the doorknob, he can only return to the window and watch through the curtains. The officers are trying to stuff his brother into their car now, using their night sticks. His brother is resisting maniacally, fending off the blows. "*Tuez-moi!*" he screams.

8:47 A.M., TOWN OF MOUNT ROYAL:

The girl looks at the kitchen clock, tries to convince herself that she can still get to school on time if she runs forty steps, walks forty steps. Her eye is caught by the newspaper that, for some reason, is floating on the dishes in the kitchen sink. Her attention is drawn to the front-page photograph. From a distance, it appears to be a close-up of a newborn baby's moony face, the cheekbones puffy, splotchy, the closed eyelids bulging. She smiles, looks more closely, and discovers that she is entirely mistaken, entirely. It is as though a match is struck against her brain, causing her brain to burst into flame. Her brain burns for the merest instant, and then it is her brain again, curious, inventive. She reads for the second time the caption under the photograph: *Passage à tabac : Le chauffeur de taxi Robert Lanteigne gît dans un état comateux à la suite d'une interrogation menée par des agents de police de la CUM.*[*] She is intrigued by the expression "*passage à tabac*," "tobacco passage," which she has never heard before. She imagines, facing each other, two columns of identical, moustachioed policemen with polished bells on their heads, holding out giant tobacco leaves. She sees the man in the photograph stagger between the columns, stumble against the leaves, and then fall, floatingly, into a bed stamped with the word "coma."

List: inquest findings — police officers, in alphabetic order, involved in the interrogation resulting in the comatose state of Robert Lanteigne

    JA
    LA
    AK
    SL
    CM
    PM
    VM
    PR

The girl scowls, decides that, seeing as she is going to be late for school anyway, she might as well look up "*passage à tabac*" in the *Grand Larousse* dictionary in her mother's office. She walks down the hall, enters the room. There is a book of matches on her mother's

---

[*]A brutal beating: Taxi-driver Robert Lanteigne lies in a coma after being interrogated by Montreal Urban Community police.

desk. The girl stops, perplexed. She has completely forgotten what she has come for, does not have any idea why she is there. She is amused by her own bewilderment, and shrugs, as though looking at herself in an imaginary mirror. When she leaves the room, the matches are in her hand.

Sub-list A: Inquest findings — injuries sustained
  by AK: hair pulled out
  by SL: bitten hand, bruised testicles

The girl is intrigued by the manner in which the black fabric burns. Initially, when she touches a match to it, the fabric melts, creating a small hole. The hole expands rapidly, its perimeter glowing red, until it is a centimetre, roughly, in diameter, at which time the redness abruptly disappears, the fabric stops burning. When she uses two matches held together, the fabric flames for the merest instant. But the final hole is not necessarily any larger. It does not seem possible, with simple book matches, to burn a hole greater than, or indeed less than, a centimetre, roughly, in diameter.

Sub-list B: Inquest findings — injuries sustained
  by Robert Lanteigne: broken nose, road burns to knees,
  cracked ribs, fractured cheekbone, collapsed bladder, pinched
  trachea, positional asphyxia causing brain damage and coma . . .

The girl puts her father's pants on under her school tunic. She stands with her back to the tall mirror in her parents' bedroom, her feet well apart, and bends over until she can see herself between her legs. She is delighted by the pattern of holes she has burned into the seat of her father's pants and through which she can see her floral *bobettes*. She puts the pants on over her head, looks through the holes, sticks the tip of her tongue into them. She wonders, hanging the pants up again in his closet, what her father's reaction will be when he discovers the holes. This will not likely be anytime soon, seeing as the pants are formal pants he almost never wears. Trousers, he calls them, tending to say "trowssirs" due to his mild French accent. They are part of his uniform. His dress uniform.

. . . undetermined internal injuries causing hemorrhage and death

The girl's father is a policeman.

—

MY FATHER. The beau beside whom my happiness snored. His hair made of solid basalt, eroded by time and daily grooming, its irregular surface smoothed, etched with interlinking, sinusoidal waves.

See him, Papoo, a silver hairbrush in each hand, stooping slightly in front of the mirror, feet apart, eyebrows arched, inspecting his coiffure. Perfect, as always. See him have at his basalt with both brushes in a flurry of redundant, reciprocating-action strokes. See him pause, tilt his head to re-inspect. Perfect, still perfect. See him have at his hair again briefly and then press the brushes together by the bristles and place them on his dresser.

My father. My defector. Out the front door just as I was waking up. Gone, gone. Plunge, I did, into the bathroom still rife with his weather: the tiles still drenched from the monsoon of his shower, the balmy air high with the spring thaw of his stink. Gone, already, to work. And not to be back, either, until eleven or later.

"I don't know how he functions," says my happiness, her coffee growing cold, "on so little sleep." She exhales smoke languidly, her indolent housecoat falling open, the tip of her index exploring the rim of her collarbone. A shudder grips her roughly by the shoulders, she closes the housecoat quickly, shields her breasts behind her arms. "But he certainly," murmuring, "does function."

My father. My language. Josée Bastarache I am, and he, Paul-François. Though his wife is Hinglish. Was. Sandra Beck from Lennoxville. When I first met them, they were speaking French to each other, so I naturally just joined in.

French, my father tongue.

Was there a room in the house where my father's presence was not palpable? Was there?

You only had to hold one of the crystal highball glasses up to the light over the bar in the living room to hear the irised swirling of his conversation, only had to feel, in July, against your tongue, the damp of the cold fireplace to see him, the firewatcher, sitting on his heels, throwing on a frostbitten log from the outdoor woodpile, dodging the flight of startled, indignant sparks.

The toaster grumbled peevishly as it underdid the breakfast bread of its absent master's mere underling, me.

The refrigerator brooded when he was not there, longed for the search of his gaze, consoled itself with the echo of his big laugh jammed permanently into the corners of the kitchen ceiling.

And everywhere, everywhere you could hear the swish of his gabardines, as he called them, his work pants, shapeless, beltless, spattered with paint, barely clinging to his boxer shorts, gabardeens, he called them, did I say that? and put them on dutifully before performing even the most minor, unshaven, Saturday repair.

"*Fais-moi un dessin, Papou.*"
   "*Chu pas bon, Josée.*"*

---

*"Make me a drawing, Papoo." "I'm no good, Josée."

The newspaper comics my father reads. Terry and the Pirates. Steve Roper. Studies them, examines every frame, squinting with concentration, as though looking through snow glasses. And I, in my seven? my eight?-year-old candidness, I impute this fascination to an aptitude for drawing. I assume. I insist.

*"Oui, t'es bon! Fais-moi un dessin. Papou!"**

He's in the velveteen armchair, legs crossed, a patch of Crisco calf showing. He's got me tucked into the crook of his left arm. The newspaper is lying on his knee, partially overlaid with a brown paper grocery bag. In his right hand there is a Mirado pencil, as orange as a Japanese lily.

He's copying a frame from Steve Roper onto the grocery bag, erasing far more than he's drawing, brushing the eraser filings off the paper and onto himself, off himself and onto the carpet. And I, I am falling into my father, into the inner space of his body, his nebulae and distant stars, his blue dwarfs and red dippers. Far, far above me I see what can only be the petals of the Mirado pencil, floating. And flowing out from the stem of the Mirado flower I see my father himself, the air of his body, his oozing, basalt bones, his adult breath and high winds.

My father. My very atmosphere. Palpable his presence was. In every room. Because. He was. Do you think? So seldom present himself, to be palped.

Paul-François Bastarache. *Inspecteur* Paul-François Bastarache.

Yes, yes, the girl's father is a policeman.

A fucking policeman.

—

UNLIKE ME, WHO SPOKE ENGLISH because my parents insisted I speak English, Marie-Noëlle spoke English because her parents insisted she speak French.

*"Yes, you're good! Make me a drawing. Papoo!"

"Josée," she said with her usual bullying directness, "why weren't you in school? Are you sick?" Like a sunflower caking pollen onto a novice bee.

Am I sick? I'm in jail, manacled, bruised. I've been there all day. The inside of my nose smells of my father's flame-proof *trowssirs*, my father's uniform skin, melting. The walls are rushing at me from all sides. Or else it's time rushing at me. I have to keep dodging, dodging. I don't dare stop. I've no air. Does that mean I'm sick? No air and no time even to look up at the ceiling, which is painted with Robert Lanteigne's babyful face looking down at me. Or not looking. Looking like it's looking. Robert has no time either, in his lungs. Coma coma down doobeedoo down down, waking up is hard to-oo-oo do.

"No, no, I'm fine. I'll be back at school tomorrow."

Silence. Inadequate response.

"Did you see," I said, attempting, ostensibly, to distract Marie-Noëlle from her inquisitional intentness, but hoping, inwardly, hoping . . . , "what the cops did to the taxi-driver?"

"Are you on the rag?"

"You didn't see?"

"Are you on the rag? What taxi-driver? No."

. . . she would say exactly that. *Merci*, Marie-Noëlle.

I could squeak into the phone, at the top of my lungs, that somewhere, somewhere in this city, is the last person to have been in Robert Lanteigne's taxi. That I need, absolutely, to know who this person is. If only it had been me. That I keep trying to give new eyes to this person, new clothes, a new history, and yet the person is always the same, a young boy, always, leaving one party and going to another. That I was not the last person, although I wish, I wish, to see Robert Lanteigne before he went gonzo, went sailing over the foaming waterfall onto the sunny rocks below, stamped with the word "police."

I could squeak, I could just squeak. And would Marie-Noëlle hear me? No, she would not.

"Marie-Noëlle, what does your father do?"

"My father? What brings this on? I don't know. He works. Something to do with exploration."

"Exploration."

"Yeah."

Thank you. It is possible to rejoin the girlgoyle regiment, with our pink-eyed knees stretching out from under our hiked-up, pleated tunics. We can be depended on to never step outside the eyeliner of our lives. It is possible. I can still be like us.

"Exploration of what?"

". . . tungsten maybe?"

Possible, easy.

She read me our homework from her prized, oat-fed agenda. I could see her cauliflower handwriting as she read.

"*Français.* Composition for next Friday. *Huit cents mots.* Eight-hundred words. *Bâtard!* Write appreciation of film *Les Ailes brisées.*[*] Examine nature of relation *homme/animal.* The film was about this Japanese man who collects goose eggs he finds abandoned in marshes, keeps the eggs in a drawer until they hatch, feeds the babies, sleeps with them, teaches them how to fly."

"Mr. Nishimura," I said.

"Yeah! Mr. Nishimura. How do you know that?"

"I don't know how I know."

No, and yet I could see, in my mind's eye, Mr. Nishimura, as plain as punch, wearing his rubber boots. I had seen him somewhere. I had.

---

[*] *The Broken Wings*

I searched and searched, I rifled through every book, magazine, and newspaper in the house. I panted, raved, opened every cupboard, every cabinet, I even ransacked all the useless, neglected crud in my room.

And suddenly, there it was. My lungs froze.

I held it in my hand.

No, not the letter from *Reader's Digest* with the picture of Mr. Nishimura sleeping with geese. The key, the key, the key. I ran my finger over the miniature mountain range of its teeth.

"Did you find what you were looking for?" says the policeman, reading his paper, eating a carrot.

"Yes, thank you." The key. I drove its honey-coloured tip into my palm hoping, stupidly, the pain would shut the policeman up.

"That's a relief. Where'd you find it? Funny how you always find things in the last place you look for them."

The key. That had not forgotten about me.

Danilo's key.

—

I SAT ON THE FLOOR with my back against Danilo's door.

There must have been a vent somewhere in the dim, murky corridor, through which an anaesthetizing gas entered. The stuccoed walls were asleep on their feet, the sentinel doors slumped. Only the exit light over the stairwell resisted the fumes.

It had taken me less than nine minutes to get to Danilo's apartment. I knew because I had the policeman's sport watch with its black, rubber strap in my pocket.

The policeman was asleep less than nine minutes away. With my happiness. Danilo was asleep on the other side of the door.

Only the exit light and I were awake. And the light stared, red-eyed, insomniac, longing for daylight. Whereas I . . .

My cheeks were on fire, my pulse fluttered in my lips, the turbine of my heart could barely keep pace. My blood swept up my shins, poured down my thighs and crashed into the bottomless reservoir of all my absurd, unknown expectations.

I could not bear such intensity. I hurried home, my head tucked under the hood of my black sweatshirt, lay on my back in my bed with my knees up, my face in my hands. My slit, lippy though it was, could barely make itself heard over the torrent in my arteries.

It *is* possible, I thought, terrified. Easy.

—

I SLID THE KEY INTO DANILO's DOOR. The delighted lock yielded with a muted, oily *t't'ck*. The door swung open, obsequious, silent.

I.

Entered.

Shhh.

The washroom, there, on the left, a puff of scented, ceramic dampness in my mouth.

Had I been in this apartment since the day Danilo moved in? No. A day of empty rooms, of sky-blue windows and boxes bigger than me.

The kitchen on the right, pulsing with darkness.

A day of Danilo in his chequered shirt, officious, sweating, his good cheek streaked with pizza sauce. Which was his good cheek again?

And here, in the living room, the darkness spacious and broad, a faint draft of light drawn in through the tilted slats of the blinds.

I floated from armchair to sofa, sat in each one, tucked my feet under myself with airy primness as I made idle conversation with Danilo's invited guests, unmoved by their sophistication. I held my glass cupped in both palms, assured them there was more wine, if they would like some. As long, that is, as they weren't driving.

I did not so much as think about, I thought only about, the door. That was slightly open. That led to the bedroom. Where my beau lay sleeping by himself.

"Danilo once told me," I told them all, "that the more a painter paints, the more he paints with sincerity. Whereas the more a writer writes, the more he lies."

"Ooo," they all ooed.

"And so I said to him: spoken like a true musician."

"Oooo!" My delighted urethra sparkled with pleasure, I rushed into Danilo's washroom, wiggled down my ancient, black snow pants and my red pyjamas. I sat on his toilet, pressing my chest onto my thighs, to stifle the sound.

Do I dare flush? Do I?

"Snow pants?" said Danilo, groggy, squinting. "Isn't it May, or April, or something?"

He was sitting at his kitchen table, the side of his head resting on his arm. He was holding a flashlight, which he had just clicked on, the beam so feeble and yellow it barely clung to me, staining my black sweatshirt a slimy green as I stood in the kitchen doorway.

"You weren't worried I might have been a burglar?"

Silence.

"Because I might have been."

He sat up, rubbed his eyes with the knuckles of his index fingers. "I did think maybe you were, three nights ago. Which is why I didn't move a muscle. Nothing here worth getting in a huff over. I didn't figure you were a burglar last night, or the night before." He blinked rapidly, his ocular nerves not seeming to be firing in the proper sequence. "Burglars don't tend to show up every night a little after two. Also," he pulled at his lashes, "they take stuff. Whereas you . . ."

"I?"

"You have a wee pee, as La Beetch would say."

An incandescence of words flared up my spine and surged into my brain. So many and scorching they turned my tear glands to ash and fused my voice into a silent lump.

I ran.

"Vieux con!" I rasped into the spring night, when I was outside. "Fuckhead!"

The words started to dribble out of my head then. For days they dribbled. They dribbled out of my head the way cake batter dribbles out of ovens in cartoons, on and on in absurd exaggeration, filling the kitchen, filling the house, bursting through the roof. I told Danilo off a quintillion times, delivering up endless variations of the same salient points until I was dry, spent, my house completely enveloped in cake.

I opened the door then, with astonishing ease, stepped outside, and looked back at my battered house. I realized what of course was obvious to all, that my anger had not been directed at Danilo, but at myself.

Such appeasement. I knew he hadn't heard a single word. Not one. Weak with relief I was.

List: The salient points

1. I had known all along that the key hadn't been given with the idea of its ever actually being used.
2. If black snow pants were the very thing for night prowling, hard to see and quick to put on over pyjamas, their comicality

was perfectly apparent and not, to quote a friend, worth getting in a huff over.

3. It was high time my baby-faced, wee-peeing bladder grew up.

4. Given #1 above, I was a gnithead to have expected, on Danilo's part, something surprised, generous, something effusive.

—

I SLID THE KEY INTO HIS DOOR.

It was almost three. The apartment was saturated with stillness. I had the impression that if I moved too suddenly, the faint draft of light in the living room would crystallize and fall to the floor in chinking flakes.

I got down on my stomach, nudged open the bedroom door with my trout nose, swam across the floor, my gills filled with the salty smell of Danilo sleeping.

His clothes were floating in a clump beside the bed, his shoes beside the clump. I tied the shoes together by the laces and swam out with them hooked over my fin.

Outside the bedroom I shook myself off, slunk back to the washroom, untied the laces, yanked them out, and deposited the shoes in the toilet bowl.

I sashayed home then, singing to myself in time to the nylon swish of my snow pants, "In *On*tario, ee-yo ee-yo, when the weather gets hot, ee-yot ee-yot. . ."

I got into bed.

"I'm going to sleep now," I said to the jury of my dolls. "For fifteen hours." They looked over at me in unison. "No more night prowling for this kid. No more Uncle Danilo. Happy now?" They nodded their bandy heads vigorously, clapped themselves on the back.

I slid the key into his door.

Faint I felt, nauseous. My hands were ice cold, bloodless.

I moved through the living room, as skilled at silence as a conger, an eel. I nudged open the bedroom door. I could see the clump of Danilo's clothes. Beside it the tall pair of rubber boots, stuffed with flowers, waiting up for me, warning me, their white petals glowing mysteriously, enticingly, in the darkness.

"Rubber boots," I said to myself. "That's very good, Danilo." I imagined hiding out until he left, sliding under the limp sheets that would be barely warm and that would still smell of his enzymes. "Just not good enough."

I left without a sound.

Every night I got up at three and shut off the alarm clock before it sounded. The alarm itself would never have made much of a dent in my dreaming. But the fear that its going off might wake the policeman and my happiness infiltrated my sleep with sidereal precision, growing in insistence until it jolted me into consciousness with mere minutes to spare.

I slipped on my snow pants and strode over to Uncle D's.

Fine work, Josée. Argument well developed and well researched. Some aspects of Charlemagne's life I wasn't aware of myself. The chief pleasure of teaching, you may be surprised to know, is learning from one's students. I am happy to say that you have been showing — lately, at last — an application and sense of purpose worthy of your considerable talent. Now we both *know what you are capable of. A+*

He impressed me, Danilo did. He put his rubber boots out, stuffed with flowers, every night. And every night I left without a sound.

Until at last he gave up, said "uncle." My heart leapt with delight at the sight of his shoes, again beside the clump of his clothes. I swam in, swiped the shoes, and dropped them, laces and all, in the toilet on my way out.

"Josée," says my happiness. "Come with me to *An Officer and a Gentleman*. It's playing in French at Cinema V. Tonight only."

"Richard Gere speaking French? No way."

"Never mind the Gere-box. Debra Winger is wonderful."

"I've got an exam tomorrow. I need to get to bed early."

She looked over at me, concerned, neglected, the waylaid mother trying to gain a foothold in the life of her capable child.

"*Qu'est-ce qu'il y a, ma puce, hein? T'as changé. J'te reconnais plus. Tu travailles si fort. T'es tellement disciplinée. Y'a autre chose dans la vie que les super-bonnes notes, tu sais. T'as besoin d'un break. Je veux que tu viennes au film. Alors tu vas venir, c'est tout.*"*

"All right. If you tell me to, I will."

"Ah, Josée. Aren't you going to put up any more resistance than that? And why don't you want to speak to me in French anymore?"

I knew he would be waiting up for me. But how, but how? Not the flashlight-in-the-kitchen caper. Not the boots and flowers.

Would he be sitting, slippered, in the living room, wearing a silk dressing gown and smoking two unlit Tiparillos?

Would he be wearing his chef's hat and his duly rude apron? Would he be making curried eggs with whipped cream? I hope, I hope.

No, he would be hiding out, in the corridor. He would sneak up on me from behind as I was opening the door. That was *it*.

---

*"What's up with you, Josée? You've changed. I don't recognize you anymore. You work so hard. You've got so much discipline. There are other things in life besides great marks, you know. You need a break. I want you to come to the film. So you're going to come, that's all there is to it."

I did *not* look behind me as I slid the key into his lock. I knew he was going to attack, I knew. My urethra was sparkling, my shoulders were already tingling with the touch of his hands.

I wheeled around. No, he wasn't there after all.

Would he be lying on his bed then? With his hands behind his head? Wearing a giant pair of clown shoes too big to deposit in any toilet? Oh, *that* was it! *That* was Danilo, I was sure of it, sure of it, I turned the key recklessly, the happy lock yielded, the door swung open, and there he was, his navy blue trench coat buttoned up to the icy white collar of his shirt, his pagan hair combed with black honey.

No, Danilo. Not good enough.

I wanted the clown shoes. I did. I wanted to be right.

But he bent down, turned his good cheek towards me, his birthmark, his port wine stain, his *nevus flammeus*. And so he received what he had no doubt imagined, expected, from me: something surprised, generous, something effusive. I threw my arms around his neck. I kissed him there, I only kissed him there. I felt the ardent redness of his birthmark staining my lips, staining my throat. I pressed my well-tuned twin carbs against him, kissed him, kissed him there. I kissed him and kissed him. I sobbed and sobbed.

—

IT NEVER RAINED WHEN I went to Danilo's, never. But the best nights were when it had been raining earlier. When, that is, the black, humid air still smelled of straining weeds, and the puddles were so smooth they looked like holes in the asphalt, through which you could see the stars.

Danilo did acquire, somewhere, a pair of giant clown shoes. He put them on his hobbit feet. I sat on his midriff and taught him hand-clapping songs:

> In *On*tario, ee-yo ee-yo
> When the weather gets hot, ee-yot ee-yot
> I take off-a my clothes, ee-yose ee-yose
> And jump into the water, ee-yotter ee-yotter

We were ace together, ace. If I leaned back I could feel, under his clown suit, his *pénis*. What he referred to as his "peenits."

> My mother saw me do it, ee-yooit ee-yooit
> Take off-a my clothes, ee-yose ee-yose
> She beat me black and blue-it, ee-yooit ee-yooit
> She break-a my nose, ee-yose ee-yose

> The very next day, ee-yay ee-yay
> On *thuh* highway, ee-yay ee-yay
> Who should I see? ee-yee ee-yee
> El*vis* Pres*ley*, ee-yee ee-yee

(But I wasn't in love.)

> He wanted to get married, ee-yaried ee-yaried
> The very next day, ee-yay ee-yay
> What did I say? ee-yay ee-yay
> Just go a-*way*!

(Not with Danilo.)

He stood in the kitchen wearing nothing but his duly rude apron, up to his elbows in *papier mâché*.

His skin was evenly covered with lifeless black hair. So much so that he looked like he was going bald, everywhere, as if he had once possessed a full pelt of fur, without commercial value, perhaps, but a full pelt nonetheless, that due to some disease or nervous disorder was falling out. He looked like an unassuming woolly biped, with mange.

He applied the strips of glue-soaked newspaper to a chicken-wire form that he had twisted, bent, and pounded into shape.

"How can you tell what it's going to look like when it's finished?"

He shrugged, not wanting me to see that he was wanting me to see that he was pleased by my admirative tone.

"So what's it going to be when it's finished?"

"A spotted hyena."

"Yeah, but it looks to me like it's got, like, six leg things. Hyenas don't have six legs."

"This one is the tail."

"Yeah, but they don't have a tail and five legs either."

"You'll see."

And I did, much to my rejoicement. A spotted hyena it was, with no spots, yet, but with a cackling snout, a tail, and four fine legs straddling a considerable peenits.

"Can we call him Gérard? Can we? Gérard, *marquis d'Hyène*. Or Jim? Julian!"

"Her," said Danilo.

"Her?"

"Her." He looked at me. I have seen a sort of similar look in the eyes of other men. When their unbuttoning of the first button meets with an inability to resist. When, that is, they begin to lose interest. "That's her clitoris actually. You know what a clitoris is, do you? I *think* it's the same word in French. Cleetoreece?"

But it was a peenits, it was. As much a peenits as Danilo's own.

"You *don't* know what a clitoris is? I'll have to show you then. Jump up here on the table."

"You *know* I know what it is. And it's not *that*."

Danilo's hobby, apart from me, was animal sex. The sex of animals, I mean, how they do it. His apartment was full of *papier mâché* sculptures of creatures whose reproductive strategies excited his curiosity.

"This," he might say, fingering a strangely contorted creature perched on his piano, "is a paper nautilus. A mysterious animal. Tonight is paper nautilus night. Ready?"

He threw a sheet over my head and tied it at my waist. I should maybe say I wasn't wearing anything underneath.

"At one time, people thought that female paper nautiluses were afflicted with parasitic worms."

He cut out a hole for my face and another hole lower down and then he tied some pink-ribbon tentacles around me because paper nautiluses are actually octopuses, despite the fact that they live in paper-thin shells that are really very beautiful.

"Then they realized that the worm in question was actually one of the male's arms, which was also its peenits. They thought it broke off after the nautiluses intercoursed."

He put a sheet over his own head, and tied some tentacles around himself.

"Then they discovered that the male actually shoots his whole peenits into the female, harpooneer style."

He cut the point off a sugar cone. Then he got me to lie down on my back, spread my tentacles and inserted the cone into my slit.

"So that's how we're going to do it."

He lay down on his back too.

"Hold the cone upright."

He had a bunch of small tubes filled with coloured pellets, cake decorations actually, imported from Holland. He broke the end off one, held it against the rigid catapult of his peenits, and fired. He was not a crack shot.

Oh, he did make the occasional hit. Overall, though, my face-hole received considerably more decorations than my sugar-cone hole, so I was not in any great danger of getting fertilized. Nevertheless, Danilo inspected me closely when we got up, licked his index, and carefully removed any cake decorations that hadn't fallen out.

"Goodness," he said, as I hurried on my snow pants, "your ears are just as red as red."

I have to write a poem for French. I do it in a minute and a half during recess. Sitting on the can. All I want is to go to sleep.

I get the poem back:

Ton poème est charmant, Josée. Je m'offre le plaisir de recopier ces quelques vers, que j'ai adorés:

Ma vie
est un croquis
dessiné sur, oui,
du bon papier,
trouvé là, sur la plage,
un caillou à chaque coin

C'est beau. A++++[*]

What a joke.

Danilo stormed and trumpeted, flapped his triangular ears, slashed away with his floppy trunk. He had big green tears painted on his cheek under his good eye.

"The male elephant," he roared, his voice, due to the toy proboscis dangling in front of his mouth, seeming to come from somewhere behind his head, "enters a state of vicious frenzy called musth, characterized by the exudation of a dark green ichor."

"A wha'?"

"A ichor. A body fluid. Ichor is what the Greeks called what the gods had instead of blood. So. Musth. Characterized by the exudation of a dark green ichor under the eyes and over the generative organ."

He had big green tears painted on his generative organ too. He ranted and puffed, overturned the kitchen table, spilling the dishes and dried flowers, leaving the salt shaker spinning on the floor. He grabbed the shaker and sprinkled himself liberally.

"*Mwaaa!*" he brayed. "Come, female, and snack on my salted peenits."

"Oh, Josée," says my happiness, fingering my intermediate algebra text, smelling of gin, smoke, and indolence, "a boy wanted you to call him back."

---

[*]Your poem is lovely, Josée. I can't resist the pleasure of rewriting it, it's so short and I enjoyed it so much:

My life
is a sketch
drawn on, yes,
good paper,
discovered on the beach,
a stone at each corner

Beautiful. A++++

"*Who?* When did he call?"

"Yesterday, I guess. I forgot to tell you. I'm sorry."

Her small, unsubtle ways.

"He said his name was Sébastien."

I roll my eyes with disgust. Sébastien has a dimple in his chin so deep you can only think that it was where the umbilical cord was attached when he was a fetus. So deep you can't help but see yourself being sucked into its vortex. My disgust is genuine. I'm not trying to soothe my mother's sense of ascendancy.

"Mmn," she says, her sense of ascendancy soothed nevertheless. "I know what you mean. The thing about boys is that the vast majority give the rest a bad name. You're smart not to let boys get in the way of your good years."

Danilo, like me, was an only child.

"What are you making?" I said.

"I'm melting chocolate. Tonight we're going to be spiders. Okay?"

"Okay. But what's the chocolate for?"

"Well. The interesting thing about spiders is that the male produces his sperm in one place, his abdomen, and his spermatozoa in a completely different place, his pedipalps, which sort of stick out from his mouth, like hollow antennae, like straws. First he spins a small web. He deposits a drop of his spermatozoa-free sperm onto the web. And then he sucks it up into his pedipalps, where it gets mixed with the active ingredient. After that, he inserts the pedipalps into the female. Got it?"

"Sure. But what's the chocolate for?"

He was adding cream to the chocolate, stirring like sixty. He slipped off his shiny white housecoat, folded it, and lay it across my ribs. I was lying on the kitchen table. I didn't say that, did I?

"The chocolate is the spermless sperm." He was back to stirring. "I'm going to deposit it, when it cools, on the housecoat, which is silk, so there must be a spider in its past. Then I'm going to take two of these excellent flexible straws, that I ripped off a hospital actually, and use them, pedipalp-like, to suck the chocolate cream into my mouth where it will get mixed with my active ingredient. Then I'm going to insert the straws into you, which I trust you will enjoy."

"And how, may I ask, will your active ingredient find its way into your mouth?"

"Oh, we'll think of something. We'll think of something."

We were only children, Danilo and I. Playing.

"What's this?" I said.

"That?" said Danilo. "Where'd you find that? Been rooting around in my shit, eh? It's a report I got from a specialist way back when. I think I was about your age, in fact. There must be a date on it somewhere. Translated into straight English, it says that I have a birthmark, a *nevus flammeus*, that I need glasses, but that I'm not wonky."

The patient was born with a left-sided facial nevus flammeus *(port wine stain), involving the cheek, upper eyelid, and left side of the nose. This is a benign, vascular lesion, medium purple, that can be expected to deepen in colour over time, as well as to thicken and become ridged.*

"Neeevis," I whispered, calling. Calling it. "Neeevis-sonneeevis. I am your kelpie, neevis."

"Khiss me, khelpie," it murmured, answering. Answering me. "Khisss."

Its cobbles caught on the ridges of my lips. The masking cream's fading sheen clung to me, its perfume mingling with the odour of my own poisonous braces-breath, scorching my nostrils. I navigated the neevis's coastline in my lip-ship, sailed the eyelid, plied the nose.

"I am dry, kelpie, dry. Hideous to look at. I am thickening and ridged."

I traversed the neevis's grainy moraine with my tongue-tip's pink nib, making my mouthwater trickle into its fissures.

The neevis softened, shuddered.

"Khiss," it murmured, "khiss only me."

His left eye is hyperemic over the bulbar conjunctiva. He also has anisometropic vision with a hyperopic, astigmatic left eye, causing blur in that eye.

"Kelpie, kelpie," murmured the neevis, calling. Calling me. But my throat was too thick, too rigid to answer.

I licked the damaged left eye, the misgrown lashes. I breathed on the neevis my putrescent breath. The neevis gasped, grew.

"Breathe on me, kelpie, do. Please, please. Your breath stinks, it is alive with rot, your breath, alive." I breathed on the neevis, scrubbed it with my forehead, buffed it with my hair. Its medium purplicity shone, shone.

Fundal examination of the eye revealed the presence of left choroidal hemangioma, well circumscribed, slightly raised, affecting the left foveal region.

"I, I am your kelpie, neevis. Only I." The neevis blushed. I could feel my brain collapse, my insides yield, until I could no longer tell my surface from my spirit. I wanted to slither over the neevis's gleaming fleshlets, to sing, to sink into its deep purplicity.

> *The nevus flammeus involves the ophthalmic and maxillary divisions of the trigeminal nerve, and the choroidal hemangioma has the characteristics of those associated with Sturge-Weber syndrome. Nevertheless, the patient does not suffer from seizures.*

The hard, piglet snouts of my nipples nosed the neevis, sniffed its wattles. I breathed through my piglet snouts, breathed the neevis into every part of me, my pancreas, my slit, my liver and lungs. How it shone, the neevis did. It shone like liver, shone like lung.

> *He has no apparent neurological deficit.*

"Neeevis-sonneevis-sonneevis-sonneevis," chanted my slit, my *conne*. I kissed with my clit, with my clittlekiss, the neevis, cleaned it, scoured its nubs with my slit, my *conne*, so it shone, the birthmark, shone like my slit, my birthmark, my *conne*. I scrubbed the neevis, the neevis-sonneevis, the neeevis-conneevis-conneevis-conneevis.

Until I was sick to my slit.

Sick with such pleasure.

—

I SLID THE KEY INTO DANILO'S DOOR.

I could feel him looking at me, from the other side.

It was so easy to look into Danilo's eyes. He knew how to let his gaze be absorbed into mine. How to let me win.

But when he had his back to me, when he was in another room, then I could feel him looking, looking, his duly rude gaze fingering me, feeling me up, making me squirm. Then I wanted to run to him. To make him look at me. So he would not look.

I could feel him, on the other side, looking.

I slid the key out of his door.

I learned this from Danilo:

The spotted hyena was once thought to be a hermaphroditic animal. It is difficult, in fact, to determine the sex of an individual hyena because the clitoris of the female is virtually identical to the penis of the male. Both organs are fully erectile. Both are used for urination. The vaginal lips of the female, moreover, have melded together and become infused with fibrous tissue to form a false scrotum containing false testes.

Having no vulvar opening, the vagina can only be accessed through the urogenital canal, which passes through the clitoris. Mating is achieved by the male's inserting his erect penis into the female's relatively flaccid clitoris. Clitoral erection occurs at earlier points in the mating ritual, and during exchanges, often aggressive, between females.

The female must also give birth through this same urogenital canal, through the peniform clitoris, which ruptures during parturition. The wound is severe and slow to heal. The mother does not always survive.

If I could, I would grab the female spotted hyena by the shoulders and shake the daylights out of her. I would scream at her, "Stop it! This is lunacy, an aberration. You can't have fake balls! You simply cannot give birth through a prick! Stop it. This is not who you are."

But it is, isn't it? It is.

The female spotted hyena is, to me, the most terrible of animals, the most forthright, the most chastening.

I slid the key out of Danilo's door and let it drop onto the rubber mat. I took off my snow pants and kicked them down the corridor.

And then, in my ratty, red pyjamas, I walked out into the warm suburban night. I listened to the conspiracy of trees, the ominous, unruly council of leaves hissing behind the huddled streetlights.

And far ahead loped the spotted hyena, her snout high, her back sloping. She stopped to sniff the air, looked back at me, harried but not impatient, unassailable.

"*Grouille-toé*," she cackled. Get your ass in gear. "*Conne-que-t'es.*" Idiot-that-y'are.

The hyena had the right name for me. Cunnkitay. I ran after her, doing the best two-legged lope I could muster. She shook her head with disgust, turned and set off.

And so I thought about all my young loves.

About Marie-Noëlle, in class, her left arm raised straight up, elbow locked, palm flat. Ready, should the walls give way, to hold up the ceiling.

About my mother, sitting at her vanity, her crutches hooked over the top edge of the mirror, leaning forward to suck the life out of a cigarette pinned between the mirror panels, her hands close to her shoulders, like stubby wings, the feathers of her fingers rippling to hurry the drying of her blood-red nails.

About my father, in the velveteen armchair, a patch of Crisco calf showing, the comics lying open over his crossed knees, snores billowing out of his mouth in clouds of thick, black smoke, etched with the word, "Papoo-eeyoo-eeyoo."

About Danilo, detailing my sexual comportment to his assembled girlfriends, with little enthusiasm.

About my one true love. The neevis-conneevis. At the thought of which, every beat of my heart hurt.

I gave up loping, stopped to sniff the air. The wind was slick, the trees were rearing, tossing their heads. And I was free at last of all my young loves, free, the hyena having disappeared in the distance, free to be the idiot that I was, Cunnkitay.

"Hi." A cop, looking up at me coyly through his window, his car inching along beside me. A fucking cop. "Give you a lift?"

Free? Me? How many nights had I trundled over to Danilo's? With never a cop in sight. And now, on this night, a fucking policeman. I ran. I did. I could see myself running, head high, back sloping.

The cop reached over the back of his seat, pulled on the rear door handle, pushed the door open. I ran for all I was worth.

"So," he said, settling back into his seat, adjusting his rear-view mirror in order to be able to see me. "Where to?"

I ran, I did. And yet I was sitting in the back seat of a police car. We were pulling away from the sidewalk, driving down Graham Boulevard. We drove right past the hyena. She cackled out every slavering obscenity at me.

"If you don't give me an address, I'm afraid I'm going to have to take you to the station."

—

THE WALLS OF THE POLICE STATION were turquoise. High and flat and turquoise. No sooner was I in the door than I was confronted by a polished countertop at mid-lung. Behind the counter there was a wall clock that said three forty-two. And still does, as far as I'm concerned. There was a large map of the Town of Mount Royal. A portrait of the Queen of England. She was gift-wrapped in a blue sash.

And there was a policewoman, behind the counter. The policewoman's gardener had rigorously trimmed her hair until it had adopted a dwarf habit of growth. Her tiny earrings made the corneas of her lobes look like they had white pupils.

My cop leaned his elbows on the countertop. "What are you working on?" he said to the woman, observing something I could not see.

"I'm making a collage for my niece," she said.

I could see the scissors in her hand. I remembered Danilo, leaving a trail of blood spatters all the way to the front door.

Later on, the policewoman made a collage for me too. When I was in the hospital. She was actually quite well-known, famous even, as a collage artist. And still is, as far as I'm concerned.

My cop watched her work for a brief eternity, just to make me shit.

"This," he finally muttered, nodding conspiratorially in my direction, "is the unidentified individual. Highly untalkative. She wants us to believe her name is Cunnkitay." He pronounced the name with the same quiet precision a bat might apply to eating an after-dinner mint. "Leave her in your able hands?" He watched some more. And then he strode out of the station, dragging his hand over the countertop, his voice booming past me, "Your niece is going to love the collage."

The policewoman continued cutting for a while, just to make me shit. She hadn't so much as glanced in my direction. And didn't do so either when she said:

"You're Josée Bastarache."

An incandescence of words flared up my spine and surged into my brain. "Fuckhead!" I hissed, and ran for the doors.

The door locks cracked shut with a sound that made the turquoise air reverberate. The policewoman came ambling after me.

"Josée. I know your father, that's all. We all do. Half of Montreal knows him, which can't be easy for you. I saw you with him once somewhere. I know. The Montreal marathon. Yeah. We even talked a little. You wouldn't remember that."

I dodged past her, ran back along the counter, grabbed the scissors in one hand and her collage in the other. She was quick, though. She leapt at me and snatched away the collage as she was falling to the floor.

I ran back to the doors, the scissors in my hand. The policewoman got to her feet. Her shirt was torn, one of her bra-cups peeked out like the blind nose of a white rodent.

"Josée," she said, her voice calling me with a soft, steadfast authority I knew I could not resist.

I started cutting the braces off my teeth then. With the scissors. Which were very pointed, and very sharp. Also, I hadn't thought to bring along my folding pocket mirror. Very thankful I was when the policewoman got the scissors out of my hand. I thrashed and pummelled then, my excitement fed by the pain that splashed up my face every time a broken wire pierced my lip.

Eventually, I was sitting at a table in an adjoining room, this one pea green, my heart racing, my mouth as though having dropped out of my head, sweat trickling out of my hair, my wrists handcuffed.

The policewoman stood over me, radiating heat. She was panting, the nose of the white rodent was bobbing, sniffing.

"I would have just driven you home, Josée."

Oh sure, tell me another one.

"But I'm going to have to call your father now."

"Handcuffs!" shrieked Papoo. "She's only thirteen for fuck's sake!"

In the first place, I could probably have squeezed out of the handcuffs if I'd really wanted to. In the second, "fuck" in his voice was as vomitative as "registered savings plan" in mine. In the third place, I was like seven months shy of *fif*teen.

"She took my scissors," said the policewoman, "and tried to cut the braces off her teeth." Her arms were tightly crossed over her midriff to close her torn shirt. There was blood on the shirt. "I'm all alone here."

Papoo's allegiance to me, tenuous at best, swung with a clang over to his co-cop.

"I was just walking around!" I protested, trying to swing some allegiance back, knowing it was gone, gone, and not to be back either. "I wasn't *doing* anything!"

"You weren't doing anything? I should hope you weren't doing anything. What *would* you be doing at four o'clock in the morning? And who would you be doing it with?"

"I wasn't doing *any*thing with *any*body. Okay? I was just walking. I hate it when you say fuck. I fucking hate policemen! O*kay!*"

"You just *shut* up!"

The policewoman strode around behind me then, took my chin in her palms and wedged my head up under her rodents.

"There's a pair of needle-nose pliers," she said, "in the third drawer. You should be able to break off the wire with them."

The policewoman's hot palms held my jaws, her thick fingers separated my bleeding lips. I was strapped into a helmet of flesh.

"No? Try the next drawer down, then."

It was no ordinary helmet, though. It must have contained fine tubes through which an anaesthetizing gas penetrated my skull and washed over my brain, making it start to revolve slowly inside my head. A shudder rippled through me, a spectral, mischievous thrill. "That's right, Josée, that's right," clucked the policewoman, her voice trickling down my face with a quality not unlike the unhurried persistence peculiar to blood, "go to sleep, dear, go to sleep. Shhh. Everything's fine. Sleep now, sleep. Have you got the pliers, Paul-François?"

—

"ARE YOU SLEEPING, JOSÉE?"

The sick girl wonders if she is dreaming. Her happiness is talking to her.

When she moves her head, she can hear the crackling inside the pillow filled with dried herbs and twigs from the seventeenth century, in England. She is looking towards a bare window whose panes are separated by pieces of wood painted with thick, white icing. The panes are black, so much so their glass must have been manufactured with octopus ink. Or else the hospital room must be lying in very deep water.

"Have you any pain?" says her happiness. "You look better. Your colour is up."

The sick girl cannot speak. Her voice has evaporated. She has to answer in code: her eyelids twitch, close slowly, open quickly. Yellow subtitles appear in the air above her. "I'm fine, Maman," say the subtitles, "I'm fine." The sick girl wonders why it is that the hale and hearty require such reassurance, when it is the sick who are sick.

"You haven't eaten yet? Would you like me to go see where the nurse has got to? I can't understand why she's always late with your meals."

The girl holds her breath, releases it in an inaudible sigh. Yellow subtitles spill up into the air. "You insist on coming to visit me, Maman, but when you're here, any excuse is good enough to leave the room. The nurse is never late."

"You must eat, Josée. I'm going to go speak to the nurse."

The clear thread joining the sick girl to her mother snaps, tossing droplets of vapour into the air. The thread falls wetly across the girl's face, making her close her eyes.

The black, magnifying eyes of the fever cow are looking right at her.

"Are you back?" says the cow. Her teeth are rotten, her breath gastric, fermenting. So much so it makes the sick girl's head spin with laughter.

She has a brown, scraggy body, the fever cow does, attached to a muchtoobig head with horns that spiral and droop. Her back has been ironed perfectly flat. It is just wide enough for the sick girl to lie on.

Together they explore the ceiling. Not that the fever cow can fly. Her hooves are, in fact, planted on the floor. But her back does not necessarily bear any relationship to her hooves. The ceiling is covered with square, perforated tiles, white once, but greyish now, like the enamel of the sick girl's mother's filled teeth.

"What's twenty-two times twenty-two?" the girl says.

"No, no," says the fever cow, "I'm afraid of numbers."

". . . 484. Holes in every tile. Times the number of tiles." The girl begins counting. "One, two . . ."

"No, no, no," says the cow, panting, her nostrils twitching, "I mean it, I'm afraid of numbers. I'm getting out of here!"

She sails headfirst through the transom into the hallway, looks left and right, plunges towards the large window at the far end.

The girl bounces against the fever cow's hard back. "Owww!" she says, "Take it easy!"

The cow stops abruptly, the sick girl is thrust against the muchtoobig head. Her abdomen is flooded with pain. She howls.

"Sorry," says the fever cow.

The girl sits with her back against the head, her knees apart. She reaches her tin hand into herself, bails out the pain and tosses it overboard. More pain enters as she bails. She bails and bails.

"Get it all?" says the fever cow.

"Yeah, I think so."

"I don't," says the cow. She bucks.

"Ow. Stop it."

The cow bucks harder. The girl's abdomen is flooded with pain again.

"Sorry," says the fever cow. Her eyes are as black and mournful as camera lenses. She plunges her nose through her legs until she is bent in two, taut as a spring. *Sproing!* She catapults the girl-cowalier down the hallway and back through the transom.

The sick girl discovers that her bed is so far below her she has to squint to see it. So far she will not land for hours, surely. For days.

And yet she is falling so quickly that the bed is already perfectly visible and as though growing. The pain will be terrible at the moment of impact, terrible.

But it is not the bed the girl lands on. It is the voice of her happiness.

"You go ahead and cry, Josée. *Ma douce.* It hurts, I know. Cry, cry."

The girl's forehead crinkles, her tear glands turn themselves off. Yellow subtitles appear: "It only hurts when I'm awake, Maman. I'm fine now that you're back and I'm dreaming again."

"Try not to move around in bed so much," says her happiness. "You're liable to pull out the IV. I spoke to the nurse. She'll be here in no time."

The sick girl is sure she smiles, that her smile is open, appreciative. And yet the subtitles that appear are not yellow, not coherent. They cannot at all be what she meant her smile to mean. If she did smile.

"I'll stay with you until the nurse comes. And then I'll let you eat in peace, and go grab a bite."

—

"JOSÉE," SAYS THE DOCTOR.

The sick girl is sitting up against the silent pillows. She is wearing the white robe her mother made for her. The material is buoyant, spongy. She has the impression that under the robe, her outer body is smaller than her inner body.

"How are you feeling?"

The doctor's skull appears to have gone through a rapid growth spurt. It has burst up through his hair, leaving him pristinely bald on top, but with rich, black hair on both sides.

"What would you say to the idea of sleeping in your own bed tonight?"

His eyes are as brown and frothy as dark beer and make the sick girl forget that her mouth tastes like it is filled with dried herbs and twigs from the seventeenth century, in England.

"I've talked with your parents. I was, ah, a little vague. Parents aren't really interested in facts." He smiles, although not with his mouth. "The truth is, Josée, we would need to do some further tests to pin down the infection exactly. But you've responded well to the antibiotics, so I think we should just get you out of here. Which is not to say that this sort of infection is not a serious matter. PID, right? Pelvic inflammatory disease. There are more specific names depending on the location of the infection, the uterus, the ovaries, whatever. If it's in the Fallopian tubes, it's called salpingitis — I'm not saying that's what it is in your case necessarily — but salpingitis *is* a principal cause of sterility."

The not-as-sick-as-she-was girl bats her attentive eyelids wisely. Yellow subtitles dance around her head: "Salpingitis-salpingitis-s-SA-s-salpingitis."

List: 88 anagrams of "salpingitis"
1. pissing tail
2. git painliss
88. I slings it, Pa

"Now then, Josée, we did of course do a mucus swab. Right? We didn't find anything that we might have been looking for in the way of unwelcome micro-organisms. But we did find some . . . unauthorized stuff."

She looks petitely at her clasped hands lying on the pastel hospital blanket. Yellow, italic letters flash across the screen. *The Continuing Adventures of Dr. Mucus Swab, Veterinary Guy-necologist.*

"Doctors are not always interested in all the facts either, I'm sorry to say. They don't have time. But you're an intelligent girl, Josée. Your body is not a toy. Treat it with respect. Now that you've had PID, which is okay, girls your age get PID — girls your age don't get PID too — but now that you've had it, you'll be more susceptible in the future and, as I say, the consequences can be very serious. So treat your body with respect. I don't want to see you back here."

"'kay." The girl is repelled by the vomitative sweetness in her voice.
". . . Okay then."

—

THE BARELY-SICK GIRL SITS IN THE emergency room of the hospital, waiting for her mother to pick her up. She inspects the people in the room with unabashed frankness, observes how each one deals with the gregarious solitude of waiting.

She becomes aware, suddenly, that the lights are brighter, distinctly brighter, than they were. There is a nameless, hesitant expectancy in the room. People are murmuring, standing, moving towards the windows. The girl turns in her seat to look outside and is struck by the fact that it is not the lights that have brightened, but the sky that has grown dark. It has become a perpendicular cliff of black cloud on which the sun, from somewhere, continues eerily to shine.

She resists the desire to jump to her feet and be the first to reach the windows. She is not supposed to display eagerness, spryness, apparently. She is sick, or has been. Her body is not a toy. Apparently.

By now the occupants of the room have transposed their solitary gregariousness to the area in front of the windows. The first hailstones crack against the glass with startling force, sending a current of anticipation sparking through the onlookers.

The girl turns away. She is the only one still seated.

It is not easy after all.

The rhythm of hailstones quickens.

Not easy. Not even possible, apparently.

The assault is underway, the onslaught, the plague of hail. The windows rattle intolerably, the girl covers her head with her arms. She imagines the spotted hyena, beaten down by the hail, staggering to her feet, snapping furiously at the pelting stones. The din increases, becomes overpowering, nauseating, it penetrates the girl's clothing, shakes away all the loose-fitting scales from her body, all the distracting bits of colour and curiosity, until all that is left is the hidden, fibrous pith of her white self, starched with antibiotic, cured, consenting.

And disappointed. Utterly disappointed.

I had been so proud of my body.

So proud of how it could emerge from the swamp of sleep even before the alarm sounded and step out in time to the scissor-swish of my black snow pants.

Of how it lurched and glowed under Danilo's disciplined, playful, buoyish touch that kept me floating out of sight of myself.

Of how it loved his cheek. His birthmark, his *nevus*. And always will.

Of how it collapsed, exhausted, on the can in the girls' washroom and wrote ninety-second poems that fooled them.

Of how it gurgled and cramped and still hurried to do the bidding of all my young loves.

But it was not possible. There were too many of them. It was I who failed my body.

There were just too many of them to love. Too many busy policemen, too many happinesses. Too many licorish shticks. And not enough birthmarks. Not enough hyenas.

—

The sky is stark-raving blue again, having been well scoured by the storm.

List: Decisions taken by the barely-sick girl on this the day of the hail

1. That she will ditch the Town of Mount Royal, Montreal, Quebec, Canada, North America. Not right away. First there is the little matter of scaling a perpendicular cliff of black cloud, i.e., high school, *bâtard*, *cégep*, fluck.
2. That if it is all right for the spotted hyena to call her Cunnkitay, a.k.a. Idiot- that-y'are, for committing the weirdicity of falling in love with a grown man's birthmark, it will never be all right for herself, in woman form, at any age, to do so, ever.
3. That love is for survivors, which is all right too. And that she is not a survivor, apparently.

The girl catches sight of her mother on the paved walkway that leads up from the parking lot to the revolving door of the emergency room. She is walking with her characteristic swinging and determined gait, eyes dead ahead, advancing at a pace few can keep up with. She reaches the revolving door, which is in motion, and slides in sideways. The door loses momentum rapidly, stops, trapping her inside. She pushes and bangs on it, but the door refuses to move. One of the people waiting, a lumbering man with ill-looking, caramel-coloured skin, plods over and lunges against the door, jerking it into motion and setting the mother free. She waits for the man to stumble around in the revolving door and re-enter the room, and thanks him with effusive directness in French and English, "*Merci, merci énormément*, thank you very much." She extends her hand to him, which causes her to stagger slightly, which in turn causes one of her wooden crutches to fall to the ground with a clatter.

A minor event, but, to the barely-sick girl, a revelation.

How many times has she said to her mother, in a tone of sweet-tempered daughtership, that she never even notices her crutches, could not possibly imagine her without them? And now she has crashed into the cold truth of this statement.

The mother has been using crutches since before the girl was born. They have been to the girl nothing more than an aspect of her mother's physical presence, like her long, moss-green skirt, the mole under her eye, the clinking of her screw-on earrings, or the trails of smoke catching on her hair. Or even the rounded stump of her footless left leg, which, although she has never dared say so to anyone, has always made the girl think of a giant eraser. Granted, her friends have always ooed and awed on seeing her mother navigate with effortless skill, but the girl has always secretly found their attitude unwarranted and even childish. They have thought of her mother as a normal biped unluckily stricken with a devastating disease, instead of as someone who simply lived her life on crutches, cooked, shopped at Ogilvy's, peed, painted bedroom walls, on crutches, all day every day.

And now it has dawned on her that they were far more right than she had ever realized, and she far more wrong.

How simple and unremarkable this idea is: that there was a time when her mother was not her mother, when Sandra Beck was not *this* Sandra Beck. A time when she had two perfectly good feet, when she could barely even stand on one foot alone without putting the other one down. How perfectly banal. And yet how inconceivable, excluding, how laced with betrayal.

—

THE MAN PICKED UP THE CRUTCH — eagerly, seeing as doing so released him from the obligation of shaking the mother's, my mother's, hand. He and she did not, after all, belong to the same species.

He was an oversized gnome with yellowish skin, and she, although she didn't know it herself and I had just found out, was a heroine.

She re-adjusted her crutch under her arm and looked around the emergency room in search of her barely-sick daughter.

Our eyes met, the emergency room broke apart like a painted egg floating on the ocean, the pieces drifted away, leaving only me and my happiness, together, newly hatched.

The game was on, a complex and difficult game. I must not move now, not until she reached my seat. If I so much as blinked or twitched a shoulder, my happiness would congeal, become dry and white. My mother would turn into a statue of salt.

She was walking towards me with her characteristic swinging and determined gait, eyes dead ahead.

I must not move. Not yet, not yet. She was coming, she was. I must not move!

She stood above me, my happiness, radiating cold.

Ahhh. Weak with victory I was. A dangerous game, never to be played again. Never.

CRUTCHES

INSPECTEUR-CHEF PAUL-FRANÇOIS BASTARACHE, the visor of his police hat gripped lightly in the fingers of his right hand, the hat itself, like a bouquet of flowers, held against the left side of his chest, stood to attention. The black serge of his dress uniform coat was so skilfully tailored and hung so perfectly that it gave the impression of enclosing no substantial, living body at all. So that, had a hook-nosed pirate wearing a lime-green bandana, say, rushed up and run the coat through and through with a rusty, chipped sabre, *inspecteur-chef* PF, unbothered, would simply have continued as he was, watching the voice of the Reverend James Patriquin swirl gently over the heads of the assembled mourners, drift upward against the intense, charitable green of the cemetery fir trees, and disappear into the sky, which was sagging with rain cloud.

The odd intelligence-gathering drop landed on the brass hardware of the coffin with a soft *toonk*, or startled the back of a hand.

And then the clouds launched their offensive, the onslaught drowning the end of Reverend Patriquin's closing prayer and sending the elegantly, if sombrely, dressed party scurrying for the parking lot. *Inspecteur-chef* PF felt an arm slide under his arm, observed a black-gloved, feminine hand remove his hat from his fingers and put it approximately on his head. He felt himself being propelled by the feminine presence towards the parking lot, more particularly towards a white minibus parked there like a queen termite among her offspring cars. He heard, through the clatter of rain, a certain amount of drenched, playful laughter.

". . . hard to believe, you know, there's an actual body inside. You just get this, this impression there's nothing but rocks and a bunch of old newspapers."

"Or a wax copy. The original having been sold for a small fortune to the Society of Necrophiliacs. Oh, Chief Inspector! Sorry. I didn't see you. No, no, after you. Get in, get in. It's raining out."

"When my turn comes," said *inspecteur-chef* PF, climbing into the back of the minibus and brushing off his wet shoulders, "I'm going to bring along a little reading light," although his own, ancient blue LeSabre was parked not far away, "and all three volumes of *Le Comte de Monte-Cristo*."

"Dumas! Just the thing for the afterlife. Great stuff. Did you know the guy was black?"

"Yeah, I think I — " He broke off suddenly, turned to the damp, feminine presence seating itself beside him, "When did you say Josée was going to arrive?"

The woman looked at the inspector for a moment with an air of secret entente. She then spoke with capable solicitousness, quietly, distinctly, as though she were transmitting a message that PF was in turn to transmit. "She was still in Bogotá the last time I spoke to her. She couldn't get into Miami because of the storm that's affecting the entire Eastern seaboard. She hopes to arrive later today. It's twenty-two hours from La Paz at the best of times."

The inspector nodded consistently, alertly.

"But," went on the woman, "she's coming. To be with you."

PF stopped nodding.

He inhaled deeply.

"His mother was black," he said, returning to the Dumas conversation. "She was a plantation slave."

"His mother? I thought it was his grandmother."

PF pouted in a way that suggested this may have been correct.

"And where," he said, turning back to the woman, "did you say you've got the reception organized?"

"The Lennoxville . . ."

"Golf Club. Right, right. I knew that of course, sorry. I'm just . . . I don't think I'm going to go."

"But you can't not go."

"Oh, I'll put in an appearance obviously. For sure. But I'm . . . I won't stay. I'm awful keen to get back to Montreal."

As a prominent member of Montreal society — a high-ranking officer increasingly concerned with fostering a spirit of cooperation and respect between police and the public at large, as well as the host of the popular television program *C'est la loi/It's the Law* — *inspecteur-chef* PF was invited, indeed required, to attend a fair number of funerals, both private and public.

And while he was unfailingly moved by the austere, genuine, and, in a strange way, living history of cemeteries, as well as by the high feeling of funeral ceremonies, he was not, simply stated, a man inclined to grieve. He avoided, therefore, such tributary activities as casket viewings, commemorative services, and post-funeral receptions. "It would not be unfair to say," he might say, "that because of the work I do, I've had more contact with death than many people. Maybe my skin has gotten jaundiced. I mean, it's easy enough for us to convince ourselves that we regret the promising life cut short, or the well-lived life that's come to its inevitable end. But who can honestly say that they regret the dirty little life that stretches on and on before snuffing itself out at last, after costing us a fortune in penitentiary and health care expenses? My point is, we don't really grieve for the dead, we grieve for the living. For the survivors. Ourselves, basically. We grieve for what we presume we no longer have time to become, and what we know, ultimately, we must become: either black earth or grey ash. We grieve for having to continue on alone. We're a little resentful in our grief. A little jealous."

And so, having put in his appearance at the reception, having gripped any number of hands, some limp, some sturdy, some fleeing, some undeniably suggestive, having remarked that people reveal a good deal more about themselves when they touch you than they do when they look at you, every face, including his own, likely, having been a fitted mask of genteel earnestness, having slipped out through the kitchen and threaded his way through the dented and overflowing garbage cans to the parking lot, Paul-François was, now, driving back to Montreal, on the Eastern Townships Autoroute, sitting in the familiar seat of his blue LeSabre, relieved that the rain and the Lennoxville Golf Club were well behind him. The dashboard gauges observed him steadily, evenly, monitored his attentiveness, his degree of detachment and level of anxiety, using the data to attempt to forecast his responses.

On his right rose Mont Orford, a small-headed beast with green, knotted fur, disdainful, silent, threatening at every instant to shake itself, to throw off the irksome autoroute cutting into its flanks and send the puny vehicles flying.

Inspecteur-chef PF made no attempt to marshal his thoughts into a coherent sequence. He made no attempt to think at all.

He had, during the course of the morning's funeral, made a resolution. Not a noisy, New Year's kind of resolution, but one so solemn and steadfast he had not even formulated it in words, knowing implicitly that to do so would only weaken his resolve. He simply wanted the resolution to hang over his head and track his every move, like the red arrow that indicated which player was being controlled in the electronic hockey he played ineptly during his Christmas visits to the Children's Hospital.

What he wanted, *inspecteur-chef* PF had decided, was to grow up.

How many years had he been married to Sandra Beck now? More than twenty-five, anyway.

During most of which time Sandra had worked for, or with, or herself been, the manager of the world-renowned and frequently recorded Orchestre Symphonique de Montréal.

And when he had married her, *agent*, or was it *sergent* by then? PF had not realized, that is to say he *had*, obviously, been aware that she was attractive, very much so, in a fur-trimmed, Bishop's University Winter Carnival kind of way, queen of which she had in fact been, much to her subsequent embarrassment, and how could he not have been aware, seeing as he had been completely in love and had wanted to live the rest of his life with her and all the rest of the tra-la-la, but he had *not* realized, when he married her, that Sandra Beck was, in fact, a beautiful woman. And perhaps, when they got married, Sandra had still been too attractive to be beautiful. That too was possible. That she had not herself been aware yet of the authority of her lips which, due to the slight upturn of her nose, remained parted even when she was silent, an infrequent occurrence admittedly, lips that seemed, therefore, constantly on the point of murmuring one of the expressions of tenderness they never actually did murmur. Or almost never. Which only added to their authority. Or the eminent influence of the mole under her eye, which was no more than a mole, but which was also an ever-present, a melancholic promise of intimacy. "Like a brown tear that never runs down her cheek," as Josée had once said, Josée being their daughter, who was coming, arriving later that very day perhaps, coming to be with him. It was a long flight from La Paz at the best of times, and these were not the best of times, no. Not with the tropical storm off Florida. A long flight, with connections at Arequipa, Bogotá, and Miami. When Miami was open. PF knew because he had made the flight himself not so very long ago, with Sandra, to see Josée.

Twenty-two hours, from Montreal to La Paz. Twenty-two hours during which PF and Sandra lived in the state of suspended personal accountability that characterizes the traveller, their engagement with their own destiny limited to the occupation of the right seats in the right airplanes, and to the satisfaction, within air travel constraints, of their bodies' requirements for nourishment, elimination, and sleep.

It did not start well: Josée was not at the airport to greet them.

And so they waited, wearily, for their luggage at El Alto airport on the *altiplano* above La Paz, the highest airport in the world, higher than any point in British Columbia.

A group of young backpackers approached PF and asked if he could help them find Plaza Murillo on their map of the city. Being a constabulary citizen whatever the country, PF was only too happy to be of assistance. Plaza Murillo was found.

He was bolstered by this small triumph. And his sense of having been abandoned by his daughter was further mollified by the appearance, at last, of his suitcase breaking through the hanging rubber straps screening the baggage entry. The suitcase wobbled towards him, concentrating on keeping its balance, as though just learning to ride the conveyor. And then, when it was so close that PF could clearly read the words "American Tourister," it suddenly and of its own accord leapt right up into the air. PF, for an instant, could not believe his eyes.

"Excuse me!" he called out, "I think that's *my* suitcase."

"Allo, Papou," said Josée Bastarache.

There followed a vigorous round of tripartite and joyous embracing, after which a radiant PF felt something peculiar about the way the dress-uniform coat he had decided to wear re-sat itself on his shoulders. He checked all his pockets.

"F'ck!" he hissed.

"What?" said Sandra.

"The backpackers. They swiped my wallet."

Sandra broke out into peals of laughter that suggested events of this nature were a bi-weekly occurrence with PF. "So how much," she said, "was in it?"

PF shrugged indifferently. "Oh, not that much," he lied, having been warned that it was not always easy to use traveller's cheques and credit cards in Bolivia.

No, and it did not go well after that either. The altitude made them feel queasy, breathless, apprehensive, as though some smoking taxi were about to leap out at them every second. Sleeping was a hallucinogenic experience from which they woke clammy and disoriented. Sandra tired quickly walking the sloped, crowded streets on her crutches. She was assailed by the constant, hectoring animation of La Paz which, in her view, was little more than the largest flea market in the world.

"I'm going back to the hotel, PF."

"I'll come with you."

"No. Don't."

And Josée.

Josée was in Bolivia, or had gone there originally, to do theatre with the children of the San Pedro prison, a project she had worked up herself. By some mysterious process, she had obtained an interview with a benefactor in Rhode Island and received funding through his private foundation. The benefactor, however, died during Josée's first year. His foundation's accountability was then discovered to be in complete disarray, a receiver was named, and Josée's project was dropped. Therefore she was getting up at four-thirty every morning to bake bread in a *panadería*, and then working a street stand in the afternoon, making *buñuelos* and *pastelas con queso* by the hundreds.

Of most of this, until they arrived in La Paz, her parents were unaware.

She was also writing a children's play for the next school season, in the summer.

Each time he heard his daughter rattling away in Spanish, PF was as though starstruck by her autonomy and resourcefulness. She not only had ideas, she knew how to make them work in the world.

Sandra, on the other hand, was not, or would not allow herself, to be impressed. She was hurt that Josée had never told them about her funding being cut, never allowed them, that is, to be of help. Above all, she wanted Josée back in Canada.

"She doesn't belong here, Paul-François. Everything's made of stone. All these haggling women with their crinolines and their tiny bowler hats, and their faces made of stone too. It's wonderful experience for her, certainly. But . . . Oh, PF, we *need* people of Josée's stripe in Canada."

"She's happy, Sandra, healthy. She's put on twenty pounds."

"Which in Josée's case means she isn't eating. I don't agree she's happy."

Josée had stuffed the room she rented with trinkets — the sort of trinkets on sale at every third street stand in Plaza de los Héroes — with *bibelots*, novelties, figurines, and every sort of miniature bird made of glass, of porcelain, of varnished paper, plastic beads, pipe cleaner, felt, wicker, of china and clay, and one gruesome, hanging sculpture in *papier mâché*, made by Josée herself. It was of the bleeding, decapitated head of Bartolina Sisa, wife of Tupac Katari and leader of the last Aymara siege of La Paz, whose body, as Josée recounted with fierce delectation, was cut in pieces by the Spanish, and whose head was carried on a stake from town to town for exhibition.

No, and it never really went much better until their last night in La Paz. They were sitting, the three of them, in a club called Malegría. A young boy had come up to their table earlier, handed PF his wallet, and waited dutifully, silently, for his reward. "Give this kid," PF had said to Sandra, knowing better than to look to see who might have sent him, "a hundred thousand bolivianos." And then an Afro-Brazilian band had played salsa music, and now a lone singer-guitarist was singing sad songs and sad songs only, "you taught me everything about love except how to live without yours." There was a vaporous warmth in the club which was the exact antidote to the nocturnal, lonely, Andean chill outside.

It was also high time the waiter cleared the table of its empty Paceña beer bottles.

"So what's the title of your play going to be, Josée?" said Sandra.

"*Tsunami*, for the moment. Okay title you think, Mamooshka?"

"*Tsunami!* In the middle of the Andes, the most pretentious mountains in the galaxy. I love it. I tell you I'd give an entire range of rah-rah mountains for just one, useful tree."

PF looked over at his daughter. He wondered if she realized that her mother was close to tears. He decided to intervene.

"Your young actor, Paco, gave me the tour of the San Pedro prison today, Josée. Eleven is he? A little young to be toting a shotgun, I'd say."

"It's just for show, Papa. He doesn't know how to use it."

"So say you. You should meet this guy, Sandra. He's got a coca plant nursery going in each pocket. He stuffs this good dirt into his pockets and plants the seeds in it. Keeps them well watered until they sprout, and then he sells them. Good actor, Josée?"

"Yup. Very."

"I believe you. And I've got to say that his prison home is a little different from the average medium-security Canadian institution. I mean first, you have to *buy* your cell from an inmate who's moving out. If you've got the bread, and some of the inmates most certainly have the bread, you can get a nice place and renovate it to your liking, you know, put in a bath, kitchen appliances. If you're out of jack, like most of the prisoners, you have to find a free spot on the floor in a corridor somewhere. One older fellow is well-known, kind of a tourist attraction actually, for having carved himself a sleeping niche in the wall over the years. With a tablespoon.

"Paco doesn't sleep there, though. Wives, children, and girlfriends are allowed free access, but only during the day. They bring produce and stuff in from outside and there's a sort of market thing that happens in the central courtyard. The whole place is kind of a cocaine brokership too. Paco says he wouldn't touch cocaine."

"I've never been in the prison, Papoo," said Josée, having apparently discerned a challenge in her father's tone. "What interests me is what Paco does when he's outside the prison." PF raised his hands, palms outward, signifying that no such challenge had been intended.

There followed a woozy and collective silence, as though the acidic, Bolivian beer had risen to the brains of all three simultaneously.

After a time Sandra suddenly said, "I want you back in Canada, Josée."

More silence.

"Look at me, Josée. You can't be happy here. Not because it's a heap of rubble, which it is. But because . . . I mean, what do you do for affection?"

"Affection? My kids *adore* me. And I adore them. I've more friends than I've ever had. Way more. Affection. Wow. That's the best reason to *stay* here."

"Yes, but I mean . . . af*fec*tion."

More silence.

"Maman. Af*fec*tion here is just the same as af*fec*tion in Canada. Just as easy to get. And just as hard to come by. Although . . . The men are *man*ly, and do they ever believe in God. In other words," she reached out and placed her hands over her mother's, "women rule."

And so they walked through the streets of La Paz. There was no point in Josée going to bed, seeing as she would just have to get up again in two hours. It was cold, so PF and Josée were each holding one of Sandra's crutches with their outside hands, and holding Sandra with their other hands. A popular song had lodged itself in Sandra's head, a song to which the Paceña beer seemed to have erased all the lyrics from her memory, except for one approximate line. This line she was launching into the breathy, LaPazian night at such piercing, regular intervals, it was as if she were emitting a municipal warning. For an impending tsunami, perhaps. "Uptown eecheemee doomai Tiananmen."

Eventually, they found themselves in Josée's *panadería*. They sat there for a time in silence. The old, grey-tiled floor had an appearance of being encrusted with years of dirt and yet rigorously scrubbed.

And then, without a word, Josée took hold of a rusted, cut-down shovel that was used to scrape ash out of the oven, and disappeared outside. PF and Sandra, left alone, drooped, breathing in the fumes of sleep.

Some time later, Josée re-entered. PF by now was making a sound like the idling engine of an ancient blue LeSabre. "Mamooshka," she whispered, "Mamooshka." She took her groggy mother by the arm and led her, without her crutches, outside.

She had dug a hole in the hard dirt behind the *panadería*. It was not a large hole, less than two feet in diameter, only inches deep.

She made her mother stand in the hole.

She took out of her pocket then a wad of newspaper that contained a new, miniature bird, made of painted clothes pegs. She placed the bird on her mother's head. She raised her mother's hands until they were beside her head, palms facing forward. She took out a ballpoint pen, licked the tip, and wrote a word on each of her mother's hands, and another on her forehead.

Sandra looked at her hands. "One" was written on her right palm, "tree" was written on her left.

"And what," she said, her eyelids slouching, "did you write on my forehead?"

"Useful."

Inspecteur-chef PF looked into the rear-view mirror of his LeSabre to establish eye contact with a non-existent passenger in the back seat. "Really, when you think about it," he said, "the characteristic which best encapulated" — note that Paul-François, who grew up speaking French, considered himself to be on very friendly terms with English, and rightly so, the proof being that English, like any good friend, was not above giving him the deke — "encapulated Sandra in the early days, and perhaps still does, was, or is, her habit of insisting on sitting beside you in restaurants instead of across from you. I mean, she'd dump her books onto the seat on her side of the booth, her coat and scarf, her earrings and bracelets too as often as not, and then she'd slide in beside you on your side. She'd lean into you, reaching for the vinegar, she'd dig her elbow into your arm brushing out her hair with her hands, she'd scrape the dry skin out of your sideburns. And even when she was at her most distant, you know, gazing off into space, her hip would still, you'd suddenly realize, be touching yours."

The blue LeSabre was making good headway. The Eastern Townships Autoroute was flowing down out of the Appalachians towards Granby, towards the calm, expansive valley of the Saint Lawrence River.

"She used to take your hand," he went on, but he was thinking, despite himself, thinking of when he was alone in bed, Sandra having travelled to Denver to interview a talented bassoonist, a talented, young bassoonist, hoping to lure him into signing a contract with Montreal for considerably less than he might get elsewhere. She'd be vaunting, no doubt, the European flavour of the city, its *joie de vivre*, knowing just how far to lean forward so that the collar of her silk blouse would open to reveal the inner palm of a breast. He was in his bed, on his elbows and knees, trying not to see the bassoonist drop his eyes and examine his cutlery, trying not to see under the collar of Sandra's blouse, the rim of her skin-coloured *soutien-gorge*, her bra, the freckles that accumulated between her breasts like early flakes of rust. But he did, despite himself, did see her reach under his jacket and pull his shirt out of his pants, place her cold palms against the spongy skin at the small of his back, explore the crease between his buttocks with a cold fingertip, exhausted he was, having worked as always until almost midnight, alone now in his bed, on his elbows and knees so the touch of the limp sheets would not excite his sleepless erection, his gin glass screwed into the pillow, trying desperately not to masturbate, to prefer the vital anguish of his adolescent jealousy to a still more adolescent release.

"She'd take your hand," he went on to the non-existent passenger, "sitting beside you in a restaurant — because she sits beside you, always, instead of across from, it's one of her distinguishing features — she'd take your hand and pin it between her thighs, as though you were what, a pair of gloves maybe, a sheet of paper she wanted to be sure not to leave behind. I mean, we are so *un*sexy at twenty-five, it didn't even cross your mind to try anything, it just wasn't there, you were just too happy with your little hand sandwiched between her cracked-wheat legs, today when she does it, and she still does, believe me, despite, you know, despite, she sits next to me, she takes my . . ."

He watched the road stream towards him and had the impression, despite the levelness of this part of the Saint Lawrence Valley, or indeed because of it, that he was descending, gradually but unmistakably, going down, down.

He felt his hand pinned between the fleshy pads just above Sandra's bare knees, the pads that he imagined were, among discriminating cannibals, considered highly prized delicacies. She was wearing a floor-length skirt, with a long, lateral opening. She almost always wore long skirts now, since the loss of her foot. He felt the strength of her thighs, not a muscular strength, no, but an atmospheric, irresistible one, like that of the cable of time itself. He felt the hotness of his face, felt himself disintegrate into innumerable, silky spermatozoa and enter Sandra through her every pore, like sleep.

He pressed the accelerator hard, the blue LeSabre leapt ahead. He released the gas pedal, let the car slow down, floored the pedal again. His impatience shimmered over his body in skating, soft flames. Again and again he sent the car lurching forward, each surge reminding him, inevitably, of driving up the exit ramp of the Place des Arts underground parking lot.

It was a memory with which he had been tormenting himself sporadically for so many years that the humiliation it caused him had become almost vital, reassuring, one of his distinguishing features. "I love," he said, turning his face slightly towards the non-existent passenger, "Place des Arts, the carpet smells so, so red. I love the warmth the giant chandeliers give off, the taste of the whisky-soda at intermission." Such an evening, June, magical, Saint Urbain Street a festival, clogged with cars and concert-goers on foot. "Once we got out of the parking lot we couldn't move, the couple in the convertible in front of us had given up, they were standing, facing us, leaning back and resting their elbows on the windshield. It was my first car with air, the Mustang." A commotion outside Sandra's window, two men dressed entirely in white, wearing Key Largo suntans and a day's growth of Nazarene-blue beard, gesticulating, trying to say something to Sandra through the window. "Visit Bill." And she, effervescent, shrugging with incomprehension, "Visit Bill?" laughing, trying in vain to lower the electric window that PF had locked from the driver's side, one of the men cutting therefore his fingertip with a knife produced from a deep, white pocket next to his groin, writing on the window, backwards no less, in blood, with surprising clarity

and orthographic conviction, *"VOUS ÊTES BELLE,"* PF storming
out of the car, the instant policeman, demanding to be shown
identification, confiscating the knife, the celebratory June evening
sapping all authority and even articulateness from his voice, the men
rolling their eyes in congenial bewilderment, putting an arm around
his shoulders, their attention never for an instant leaving Sandra. So
that PF ultimately had no choice but to resume his place behind the
wheel of his air-conditioned Mustang, beside Sandra, whose face was
wedged into the V of her palms, whose shoulders were trembling. The
couple in front were still standing in their convertible, still watching,
watching him, as were the words written in blood on the window,
"VOUS ÊTES BELLE."

"Oui," murmured *inspecteur-chef* PF in his blue LeSabre, *"belle.
Merde qu'elle est belle."*

"It's an addiction," he went on, speaking out loud now to the
non-existent passenger, "jealousy. I talked to Laliberté about it once,
they're going to make him a *commandant* if you can fucking believe
it. He said it was a question of not trusting your spouse because of
not trusting yourself vis-à-vis of other women, bla bla bla. I figured
he didn't understand what I was all about, there wasn't much point
listening. Then he said, as I was leaving, why don't you let me talk
to Sandra about it, you know . . ."

"Just the two of us," chimed in the non-existent passenger, his
voice not so much an audible sound as an electric current piercing
the back of the inspector's neck, staining his vision with a redness
like the smell of the carpet in Place des Arts.

Inspecteur-chef PF sat bolt upright. His heart was racing. The
blue LeSabre was falling at high speed down the Eastern Townships
Autoroute, which had dropped quietly, discreetly, from a horizontal
to an almost vertical plane.

He watched the on-rushing, fluid pavement for an instant, fascinated. And then he released the gas pedal, the autoroute gradually righted itself, the blue LeSabre gradually regained its original velocity, which, by contrast, seemed so exotically slow that PF, his heart beating less violently if not less rapidly, could barely keep from laughing.

Whoo, he thought, it's a good thing this car knows how to drive in a straight line. Wow. What do you think, was I going to have to get out the reading light and *Le Comte de Monte-Cristo* that time? Where was my head?

He felt almost as though he had sidestepped his own destiny, and if so, that there must be a reason for it and that surely, surely, the reason could only be that the red arrow was out there, it was, hanging over the car. A fragrance filled the interior, an optimism, like the fragrance of a reconciliation so recently ratified as still to be scented with the heady illusion that there will never again be a need for another reconciliation.

"*Bon,*" he said with firm directness, "she sits beside you, right? instead of across from. She doesn't face *you*, she faces *them*, the world, absorbs it, draws it towards her. *Tu comprends?* And the world recognizes her, recognizes that here is someone they can draw towards it. *Voilà, c'est pour ça qu'elle est belle. Tu vois? C'est la générosité de sa beauté. That's* why she's, she's *belle.* It's the generosity of her beauty."

Generous he himself felt, effusive. "The perfect crime," he went on expansively, "I had a criminology professor at the University of Ottawa who used to like to talk about the perfect crime. His name was Laliberté too, come to think of it. His theory was that the criminal soul is a humiliated one. That essentially, if the criminal defies his humiliators, it is because he *requires*, as nourishment, their chastisement. A criminal who goes unapprehended is a failure. He can brag. He cannot confess.

"So the perfect crime, and I'll give you an example in just a second, is one that allows the criminal to be apprehended, i.e., humiliated, in a manner that preserves his dignity, as *he* sees it.

"The example. Robert Lanteigne. Remember him? Taxi-driver who vandalized a church, led two squad cars on a high-speed chase for over half an hour, and then resisted arrest until . . . well, until they killed him. Using an authorized restraining technique that is no longer authorized, but still. He died. I can still remember coming down for breakfast and finding a picture of him in a coma on the front page of the paper. Christ. I threw the paper into the kitchen sink in disgust. Sandra wanted me to get myself into the inquest and crucify the officers involved. I maybe could have, I had the pull. But assuming Lanteigne was suicidal — pretty safe assumption, not that being suicidal means you want to *die* — then he did manage to get himself suicided without any of the cowardice associated with the act. No, the general feeling is that he displayed considerable courage, that he turned the cops into the cowards. The perfect crime.

"Of course, I'm not a criminal. Want to hear what my idea of the perfect crime is?

"A young kid throws a carton of milk at a downtown bus, right? This is years ago. The driver, a woman, has her window open, and the milk carton goes right, *tzang*, right in the window. She's soaked, there's no way she's going to continue driving, we call for another bus which takes for-fucking-ever. Fifty-two people on the bus. I know because I interviewed them all over the course of the next couple of weeks. No perpetrator to investigate, nobody hurt. Just ten thousand hours of paperwork to stuff myself into. The perfect crime."

To the north and behind the sparse screen of intervening trees, Mont Yamaska — not a mountain but an ancient hill, an outcrop, one of a series of such outcrops, the Monteregian Hills, seborrhoeic growths on the smooth skin of the Saint Lawrence Valley — to the north, Mont Yamaska advanced in tandem with the blue LeSabre.

Inspecteur-chef PF's enthusiasm for the subject of perfect crimes waned even as he talked. Mont Yamaska would not allow him to be distracted from Sandra Beck for long. It was braiding the delicate, coloured wires of his memory, bending them towards another incident, another time, towards the end of his stint in homicide.

He was sitting alone in the interrogation room, waiting for the suspect to be brought in.

"Nmaaahh," he intoned, listening to his voice die as soon as it left his lips, *"nmaah,"* wondering that a room so airless and mute should be considered suitable for interrogation, for verbal exchange of any sort.

Outside, the winter sky was so white and cold the morning jumbo jets advanced with difficulty, having to slice their way through the brittle atmosphere.

Sergent PF had been up since before five o'clock, having had to drive his wife Sandra to the Saint Luc Hospital for seven. She was to undergo an operation that day.

He stood, blew on his hands, tried to steady his breathing, which was shallow and tense.

An operation on her lower leg. She was to have her foot amputated. She had a tumour in the bone of her heel.

He slid his hands into his pockets. And there he found his car keys, as well as the mini-flashlight that was attached to the key ring and that, despite containing two brand new triple 'A' batteries, did not work. A thrill of disproportionate regret rippled up his arm and lodged itself in his throat. The edges of his eyes tingled.

Of course he had no intention of mentioning the flashlight to Sandra, seeing as, assuming she remembered it at all, she would simply say, "For heaven's sake, Paul-François, I have other things to think about right now. Just throw it away. It's a wonder it lasted this long, it's basically just junk."

It was Sandra who had given him the flashlight.

He hadn't had his blue LeSabre for three days even. His limited-edition LeSabre, power windows, air conditioning, vinyl roof, powder-blue velour interior. Sandra was sitting in the front seat beside him, wearing the gown she might have stolen from the back of a shimmering green anaconda. A world-renowned pianist was in the back seat, her hair so abundant and black PF could only think she used a slow-release nitrogen shampoo. Beside her sat a still more celebrated guest conductor from Belgium whose name was Patrick Bempechat.

And had he, PF Bastarache, parked the car beside a pillar whose shadow plunged the driver's seat into total darkness? He had. And could he find the ignition slot into which to fit the key? He could not. And was it, after much groping and stabbing with the point of the key on PF's part, Patrick Bempechat himself who said, *"Mettez-le au point mort,"* meaning "put it in neutral"? It was. And Patrick Bempechat who got out and pushed the car away from the shadow of the pillar? Yes. All by himself? Yes. Wearing his formal, white, summer jacket? Yes.

So that when, two days later, Sandra had said, "Oh, PF, I found a little something for you at *Pnoo Canadien*," and flipped him the key ring with the mini-flashlight, PF was far more delighted than he let on. For not only did he feel that Sandra, that is to say his life's partner, possessed a sense of humour that was as touching and subtle as candlelight, he also rejoiced in the knowledge that his new blue LeSabre would be, now, without defect. He developed a technique for turning the flashlight on, flipping it around, and holding it against the ignition key all in a single motion. He insisted on parking beside his favourite pillar.

He stood in the interrogation room, his eyes directed at his feet, his chest tight. He could not help feeling that he was under attack.

Because Sandra had other things to think about right now.

Because the flashlight that had given him so much pleasure, however boyish, had given out.

Because he was obliged, on this of all days, to interrogate an absurd woman whose body was wrapped in rolls of flesh.

And because — he whirled around — the woman was taking just the fuck of a long time — he strode towards the door — getting herself brought to the interrogation room.

He threw open the door. And of course she was right there, handcuffed, pointlessly, to Morin.

She watched PF with such distant fixity as Morin unlocked the handcuffs that he had the impression of being observed through binoculars. He dropped his eyes, stepped aside.

She entered the room, walking past him in her breathy, straight-backed, waddlingly processional way.

PF tapped the crystal of his sport watch and looked ferociously at Morin.

"Quoi?" said Morin.

"Il est quelle heure?" said PF.

"Huit heures et quart."

"Huit heures et vingt-sept!"

For all response Morin reached in, grabbed the knob, and swung the door closed.

"*Assoyez-vous,*" said the sergeant.

The woman placed her palms on the table and lowered her tuberous buttocks blindly onto the grimacing, fibreglass chair. The sheen on her forehead made PF think she had the head of a ceramic doll.

And although he sat down himself and asked her to state her name, he wished he were upstairs, outside, wished he were striding over the Arctic snow, on Baffin Island perhaps, under the immense, disciplined sky.

The woman remained silent. Her eyes were watchful, eerily so, as though she were observing the future as it approached.

"I asked you to state your name," said PF, in French.

"No, you didn't say anything."

He realized immediately that she was right. "I didn't, did I. Sorry. My mind is . . . State your name, please."

"Maude-Aimée Duclos."

He could feel the Arctic sun, warm, soothing, conspicuously and yet unimposingly brilliant. "Have you ever had dealings with the police before, Maude-Aimée?"

"Yes."

"When was that?"

"Oh, years ago."

"Under which circumstances?"

"I witnessed a street fight. I just happened to arrive at the wrong moment. Or maybe the right moment. At any rate, the guy doing the punching ran when he saw me. I tried to help the other one. He was just lying there, his face full of blood. He kept thanking me and thanking me, rubbing my arm, and giggling. He asked me if I knew that weathermen and jazz musicians were descended from angels too. I didn't know if it was a joke or a kind of test-your-intelligence question. I didn't say anything. Tests frighten me, I hate them. I had to tell all that to the police. I also had to describe the guy who ran away. I tried my best. I didn't see him very well. I don't know if they ever caught him."

Sergent PF was fascinated by the woman's voice. It did not seem to correspond with her body. It came out of her mouth certainly, but it did not seem to originate in her throat. Somewhere deep in her head perhaps. Her chest.

"Could you repeat," he said, hoping to locate the exact source of the voice, "'Weathermen and jazz musicians are descended from angels too?'"

"Weathermen and jazz musicians are descended from angels too."

"Hmn." He could not be sure. "Is that all?"

"I don't know who else might be. I don't believe in angels."

"I meant was that your only dealing with the police."

"Yes."

"Okay."

PF was eager to ask another question. And yet he could not think of one, he was disconcerted by the woman's voice. It did not strike him as being a voice that, like the body harbouring it, was smothered in fat. No, it was a warm voice, soothing, conspicuously and yet unimposingly brilliant. So that his next comment, as he realized himself the instant the words left his mouth, was utterly inappropriate.

"I'd like," he said gently, "to help you."

He had no idea what could have induced him to say such a thing in the course of even a preliminary criminal interrogation. His cold cheeks flooded with hot embarrassment.

And yet the woman continued simply to watch the future approach. As if she had not heard. As if the words had not yet been said.

"What," said PF, desperate to keep talking, his voice barely audible, as though smothered in fat, "is your occupation?"

"What is my occupation?"

He nodded.

"I'm a model."

"A model," he said with easy sarcasm and with greater confidence, sarcasm being a strong solvent for embarrassment.

"Yes," she said. "I applied for the job after reading an ad in the newspaper. An artist was looking for a woman under thirty-five years of age to pose. A corpulent woman. The ad said the conditions of work were to be discussed. But the salary being offered was about forty-seven times what I was making working at the market, selling lemon pies and maple butter and seven-grain bread. There were quite a few candidates. We were in an empty children's classroom, in an art school. It was Sunday. Horrible. All these fat women waiting, all tittery and blabbing, sitting on desks made for little children. One of them was wearing a hat with plastic grass and little baby chicks pinned to it. She made my skin crawl, she was more childish than the children who made the drawings taped to the walls. Every second I said I'm leaving, I can't stand to be here with these women. But I couldn't summon the nerve, and then the artist herself arrived and it was too late. Good-morning she said, and thank you for coming, and before we go any further I want it to be very clear that you will be required to pose with no clothes on. Oh my, I thought, my heart did a somersault in my chest. She said that anyone who was uncomfortable could leave if they wanted, and I wanted, I certainly wanted, but the woman with the baby chicks stood straight up and walked out with a nobody's-going-to-see-*my*-precious-fat look on her face, and I couldn't then, even though lots of others left, I couldn't, I would have made my own skin crawl.

After that, the artist interviewed us one at a time in another room, I think we were five or six, I know I wasn't first or last. It was so strange being in the room alone with her, I kept wanting to cover myself with my arms, I thought what if she asks me to undress, but she just wanted me to talk about myself. She said a few things to get me started, and I don't remember how we got onto the subject, she talked about earth and air and fire and water, she called them four somethings . . ."

"Elements."

"No, I don't think . . . Four elements? Maybe. And which would you want to die in, she didn't ask that, we just got onto it, I don't remember how, and I said I didn't think anybody would choose to die in a fire, to burn to death. Or to be buried under a mudslide. Drowning might be all right, fairly pleasant even. But, I said, me, I would like to die in the air, I would like to be carried away by a strong, strong wind, or fall from such a great height. Such a great height I'd die falling. I only said that because I was sure I'd never see her again, she wouldn't pick me, it never entered my mind she'd choose me. But she did. I couldn't believe it. I couldn't couldn't believe it. She chose me to be her model."

Sergent PF felt that whatever air was reaching his lungs was not, strictly speaking, air, but the woman's voice, intolerably musical, sustaining.

"Her studio wasn't part of the art school or even anywhere near it. She had to take her precautions. She didn't want any wackos. That was why the ad hadn't mentioned the no clothes. I was so terrified the first morning, oh-oh-oh, I don't know how I climbed the stairs, there were so many to climb. She was drinking tea, she drank only tea. 'It's still too early,' she said. Her first words to me. Not even 'Hello,' just, 'It's still too early.' We had to wait until the sun got high enough that it didn't shine through the windows. 'I want you to wear the light,' she said, 'I don't want it to stick to you.' But that was much later she said that. The first morning she just said, 'It's still too early,' and drank her tea. The studio was no more than a big room with four windows on one wall. Everything painted white. The walls, the ceiling, the pipes, the floor, the doorknobs, everything. No furniture. Just her stool and easel, and a wooden chair near the windows. For me. So I waited, I hid inside myself and wondered what I would do if my bladder gave out. And then she said, 'Okay, we can start. That's the washroom, you can change there.' 'Change?' I said. 'Into what?' 'Into nothing,' she said. 'Like a magician.' She didn't smile, she never smiled. But I could feel her smiling, I did laugh myself, and I knew then that it would be all right."

Sergent PF opened his mouth to ask something, to remind himself that he was in fact conducting an interrogation. The woman, however, began speaking again so quickly that for the briefest instant, it seemed to him that her voice was actually emanating from his mouth.

"When my father," she said, "had something to decide, he used to say he would put on his thinking hat. She had hair like that, the artist I mean, like she was wearing a thinking hat made especially to fit her head. Her hair was so short and black, with bangs straight across her eyebrows. She must have bought her shoes in the children's section, and she always had paint on her somewhere. She was young. Sometimes I thought she was younger even than me. I never asked her her age. The first day she told me just to sit however I liked."

Sergent PF was standing up.

"She didn't say a word, she just drew and drew, tore off a sheet, told me to sit in another position, drew some more, tore off another sheet, kept drawing, drawing, on and on and on . . ."

"Excuse me," he said, although he was not entirely sure whether the voice he heard was his own or the woman's.

". . . and then all of a sudden she said, 'That's fine, get dressed.' It had gone by so quickly. For her, I was just a sort of thing, a chair that changed shape. It was wonderful. I wasn't naked and made of fat. I was made of wood. I was being paid to be made of wood. 'Here's your copy of the contract,' she said. 'Sign it, and bring it back tomorrow.'"

"Excuse me," said *sergent* PF with purposeful loudness. "I'll . . ." He ran his hands through the corrugated side-panels of his hair. "I'll be back."

He was bent over, breathless, his hands on his knees, beside the interrogation room door, in the basement corridor, leaning against the wall. After a time he straightened, took the flashlight out of his pocket, removed it from the key ring, and looked for a wastebasket. He knew perfectly well there was no wastebasket in the corridor. Nevertheless he allowed himself to feel thwarted, cursed under his breath, and slid the flashlight back into his pocket.

"Alors," said *lieutenant-détective* Lucien Taillon, appearing from nowhere, wiping his mouth as he continued to chew, ski-tanned, well-spoken, exasperatingly capable, *"on fait des progrès?"*

"There are those," said PF, "who want nothing more out of life than to be interrogated."

"She's talking, you mean?"

"She certainly is."

"Ah." There was a note of intrigued admiration in Taillon's voice. "She hasn't uttered a single word up to now. I guess you just have the touch with the chubby ones, PF. I look forward to hearing the tape."

PF arched his eyebrows, as though to say he was powerless to explain the inner workings of events. He was thinking that while his forgetting to turn on the tape recorder was a gaffe of almost iridescent stupidity, it did mean that the words, "I'd like to help you," would, mercifully, pass into eternity unrecorded.

"So you're getting out of homicide," said Taillon.

And again PF raised his eyebrows, less demonstrably.

"Don't blame you. Homicide is bad for the head. Bad for the home life." The smooth pond of his forehead was broken by concerned, judicious ripples.

Again PF raised his eyebrows, almost imperceptibly this time.

"So the question remains," murmured Taillon, his face mere inches from PF's, "do we tell Duclos that we've found the body, or do we not tell her?"

Sergent PF heard footsteps descending the staircase. Two pairs of footsteps, if he was not mistaken.

"What do you think?" said Taillon.

"You're the one calling the shots," said PF.

Two men, and two only, did in fact emerge from the stairwell. PF congratulated himself. They continued down the corridor. Morin was one of them.

"Definitely not, then." The other was Bartok. "If we do, she's going to realize we've got nothing, that we can't charge her . . ." Bartok, an unkempt, energetic individual whose not-infrequent run-ins with the police for such things as releasing rats into his own apartment buildings in order to scare off unwanted tenants, ". . . otherwise obviously we would," seemed above all to disguise a more widespread illicit involvement.

"Pardon?" said PF. But Taillon was already vanishing just as he had appeared, wiping his mouth as he chewed.

"Bartok," called out PF. They had the corridor to themselves now, Morin having disappeared with Taillon. "Don't you ever get tired of this place?"

"Naa. I'm not like you."

PF took the mini-flashlight out of his pocket and tossed it down the corridor. "Present," he said.

Bartok caught the flashlight. "What, it doesn't work?" He held it next to his ear, shook it, started taking it apart with the eagerness of a squirrel breaking into a nut.

"You can keep it," said PF, "if you can get it to work. It's not the batteries, they're brand new."

Outside, the weather had changed over Montreal. The white sky had melted. It was filled with rainclouds now, like whipped lead. This, however, *sergent* PF did not know.

"Okay, go again," he said. He had not failed to turn on the tape recorder. Maude-Aimée Duclos had repeated all or parts of her story several times by now.

Repetition, according to the theory, breeds weariness, and weariness leads to contradiction, discrepancy. The truth, however, is the truth, inflexible, inalterable, untiring. Only the truth can be subjected to endless repetition without becoming deformed. According to the theory.

"Starting where?"

It did not matter to PF. As long as her emollient, cleansing voice continued to speak, it could recount whichever variation of the truth it liked.

"The studio."

"It was quiet in the studio," said Maude-Aimée Duclos, "calm. After the quietness of the studio, I couldn't stand the silence of my apartment, it kept yelling at me, telling me to do one thing one minute and another thing the next. And when I took my bath the silence shrieked at me, 'Oh god, do we have to look at this?' The artist drew every part of me a hundred times, every lump and fold in my fat, my butt, my belly and intimate parts, but also my ears and knuckles and toenails, even my moles and the hairs that run down from my navel. She covered every inch of paper with drawings and made drawings on top of those drawings. And then one day she said, 'I'm finished.' I thought she meant the contract was terminated, but then she said, 'Tomorrow I start using colour.'

"Things were different then. She told me what position to pose in, and most of the time it was difficult and uncomfortable. She would bend my arms and legs, twist my joints around and turn my head. She worked slowly, scraping the paint off sometimes and starting again, slowly, slowly, but I didn't dare move because she'd be upset with me. I had to cry sometimes in order not to move. She'd say, 'Stop that! I'm painting your foot.' Not to make conversation. She wanted my foot to know it was being painted, and it did, it really did, it tingled and started to swell, but swell I mean without getting bigger. 'I'm painting your knee,' and my knee had pins and needles it was so pleased and shy. And then later on, she'd ask me, 'What part of you am I painting now?' and I'd close my eyes and feel myself and say, "My shoulder blades?' and she would answer, 'Ahhh.' And then, 'What part of you wants to be painted today?' and every part of me would put its hand up, every part was eager and embarrassed at the same time and that's when she said I wasn't naked anymore, I had learned to put the light on, I was wearing the light, and I know what you're thinking . . ."

But *sergent* PF was not thinking. He was imagining himself skiing under the immense and disciplined Arctic sky, skiing backwards, watching Maude-Aimée Duclos do her best to keep up in her waddlingly processional way. He was using the artist's brush that was also a flashlight to illuminate the brown nipples of her asymmetric breasts, the breasts themselves not so much small as barely findable in the clammy, over-risen dough of her torso.

". . . but it was because I'd learned to wear the light that she said, 'I'm ready now. To paint you.'"

He was cutting her down from the leafless, winter tree through which she had fallen, the naked soles of her feet torn and bleeding.

"She was mean to me then. It was November and cold in the studio next to the windows, but she refused to stop to let me get warm. She pushed and pulled at me with her cold hands, made me hold difficult poses for so long I'd go numb, my circulation would stop, my head would fill with blood and I'd want to vomit. Horrible poses with my intimate parts showing. She knew she could be cruel because I'd learned, I always knew what part of me she was painting, and I know what you're thinking, the intimate parts especially, and maybe I shouldn't say so but yes, especially, especially . . ."

He was holding her trembling hand, murmuring encouragement, as the artist squeezed sparkling, astringent paint directly onto her eager, embarrassed labia.

". . . the intimate parts, oh-oh-oh, the other parts were so jealous and fighting until it was their turn, and when she said, 'That's enough for today,' I said, 'No, we can keep working, I don't want to go back to my silent apartment,' and she said, 'That's enough. Leave please.' And then one day she said, 'I've finished the painting. The contract is terminated.'"

He was spreading the paint on his own lips. He was posing while Maude-Aimée Duclos, with the sparkling, whipped paint, painted him, "And what," said *sergent* PF, his voice waxy and dry, "did you think of the painting?"

"I couldn't believe it. I couldn't couldn't believe it. I said I would keep coming for free but she only laughed and said she was finished. How could she be finished? I said that to her. I said, 'How, after painting me every day for months and months and months, can you suddenly say you are finished?' She laughed, and said it was in the contract. That it was up to her. When she decided the contract was terminated, the contract was terminated. She didn't even have to give me notice."

"But the painting," said PF.

"I couldn't believe it, I started to get upset, and the more upset I got the more she laughed at me. I wanted to look at the painting, to see if it really was finished, but she grabbed it and ran away from me. She was laughing, it was in the contract, she said, that she didn't have to show it to me unless she wanted to. She kicked my clothes down the staircase, and stood there by the open door, hiding the painting from me and grinning."

"You never saw the painting then?"

"No."

"Did you ever see any paintings?"

"No. She gave me some sketches, that's all. At the start."

"And so you left? Without further quarrel?"

"Yes."

"Did she owe you any money?"

"I don't know. I don't care."

"And have you seen her since?"

"No."

"Never?"

Maude-Aimée Duclos did not answer.

"Answer, please," said *sergent* PF, knowing she would not.

It was as though the silence entered the room through invisible vents in the ceiling, a wintry, intimate silence, as Maude-Aimée

Duclos, with distant fixity, observed Paul-François observing the backs of his hands. It descended gradually, the silence did, subduing the intense whiteness of the walls, moderating the garish, fluorescent light, drawing attention to the forgotten tape recorder that hummed with gentle, guttural insistence.

PF turned the machine off. "I'll tell Morin to come and get you," he said.

The interrogation room was utterly mute, airless, strangely suitable for verbal exchange.

"My wife," said PF then, his voice as though smothered in silence, "Sandra," as though struggling to wake, scrubbing its eyelids, "my wife was diagnosed some time ago. With cancer. In the bone of her foot. She's having the foot amputated today." He tapped the crystal of his sport watch lightly. "It may all be over by now. I'll be going to see her as soon as we finish here. They might be able to save the heel. She should be all right. They should get it all. But it does metastasize. Spread. Cancer. It comes back. I might, one day, I mean she might very well . . . one day. And then, maybe we, you and . . ."

He stood abruptly, shook out his pant legs, tucked in his shirt. He slid his hand into his pocket and squeezed his car keys until the metal points bit into his hand.

"I'll tell Morin to come and get you."

He was staring at the table directly in front of Maude-Aimée Duclos.

"We haven't," he said very softly, almost whispering, "found the paintings yet. She didn't keep them in the studio, as you know. No doubt she rented a garage somewhere. We just haven't found it yet. We will.

"We have," more softly still, "found her body. In the woods on Mount Royal. Hanging in the air from a tree. Very difficult to know how long she'd been there. Some animal, a fox maybe, managed to gnaw her feet. Very difficult to know how she got there. Impossible really."

He was still staring at the table.

"I'll tell Morin to come and get you."

Sergent PF was running down the corridor, turning into the stair-well. He was bounding up the stairs three at a time when he crashed into Morin.

"You just left her there?" said Morin. "You asshole."

PF was breathing so violently he could only say, "Sandra, Sandra."

"Christ, it's today, isn't it," said Morin. "Okay, get out of here. I'll look after Duclos. Go, go. It's raining out. Wait!" He reached into his pocket. "Present from Bartok. Good as new."

The mini-flashlight was slicing its way through the dry, heated air, describing an arc of considerable mathematical complexity, sailing just, even as Morin was calling out, "Sorry!" just over the outstretched hands of *sergent* Paul-François Bastarache. The mini-flashlight that was, now, without defect.

The influence of Mont Yamaska over the blue LeSabre was weaken-ing, although still considerable. Concurrently, Mont Rougemont, the next in the chain of wart-shaped growths, was starting to draw the car forward.

PF glanced at his car keys dangling from the ignition.

"Funny," he said to the non-existent passenger, "I just caught myself thinking about my car key ring. I don't know why really. Sandra gave me the ring ages ago. It had a little flashlight attached to it originally. No idea what became of that flashlight. Basically just junk. I had it for years, though. I mean like, years."

Playfully, tauntingly, he floored the accelerator, heard the undercarriage rattle joyously as the blue LeSabre surged ahead, felt the back of his seat grip him for dear life. He removed his foot from the pedal. *"Vous êtes belle,"* he said as the car slowed, *"oui, Sandra, t'es ben belle,"* a glint of finality in his voice, it being his intention to remain silent now, to just drive, to not think. And perhaps, as far as he was concerned, he did remain silent. Perhaps it was the non-existent passenger who slipped into the driver's seat.

"Yeah, it used to be," said, if so, the non-existent passenger, "a marriage was consummated the first night a couple had sex. Right? Nowadays, it's the first night they don't. We didn't that night: the night of the men with the Key Largo suntans outside Place des Arts. It was awful. Sandra slept like a stone under water, her brain anaesthetized with the realization she was stuck with a bodyguard for life. And I lay there perspiring, motionless, terrified of waking her, of being out of my depth, wanting to flee.

"Looking back, I see that that moment, in the Mustang, with the words *'vous êtes belle'* written in blood on the window, was a, a sort of consummation of our marriage, yes. Clumsy consummation. Is there any other kind? Public too, which was a little weird. I mean, we were laid bare, intimate, for the first time really. Naked. Scared. Or I was."

The dashboard gauges continued to observe *inspecteur-chef* PF closely. They had been caught short by some of his erratic decisions. But they were impressed now by his collected attentiveness and the steady resolution of his pulse.

He was at ease, PF was, comfortable in his seat, his right hand dangling over the edge of the armrest.

The white sheet was pinned around his neck, the brightly lit, glass-topped counter in front of him was covered with every kind of cosmetic in tubes, jars, bottles, and spray cans, none of which, however, Pauline appeared to use as she prepared his face for the quartz-halogen lights of the television studio. Never was PF more calm, more alleviated than when he was being made up, than when Pauline's innumerable Mexican silver rings were clicking against each other as she moistened and twisted his eyebrows, darkened his lids and the pouches under his eyes in order to give him a dissipated, investigative forlornness. Pauline Demers, who had a lax, root-like body decorated with all manner of kerchiefs, scarves, bangles, and necklaces, whose features were so accentuated with makeup they seemed to be squeezed together painfully in the middle of her face, who wore her frizzy, naturally grey hair pulled into a ponytail directly over her right ear, and who, confronted with the need to do up her jeans either above or below her toneless belly, chose a position barely three inches under her imperturbable breasts, giving her a general form so reminiscent of a cocktail shaker that PF could hardly help wondering if some nocturnal goblin did not, as she slept, tip open the lid of her upper torso, enter, amuse himself, and, before closing the lid, leave a parting gift of vibrant flowers.

"*T'es beau aujourd'hui,*" said Pauline. His right hand brushed the seam of her jeans.

"*Je suis toujours beau.*"

"*Toujours.*"

As a rule, she spoke very little as her fingertips carried on their conversation with the pudgy skin of PF's face. Today, however, she said, in her good English, perhaps because thinking about someone English brought the words to mind, or perhaps as a sort of homage, "How is she, your wife? Sandra, yes? She is, mmn! Beautiful. A beautiful person."

"She's all right, all right. As good as can be expected," said PF.

"She is very much courageous I think. Cancer is . . ."

She tried to make do with this floating, suspended expression of concern and return to her well-anchored silence. But silence, however sturdy, is a flimsy talisman against the insidiousness of cancer, with its thuggish lack of fantasy and style. Having evoked the malignant, Pauline needed the charm of words, of human, decorative words. She needed, that is, a story.

"So how did you guys meet?" she said. There was a lightness in her voice, as though she were announcing her presence outside the door of a potentially occupied washroom.

"Meet?" said PF.

"Mmn. That is the main mystery of any couple. How they meet."

"Oh, we've been together a very long time," he said, implying that the initial collision could not still be echoing very loudly in their main mystery. If main mystery there were. He was not convinced. Moreover, he was not sure that he could remember just exactly how he and Sandra had met.

"Not a *very* long time. That is not possible. You are not *old* old."

"No? Just a long time then."

"I think that's great. These days especially. People are changing partners like they are changing channels. These days, the most important is to have good batteries always in the . . . *zapette*?"

"The remote control."

Her eloquent fingers were trying to talk some colour into PF's lips. He was fairly certain that under the white sheet, his languorous erection could not be detected.

"Sandra, she was beautiful when you first saw her? Like now? Of course she was. More." Pauline paused, leaned back in order to gain an overall impression of the inspector's face. "So how did you meet?"

Mont Rougemont, distant, discreet, guided the blue LeSabre

with despotic, amused benevolence. *Inspecteur-chef* PF had the impression that the Eastern Townships Autoroute was sliding under the sky rather than flowing over the ground, and that, although it had never done so before, it might well miss the city of Montreal entirely.

How had he and Sandra met? How had they? How?

Gorgeous she was. Stunning. He followed her, followed her the way a down-and-outer, in raw weather, follows a dark-suited business-man smoking a cigarette: not to pounce on the butt, which will almost certainly be crushed under a thin-soled, Italian shoe, but simply for the nostalgic, soothing turbulence of smoke.

She stumbled. He made a move, instinctively, towards her. She caught herself, looked at him as a store owner might look at a shoplifter attempting to put a box of Fudgeos back on the shelf.

And he, whose optic nerve was wired to the speech centre of his brain so that he could not make eye contact without instantly verbalizing, said, "Excuse me, please, I am afraid I am lost." His Quebec accent stained the words so they came out, "a' am afred a' am lust."

The young woman could not help smiling at this reaffirmation of the mysteriously amorphous fact that she was unfailingly asked for directions when, but only when, she was in an unfamiliar place.

"You look lust," she said, deferring the harmless and yet deflating admission that she was from out of town herself.

"I am looking for the museum of the fur trade."

"Oh. Well you've come too far. You've got to go back along Saint Joseph to the canal, past the yacht club. It's an old stone building with two wooden doors." She knew this because, and only because, she herself had just finished visiting the museum.

"But you speak very fast for me."

She repeated herself, spacing the words, pronouncing them with exaggerated clarity, reinforcing them with hand signals that allowed, indeed obliged, the man to remark the curve of her forearm, which was like that of a theoretic and perfect air foil. He observed that her skin was inlaid with a mosaic of freckles barely darker than the skin itself, giving it the appearance of sand drying after rain. That she had a mole under one eye. Not a blemish, not at all, but a pledge of vulnerability.

"Okay?" she said. "You understand?"

"Sure I do." He attempted to convey the impression that he was doing his best to disguise his continuing perplexity.

"You don't, do you."

Successfully, apparently.

"I can take you then. It's not far."

"No, no, no. I will find it. I don't want that you derange yourself."

"Oh, I think I might already be fairly well deranged. And it's really no problem. Otherwise I wouldn't offer."

And so they walked together. Not quickly.

"It's terrible," he said, looking out over Lake Saint Louis, which was vast and choppy, "to think that men put canoes in the water here. Just canoes. To cross all Canada."

"Yes," she said, stopping. "It is terrible."

"Maybe they stand here, right where we are, here, when there were trees, and have one last piss."

He had found the right tone. The young woman was clearly struck by the playful immediacy of the thought. She could not resist a quietly dramatic surge. *"Les voyageurs,"* she said softly.

"But you say that perfectly. You speak French then. *Tu parles français.*"

"No, no. *Un peu*, that's all."

He noticed that when, as now, she blushed, her colour-fast freckles appeared very pale, relatively.

"So how long," she said quickly, beginning to walk again, "have you been in Montreal?"

"Two days."

"Your English is very good."

"I didn't learn in two days! You are laughing of me. I knew it before. I have been learning in school since grade five."

"Oh. I wouldn't have thought they'd teach English in France necessarily."

Neither, of course, would have he. But how, given that she had precipitately concluded he was from the mother country, could he refuse such an open invitation to appear interesting, to indulge in the thrill of duplicity?

"Yes, in Bretagne they do." He thought he might disintegrate, blow away like flakes of ash.

"So you're a Breton."

"I am, yes." It was his turn to redden. She liked this. She had noticed that those who had a tendency to blush when they talked about themselves had, generally speaking, little reason to do so.

"Now I understand why you're interested in the voyageurs."

He wondered if he would not have found her more beautiful still if she had not believed him.

"And you," he said, "you have lived always in Montreal?"

"Not always."

She had answered quickly, to give herself time, her mind was racing, it would have been simpler, perhaps, just to have said that yes, she had always lived in Montreal, but she did not really know the city, she had never been anywhere in Canada outside Quebec except

Toronto, and she would not say she was from Toronto. She did go frequently to the United States, Vermont in particular, Burlington, and he could know nothing about Burlington. But her silence was growing between them, over them, like the vine that grew over the walls of her father's house, covering the windows, weakening the frames, letting in the rain.

"My name is Texas," she said suddenly. "I was born near Austin."

"Texas! No!"

"I have a brother. Toby? His real name is Manitoba."

"Manitoba!"

"My father's an airport architect. He helped design the airports in Austin and Winnipeg. He used to say, 'They name dinosaurs after the places they discover them, don't they? Why not children?'"

"I must meet this father. How are you, Texas." He bit into the name as though it were a piece of angel food cactus. "My name is Paul-François."

She was exhilarated by her inventiveness, delighted with Paul-François for drawing it out of her, almost grateful. She was deciding she might call herself Texas forever. She did not, in her enthusiasm, notice that his difficulties with her English seemed to have largely resolved themselves.

And he had never felt so western, so released from the parish of his Quebec. He was thinking that the reddishness of Texas's hair was not unlike that of tall grass in mid-November. He was already imagining himself flying with her over endless plains of the same reddish grass, the two of them looking out a sunlit portal, and Texas saying that she rode over plains like that as a young girl.

"And what is it you do, Paul-François?"

"I am a artist. I paint." It seemed more truthful to continue lying. But no sooner had he said the words than it struck him that Texas herself might be an artist, and not only that she might be, but that she must, could only be. His lungs seized with panic.

"That's so . . . really . . . I mean, I know absolutely nothing about art."

He had barely enough breath to say, "Neither do I."

"No. You just do it. I'm sure you're very good."

"Ça va, Inspecteur?" said Pauline Demers. *"T'es silencieux tout à coup."*

PF had indeed fallen silent.

"Non, non, non," cried Pauline, *"il faut pas que tu pleures!"* She grabbed a Kleenex, twisted it into a point, and attempted to siphon the tears welling up in PF's lower lids. The lids, however, fluttered skittishly like highly strung moths. The tears overflowed.

"Ah, mer de merde. I'm sorry, Paul-François. I should not talk of Sandra."

And so they stood next to a mannequin wearing a red toque and furs, whose plaster face revealed not the slightest sign of strain or even effort despite the fact that the mannequin was snowshoeing in deep, Styrofoam snow and bent under an enormous load of pelts wrapped in canvas. They watched a National Film Board documentary short that, judging by its visual quality, had been running without interruption since the museum first opened in the 1930s. The film was narrated by a reboant bass voice that sounded like it was home to a nest of termites. It showed vigorous men retracing the route of the voyageurs in authentic canoes, paddling with light-hearted, staccato strokes up the Ottawa River, over Lake Nippissing and Georgian Bay, and it celebrated a Canadian wilderness that, however majestic, could not prevent itself from dozing off repeatedly and slipping out of focus.

Texas, who had just seen the film, was invoking the spirit of the voyageurs, in the person of the mannequin, to funnel the course of her life and that of Paul-François into the same, free-flowing current. She knew that, although the present moment would necessarily end, its echo would continue. For hours, days, years perhaps. Her heart was moulting, breaking through its old skin. It was a Texas heart now. She would call herself Texas forever.

She touched the mannequin's mittened hand and, with what would have been inappropriate loudness had there been other people in the small museum, which there were not, said, "My name is not Texas."

Her real name was. Texas. Now and always would be. She could, she must, go back to her god-given alias. "My name is not Texas, I've never lived in Montreal, and I do know absolutely nothing about art."

Paul-François stifled an impulse to laugh. A laugh not of mockery, but of instability, foreboding. He felt the way a roulette ball feels, losing momentum, knowing it is about to fall into the wheel.

"You lied to me."

Her colour-fast freckles appeared very pale, relatively. "My name," she said, "is Sandra."

"How are you, Sandra. My name is Paul-François."

"Yes, I know."

"But. I'm not a artist, an artist. And I've never even been to Bretagne."

She was not looking at him. On the contrary. She was squeezing the hand of the mannequin.

"So, Sandra, if you're not from Montreal, where are you from?"

"Lennoxville. It's a small town just outside Sherbrooke."

"Ah. I'm from a small city called Sherbrooke. Just outside Lennoxville."

She wheeled around, taking the mannequin's mitten with her, leaving his slender hand exposed to the bitter warmth. "Where?"

"Sherbrooke."

"Sherbrooke! No!"

Gorgeous she was. Stunning.

"I don't remember, Pauline," said PF, with as much anger as anguish in his voice.

"But it's not important," said Pauline. She had placed PF's hands one on top of the other on the white sheet. She was holding them in her own. "Your mystery has no beginning, that is all. You are just more mysterious for that reason. *Pleure pas. Faut pas que tu pleures.*"

PF felt as though he were pinned to the seat, tied down by the white sheet. His face was coated with day cream and *fond de teint*, like river silt, impervious to his tears. He could not bear the melting quality in Pauline's voice, the grittiness of the skin of her hands against his own. He couldn't remember how he and Sandra had first met, that was all. Why couldn't Pauline just accept that? Why must she find ways to dress up their relationship in mysteriousness? It was a relationship, a long one. With its good moments, and its less good. To insist on decorating what was honest and unexceptional with some sort of cosmetic magicality was a kind of untruthfulness, it was bullshit.

"Bull*shit*," murmured *inspecteur-chef* PF at the tall sky outside the windshield of his blue LeSabre. He felt an impulse to dig the tattered Kleenex out of the pocket of his dress-uniform coat, wipe his nose, and dab the corners of his eyes. He observed the endless regiment of giant, construction-toy warriors marching with rigid discipline beside the autoroute, proceeding in single file, tethered to each other by smoothly drooping high-tension cables. He glanced over at Mont Rougemont. And perhaps, for the briefest instant, he was aware of the generous influence the mountain was exerting over the progress of his destiny. Or perhaps he simply had the impression the venerable hill was lonely, listening to him.

"Yeah, the fur trade museum," he said, returning his gaze to the road, "is worth taking in if you get the chance. I took Josée when she was in elementary school. Or Josée took me. I think, if I remember correctly, I once invented a story about first meeting Sandra there for the benefit of Pauline Demers. You know Pauline, do you? She's a makeup artist at TVTS. She just had to know how Sandra and I met each other. And to be perfectly frank, I don't really remember. I mean it was a long time ago. So I made something up. Does that make me a makeup artist too? I forget the details, but it involved the fur trade museum. Total bullshit. Sandra's never been in any kind of museum as far as I know. She hates them. We were good together back then, me and my daughter Josée. We might be good together now too if we ever were together. Christ, I wish she'd get here. It's a long flight from La Paz though. Twenty-two hours at the best of times."

He glanced over to be sure that Mont Rougemont was still listening to what he was saying. It was. "What you have to understand about Sandra," he went on, "is that she won't sit across from you in restaurants. She'll sit next to you. It really is one of her defining characteristics."

It was October, early evening. Dark, pouring. Outside the heavy wooden side door of Saint Peter's Church stood, hesitantly, Paul-François Bastarache. The matted, soaked leaves were treacherous underfoot. The black, doddering trees lurked close by, drooling rain.

His mother was watching him from the car and would not drive off until after he had opened the door and entered. Enter he must.

Paul-François was a Catholic and French-speaking. He lived on Casgrain Street in Sherbrooke. Saint Peter's, on the other hand, was the Anglican church in the neighbouring town of Lennoxville. He was, therefore, in the eyes of his friends, had they known what he was up to, which they did not, in enemy territory. But it was not this that made him hesitate. Like any twelve-year-old boy, Paul-François was not short on subversive curiosity. Nor was he putting up a token show of resistance to his mother's organizing his life for him, seeing as he was still young enough to believe that a lack of such parental organization was tantamount to an authorization to do nothing at all, and this he found tiresome.

No, what made Paul-François hesitate was simply the captivating, incontrovertible necessity of entering.

His mother, considering, one, that her own great-grandfather had in fact been a Protestant and his wife, her great-grandmother, an Irish Catholic, two, that the Anglican musical tradition was a good deal richer than the Catholic tradition, three, that her son possessed a wonderfully natural and pure singing voice as well as an astonishing ability to reproduce any melody whatsoever after hearing it only once, and four, that this same son's marks in English were hardly sensational, his mother, for all these reasons, had thought it would be an excellent idea for Paul-François to sing in the Saint Peter's men and boys choir.

Daniel Hyatt, the director of the choir, was, for his part, only too willing to give Paul-François a try, seeing as his dreams of performing excerpts of Handel's *Messiah* were founded upon two smoky bases, one good tenor, and four watery trebles. Mr. Hyatt himself sang the alto part.

Paul-François did enter, necessarily, and was relieved to discover, taped to the wall, a piece of music manuscript paper with an arrow and two words written by hand, "choir rehearsal," both of which were unknown to him. However he recognized almost instantly the first word as being the English version of what was in fact a *"choeur,"* and so felt the first of an incalculable series of small awakenings that would, after a good many years, result in his achieving the deceptively simple realization that *"choeur"* was equally the French version of what was in fact a choir.

The trail to the rehearsal room was well blazed with music manuscript signs, the last of which was stuck to the door and carried the brief sentence, "Congratulations, you found it."

"Paul-François!" said Daniel Hyatt, who was in the process of pinning a music manuscript sign to his own white shirt, "Enter, enter. Welcome. I must say it's almost frightening to have a choir member actually arrive on time. This, as you of course know, is an English choir, so rehearsal starting times must be considered as mere approximations. Good. So. Why don't you come over to the piano then and we, my name's Daniel by the way," he pointed to the sign on his chest, "I'm the choir director, if such an aleatory and open-ended system as this choir represents can be said to *have* a director, why don't you come over to the piano and we'll give this voice of yours a listen-to. You like choral music, do you? It *is* a bit of, of an a-choired taste." He paused to relish the avid incomprehension on the young French boy's face. Hyatt was always pleased when one of his puns was well received, but even more so when it passed unnoticed.

Paul-François, although he remained perfectly silent, did approach the small, upright, shoe-brown piano, giving the impression that he had grasped at least the essence of what Hyatt had said. In fact, he had not understood a single word. He was simply moved by a boyish desire to reduce the physical distance between himself and the director, like any young forest animal, attracted by a shaft of sunlight. Hyatt seated himself on the piano bench and Paul-François sat down beside him.

They went through a series of simple vocal exercises after which the director, captivated by the incontrovertible grace, the imperious, almost painful loveliness of Paul-François' singing voice, beamed beatifically at his new recruit.

"You'll do," he said.

He unpinned his music manuscript sign, turned it over, wrote Paul-François' name on it, and repinned it to the boy's raglan-sleeved sweater. Paul-François was likely too young and certainly too delighted to appreciate or even notice the slight tremor in the choir director's voice, or the shyness of his fingers.

The other members of the choir arrived and each, in much the same terms, was introduced to Paul-François by Mr. Hyatt, each welcomed him in much the same manner, so that not only was he able to grasp what was being said, he even managed to summon the courage to say in English that he was pleased to meet them too.

The choristers took their respective seats, Mr. Hyatt installed himself at the keyboard, standing up so he could be seen, and the rehearsal began. The songs they worked on were printed in a white booklet written by Healey Willan. Paul-François had little trouble with the melodies, which were simple and hovered around the same few notes. Naturally, he found the English lyrics intimidating, and he was also surprised by certain words, such as *"kyrie eleison"* and *"agnus dei,"* which reminded him distinctly of Mass and which he certainly had never thought were English. It was true he hadn't been to Mass in many years, not even at Christmas, or to confession either, despite the fact that he had gone practically every week with his school class when he had been six or seven.

But what impressed him the most was how his voice, on leaving his mouth, was absorbed instantly by the voices of the other choir members, like a thread of cloud sucked into the vapour trail of a passing 737. And what was more, it, his voice, seemed to want to drag him, Paul-François, along with it, so that it was all he could do to prevent himself, if not from levitating, at least from standing up.

"Would you all stand please," said Mr. Hyatt, magically, as though he too were being swept into the vapour trail. PF was the first to his feet. They sang without the piano this time, Mr. Hyatt leaving the keyboard to come and stand next to his newest singer. This had the odd effect of redirecting PF's voice back into his own ears before it reascended.

"Very nice," said Hyatt, returning to the piano. "Really. Very. Very nice. We've added just one new voice. But effectively we've," he was beaming, "trebled our trebles."

PF was not aware of the general admiration his singing inspired, open and spontaneous though the admiration was, untainted, for the moment, by jealousy or resentment. He did feel exhilaratingly autonomous. For although he was an outsider, a newcomer, sur-rounded by unfamiliarity and Englishness, he had the distinct impression of participating, of having a function to perform. Normally he walked himself through the rooms of his house, and from his house to his school, and through the corridors of his school, with every detail and point of view along the way instantly, unfailingly recognizable. Which, he supposed, was how lives in Sherbrooke were lived. But what, besides walk himself and occasionally horse around, did he actually do? He listened, yes, paid attention, usually. But were he to attempt to observe himself walking through his own surroundings, would he be sure even of being able to make himself out?

And so he sang for all he was worth, making little attempt to decipher Hyatt's directions, simply starting when the others started and stopping when they stopped, launching his voice into the rehearsal room and watching it orbit the walls with the other voices, dimly, ingenuously aware that his sense of belonging depended on his being a stranger in a strange place.

After a time, a girl arrived. Not a man or a boy, but a girl, her straight hair painted black with rain, her chest enormous. Mr. Hyatt welcomed her with his hallmark affability, "Sandra! Enter, enter," helped her out of her formless, sodden, greyish-pink coat under which, to keep them dry, she had slid an implausible number of schoolbooks, her chest, freed of its armour and protected only by a lifeless blouse and sagging green cardigan, revealing itself to be in fact so un-enormous as to hardly seem capable of housing even an adequate pair of lungs. She could not have been much older than PF himself, if at all. She pushed up her sleeves, hooked her wet hair behind her ears, and disappeared behind the small piano out of which then thundered a cascade of warm-up exercises executed at subatomic speed.

Paul-François' face burned with apprehension. He wanted to flee the English universe in which he suddenly felt he had no part.

In the first place, Mr. Hyatt had not introduced the girl to him or mentioned his presence in any way, and he was far from having the assurance necessary to see his status as newcomer simply neutralized, to melt into the group.

In the second place.

In the second place, he knew the girl. He had seen her. Somewhere. He did not know where, no, but he was certain, certain he recognized her and more certain still she would recognize him, ask him what he was doing there exactly, why, if he was French and a Roman Catholic, he was singing in an Anglican choir. She would pick away at him. She would definitely speak French. Girls were like that. They knew things. And they had to know things about you.

Nevertheless, once the rehearsal resumed, he felt much better. Mr. Hyatt stood next to him, singing alto. The girl handled the piano accompaniment. It helped that he could barely see the crown of her head. He could not even see that if he looked elsewhere. But he did not look elsewhere.

"Break time," said Mr. Hyatt. "Five minutes. Give or give."

"Excuse me, Mr. Hyatt," said the girl over the general din. "One of the boys is singing far too loudly. Far too loudly."

It was, and would always be, a curious fact that PF had not the slightest difficulty understanding this girl's English.

"I know, I know, isn't it *vun*dairfool, my dear?" said Hyatt enthusiastically. "Come oafer here. I introdoose you to our noo-a mehmber."

"But I feel the balance of the choir has been utterly destroyed," said the girl with high artistic intent, not moving a muscle.

Paul-François examined his knees.

"Yes," said Hyatt. "Yes, and I am entirely in accord with that assessment and I assure you that I, that is together we, will work to make the necessary adjustments to create a sound that is at once equilibrious and harmoniful." He paused, looking at the girl as though over imaginary reading glasses. "Now get your fanny over here and meet Paul-François. This dood can sing."

The girl approached. Every detail of her manner expressed doubt as to the possibility of integrating this new and grandstanding treble into the small but rigorously musical unit that was the Saint Peter's men and boys.

"Paul-François, Sandra Beck. Sandra, Paul-François."

"Salut. Ça fait plaisir," said PF.

"I don't speak French," said Sandra Beck, much, much to PF's relief. Her stressing the word "speak" suggested that she did do something to the language. Grind it up and feed it to her cat possibly. She fixed her grey gaze on the new member. "I feel you are singing far too loudly." She moved on.

Mr. Hyatt put his arm then around PF's shoulders, bent down and whispered into his ear in stiff but clear French that it might not be a bad idea to turn down the volume a notch when Sandra was around. He tightened his grip on the shoulders, as though to certify PF's unstated, secret accord.

So that later that evening, when he reluctantly opened the door to his mother's car, Paul-François was starving, having rarely inhaled so much oxygen and exhaled so much carbon dioxide. His lungs and midriff were aching, and the piece of music manuscript paper with his and Daniel Hyatt's names on it glowed in his pocket like a nugget of raw plutonium. He had wished the choir rehearsal would not end until the next one began. He was in the state of lightbodied elation that characterizes young people who have encountered an older person for whom they have completely fallen, Mr. Hyatt in this case, and he could still hear, harmonizing with his own, Mr. Hyatt's piercing, falsetto voice, which sounded as though it had been cranked through a pencil sharpener.

He climbed into the front seat. His mother asked him how it had gone.

"Bien," he said, with no discernible enthusiasm.

She asked him if that meant he wanted to continue with the choir. He pouted thoughtfully before delivering his considered reply, ". . . *oui. Je pense que oui."*

And when, later still, as he lay in his bed, the enzymes of sleep began at last to break down his brimming excitement, and the melodies of Healey Willan began at long last to precipitate out of his consciousness, which was dissolving into a dream-tinged liquid, Paul-François, in the last dry crystals of his awareness, was still searching for an answer to the question that continued to taunt him with its disquieting menace. Where? Where had he seen her before? Where?

And he could feel, dancing over his skin, swirling like pigment into the oily images conjured up by his brain, the pale, grey gaze of Sandra Beck.

He loved to sing, loved the rehearsals.

But even more he loved to put the black cassock on over his stiff shirt, to do up the first cloth button at the neck, the first of twenty-eight such buttons that closed the cassock all the way down to his ankles, to put his head through the white surplice and arrange it on his shoulders, to feel the sober holiness of the garments invade him as he entered the hushed church and took his place in the choir stalls beside Mr. Hyatt, to smell Mr. Hyatt's everyday, pungent odour coated with Sunday cologne like, he thought, an onion with icing, to shiver at Sandra Beck's explosive, introductory organ chords that dispersed the silence like magician's smoke, leaving in its place the sudden presence of the Reverend Christopher Kidd, who offered the congregation his practised, rending, earnest salutation, "*Dear*ly beloved . . ." the heartfelt syllables filling PF's ears with English dignity, ". . . the skritcher moo vithussin Sunday places tooik nawlidge inkin fess . . ."

The Christmas rehearsals often going overtime, Mr. Hyatt drove PF home so his mother would not have to wait for him. He drove Sandra as well. She talked about the various piano pieces she was working on and her innumerable musical activities, often asking Mr. Hyatt's advice. PF presumed that Sandra presumed that he couldn't follow the conversation, and certainly he was doing his best to not listen from the back seat, to not understand. Fortunately, Sandra did not live far.

Once Sandra had been dropped off, Mr. Hyatt rarely stopped talking. "We, you and me and the other choir people in our black and white outfits, we belong to the uniformed élite. There's a French word for ya. We ain't the soldiers, our gear doesn't come from the army surplice store," he permitted himself a sideways glance at PF, knowing full well there was no danger of his having caught the pun, "the congregationals fill that function. No, we're the police. We enforce the liturgy, do the crowd control thing, keep the many-headed multitude thinking God. We get them to stand and sing at the right times, and sit and shut up at the right times. We fire into the air, vocally, when they start to nod off. You like singing in the choir, PF? Maybe you should think about being a cop when you're growed up."

"What you say? Me, a cop? *La police? . . . moi?*"

He cultivated the friendship of the boy who sang next to him, Stokey Leggatt. Stokey had stiff, blond hair and a nose so turned-up his ridged front teeth were always visible. PF found him strange, almost exotic. He could be giggling almost to the point of hysteria one instant, and the very next be in perfect command of himself. Stokey made it his task to discreetly teach PF a new English word every week. He wrote the word, usually with an illustrative drawing, he was very good at drawing, on a slip of paper that he glued to the back of a hockey card. He traded new cards for old ones at rehearsals, and tested PF whenever the opportunity presented itself. Consequently, among the most long-standing words in PF's English vocabulary, more long-standing often than their French counterparts, were "cervix," "vaginal wart," and "Kotex."

What gave PF the courage to endure Stokey's tasteless obsession with sexuality was the absolute necessity of having someone to talk to during breaks, in case Sandra Beck tried to talk to him. Or in case she didn't.

Sandra, according to Mr. Hyatt, was missing some molars, which was why she stifled every impulse to smile and also why her cheeks appeared somewhat sunken. She had no nose to speak of. A filament of saliva stretched between her lips when she spoke.

The first time PF heard Sandra play the organ, that is to say, the first time he saw her confront the terraced keyboards and raft of bone-coloured, push-pull knobs, her body perched on the very edge of the bench and her legs perfectly straight so she could just press the foot pedals with her toes, the first time he saw her minnowy fingers poise themselves over the keys before depressing them silently, effortlessly, and heard, not from any immediate vicinity, but as it were crashing through the far end of the church, a damburst of chord, the highest frequencies crawling in his ears like tiny insects, the lowest making his abdomen flutter, the first time, the blood drained instantly from his face. Suffocating he was, hot with amazement.

If Sandra was not much older than he was, twelve in other words, thirteen at the outside, then there were more days in her years, more hours in her days. More life in her life. Suddenly and at any time, the image of her face, contorted with the concentration of playing, might surge into his consciousness, unleashing a new wave of stifling admiration. At such moments PF would be genuinely relieved that Sandra had so little use for him.

There was something soothing, flattering, about being disliked by Sandra Beck.

"Sandra," said Mr. Hyatt as he drove, "Paul-François has this theory. He says that the choir, along with the organist of course, is sort of like a police force in church. The preach fuzz, you might say."

"I didn't say it," objected PF, "*You* say it!"

Sandra's head revolved until her eyes were directed at PF in the back seat. PF, whose eyes were directed at the weathered back of Mr. Hyatt's neck, could feel himself absorbing the pale, grey gaze. Like a wick absorbing kerosene.

"I do not," she said, "see what a choir could possibly have in common with a police force."

"They wear uniforms," offered Mr. Hyatt.

"The minnster," said PF, turning red, "is a sort of dic*tay*tor, no? Mr. Hyatt, you say it. The choir is a sort of . . . *garde du corps*."

"Bodyguard," translated Mr. Hyatt. "We're the Reverend Chrisco Kidd's henchmen, Sandra."

Sandra's gaze shifted to Mr. Hyatt. "You guys," she said, "are weird."

"At any rate," said Mr. Hyatt, "I wonder what the bleary-eyed faithful who stagger in on Sunday mornings still suffering from their Saturday nights would think if they knew that the two Depotty Chiefs in the choral police force are barely twenty-six years old between them."

"What do you mean by two Deputy Chiefs?" said Sandra.

"I mean you. And Paul-François."

Sandra returned her gaze to PF. She smiled thinly, tensely, PF caught his first glimpse of the gaps in her teeth. She was silent after that.

Loved to sing, loved the rehearsals.

But even more he loved being one of the Chrisco Kidd's henchmen.

Paul-François may or may not have believed that he believed in God, but he knew that he believed in the Chrisco Kidd. All the more so in that, apart from Sunday services, he rarely saw him.

"What is it, that noise?" he whispered anxiously to Stokey Leggatt.

Every time the choir stopped singing, he could hear a soft but perfectly distinct scraping sound coming from the ceiling of the rehearsal room.

"That's Reverend Kidd," said Stokey softly. "His office is just above this room." He said this with his usual bright-eyed tremulousness, conveying the impression that what he was revealing was not only highly confidential, but also glowing with sexual implications.

The effect of this answer on PF was profound. In the first place, he had never found Stokey's gift for salacious innuendo so repellently juvenile. He had to look away in order not to punch him.

In the second place.

In the second place, no answer could have done less to quiet his alarm. The idea of the Chrisco Kidd — a nickname that, in PF's ears, contained no trace of humour, but epitomized the minister's black and dignified presence — the idea of the Chrisco Kidd so close at hand appalled him with its intimacy. Paul-François was completely unaware of the administrative responsibilities of a Church minister, and so he presumed that if the Chrisco Kidd had an office, it was unfurnished, unlit, and was where he went to plead, in his secret, soaring language, with his God. Nor could he resist the terrifying idea that were the minister to become aware that he was being listened to from below by a Catholic, his anger would seep like an odourless gas into the rehearsal room, seek the offender out and melt his ears shut forever before he had time to scream, "I am a 'enchman! I am."

And a henchman he certainly was, prepared to walk on his knees to Canterbury were the Chrisco Kidd to lead the way. PF wandered nonchalantly through the corridors of Saint Peter's church hoping to run by accident into the minister, who would be wearing the flowing black cassock he always wore, would be tall, commanding, his hair combed over his balding head in a shiny black strip reminiscent of a warped phonograph record, would run his tongue over his upper teeth, would be smoking, holding the cigarette in his right hand, under his curled and nicotine-stained index finger. They would nod silently at each other as they passed.

But he never did run into him.

So that when Stokey Leggatt nudged PF during Morning Prayer and whispered, "I bet you don't know what Reverend Kidd's got on under his cassock?" his piglet nostrils flaring, his lips red and eager, "Nothing, not even underpants," Paul-François said, "Fuck off." And when Stokey answered, "You don't believe me? Ask Mr. Hyatt," PF hissed, "Fuck off, fuck off, fuck off," without the trace of an accent, causing Mr. Hyatt to stand discreetly and reseat himself between the two boys, the tip of his index against his pursed, restrained smile.

Christmas, Christmas Day. A quarter to two in the morning. Pitch-dark.

Paul-François sat with his mother in her car. The car was parked in the driveway, the heater on, the motor running. He could not tell if his mother was happy or unhappy. She was crying, and had been all the way home from Saint Peter's Church. Not that she was crying hard.

"Je m'excuse," she said. *"C'était beau. Vraiment, vraiment beau."*

She was referring to the midnight carol service for which her son had practised so hard, and which she had found so moving.

PF's brain, unaccustomed at this hour to either wakefulness or car heaters, had achieved a plateau of subdued, languid activity. It was replaying random selections of carol tunes, cross-indexing them with myriad impressions, the smells of hair cream and newly ironed surplices, the barely perceptible effect of the flickering candlelight on the painted panels of the church ceiling, the rustling sounds rising in a thin mist from the congregation, the occasional dry, disembodied cough.

He could not know, of course, that his mother was remembering, longingly, *"Minuit, chrétiens"** and the head-spinning Latin of the midnight Masses of her youth. She no longer attended Mass, had rid herself, or so she thought, of the nosy, insinuating Catholic Church, rid herself of a host of incessant, fussy obligations, and of the silliness of having to invent things to confess to a priest, a man who, frankly, didn't know the first thing about family life. Not hers, anyway. But why, if she was free, did she feel like a traitor for having attended, hidden in the back row, a single Anglican service? In English, obviously, which, to her, was as head-spinning as Latin. To hear her son sing. Yes.

Yes, but she'd had no idea the choir would occupy so much of his time, that he would have to attend so many extra rehearsals, that on Christmas Day of all days she would barely even see him, that he would start using, left and right, English expressions he knew perfectly well she didn't understand. But whose idea had it been that he sing in the choir? She was thwarted, gagged, by the resounding success of her own good intentions. She was jealous, she was, of her own twelve-year-old son.

"Je ne comprends plus rien," she said at last, turning off the motor, opening her door. *"Dodo."*

Paul-François, although he didn't know what there was that

* "O, Holy Night!"

needed to be understood or not understood, was only too happy to go to bed.

His mother looked up at the dependable winter stars. And again she remembered, as she had heard it, the unmistakable clarity of her son's voice, secret and soaring. Even when the organ and congregation had combined to drown out the rest of the choir, her son's voice had still been clearly audible, like a buoy, like a distant light. She felt the lump in her throat thicken.

"*Dodo, Paul-François*," she said commandingly, adding with limp sarcasm, entirely lost on her sleepy son, "Bed."

Paul-François was exploring the corridors of Saint Peter's, idly, wondering why he was wasting his time, when Stokey Leggatt suddenly rounded a corner at top speed and ran right into him. Stokey was in an advanced state of slavering, antic giggliness. PF despised him when he was like this, all the more so in that he found him difficult to resist.

Stokey took PF by the hand and lead the way, looking back continuously, almost amorously, as though he were afraid the rest of PF, apart from the hand, might not be following. They were heading, PF realized, towards the church proper. He also realized that the organ was being played, and wondered why he had not been aware of this until now.

They came to a door unknown to Paul-François. This door Stokey nudged open with experienced delicacy. A torrent of organ music surged over them, drenching them with sound. Sandra was not six feet away, practising. She had kept her greyish-pink winter coat on in the cold church. A clear drop of mucus clung to the bottom of her red nose. On the other hand, in order to reach the pedals more easily, she had taken off her skirt. Her stringy, leek-white thighs closed and opened according to the musical requirements of her feet, causing breathtaking shadows to appear under her puffy grey underwear.

After a time, Stokey closed the door as gingerly as he had opened it and tore off down the hallway, stopping eventually, panting, flushed. He collapsed on the floor. PF collapsed beside him.

"She'd let you, you know," Stokey said, his eyes dark, his voice thick with copulatory suggestiveness.

"Me?" said Paul-François. "You crazy? She 'ate' me. She can' stan' my guts. You, she let. You're the . . . sexpert."

This so delighted Stokey that he was consumed by squeals of spine-twisting laughter.

And although Paul-François laughed just as giddily himself, he was in fact harbouring, hiding, a sense of austere privilege, having witnessed what he did not believe he deserved to have witnessed, that is to say the intelligent nakedness of Sandra Beck's legs, mechanical, devoted.

"My mother," said PF in Mr. Hyatt's car, "says my voice is going to . . . *muer*."

"Break," said Hyatt.

"I woan' be able to sing in the choir no more."

Mr. Hyatt remained silent for some time, absorbed with the business of driving. He stopped unevenly at a red light, looked steadily into his sideview mirror as though he were looking into his own past.

"Anymore," he corrected softly.

The third Sunday after Epiphany.

A special occasion. Paul-François, seeing as his parents had gone skiing at Jay Peak, was spending the afternoon with Mr. Hyatt, who took him to Monsieur Patate, where the cheeseburgers were compressed until they were flatter than two pancakes, and the French fries came in three brown paper bags placed one inside the other.

"Good?" said Mr. Hyatt.

PF rolled his eyes and kept wolfing.

"Want another?" Mr. Hyatt was not likely aware that an unstated moral edict against over-indulgence hovered over the Bastarache family. That you could not, if your name was Bastarache, eat two cheeseburgers any more than you could live two days without an intervening night.

"With the slice of onion this time?" That you could not have raw onion on your second cheeseburger any more than you could pour hot fudge over your first fish.

PF watched as the jaws of his compressed cheeseburger were pried open, displaying its ferocious, stringy, orange teeth. He watched as the machined disc of onion was slid onto the beefy, greyish tongue, and as the jaws were clamped shut again.

"Good?" said Mr. Hyatt. "Our breath is gunna be some-thing-rank. Want another?"

Mr. Hyatt's apartment was a shambles. Paul-François did his best to smother his astonishment.

"I knew youzid be coming, so I straightened the place upsome. Wannawatcha da toob? *D'Iberville* is on, *je crois.*"

PF took a deep breath and waded into the swamp of comatose clothing, banjos, recorders, music scores, magazines, guitars, grocery flyers, expired sneakers, lapsed socks, and climbed out onto the high ground of a worn armchair located immediately in front of a TV filled with murky green water. He turned the set on.

"The reception's not great, I'm afraid."

Mr. Hyatt busied himself in the bathroom, leaving the door open so he could maintain verbal contact.

"It's not *D'Iberville*," said PF. "*D'Iberville* is Saturday. Sunday it's *Shell's Wonderful World of Golf*."

"Right. You play golf?"

"I am playing, yes."

"Any good?"

"Yeah not bad."

After a time Mr. Hyatt, still in the bathroom, said, "You know, Paul-François, when you sang 'Silent Night' at the midnight carol service, just you, no choir, no organ? Hey, you blew 'em away. You knocked 'em dead, kid. Dead. I won't tell you that Sandra B. said it was the most gorgeousest thing she'd ever heard, because it would just go to your head."

PF did not answer.

"You wouldn't mind," said Mr. Hyatt, "singing me a few bars while I shave?"

PF remained silent. For many moments.

And then it was as if the apartment could not prevent itself, if not from levitating, at least from standing up. It was as if the airspace were set in motion by the mild but concentrated propulsion of Paul-François' treble voice, so that even the newspapers sleeping on the floor revived, listened, and were blown away.

Mr. Hyatt placed a stool beside PF's armchair and sat down. His face was flushed, his shaved chin was gleaming, he exuded a haze of Sunday cologne. "Thank you," he said, "that was lovely." The television screen danced with sunlight and shadow, long fairways and deep skies. "And thanks, I mean, for, for . . . ah, what am I trying to say? I've had a number of choirs. None of them very good, really. We've had fun, lots, sure, me and my choirs, made good friends

. . . But Christmas was really very special this year. We even did an excerpt eh, one, from Handel's *Messiah*. Yeah." He watched for a moment. "So Christmas was great. Thanks to you. Who's that guy?"

"Frank Beard. Leading money winner last year."

"Good swing?"

"Yeah not bad. The other guy is Dan Sikes."

"I come from a practical family, Paul-François."

"Dan Sikes has a diploam in *droit*."

"A diplom*a*, a degree, in law. Does he? . . . a practical family. We practically had to declare bankruptcy. We practically won the lottery, several times, if having all the right numbers but one constitutes practically winning. My dad practically bought a cottage on Lake Massawippi. He practically totalled the station wagon once. With me in it. I was fine, but he put a dent in his back forever, which gave him a good reason from then on to do practically nothing. They must be playing in New Orleans, are they?"

A man was painting convoluted eyebrows onto a giant *papier mâché* head for a Mardi Gras float.

PF nodded. "The New Orleans Cunnry Club."

"Mmn. I've done okay, Paul-François. Really. I've spent my time failing. I don't mean failing to succeed, although I've done some of that too. I mean failing to fail. The very definition of mediocrity." He stared at the screen and was silent for a time, after which he said, "I'll let you watch."

"No, no, no," said Paul-François, "it's not nessis-airy. I can watch golf each Sunday." He got up quickly and turned off the set, looking around for some object to use as a source of distraction. He was marvelling at how the cluttered life of the apartment was relegated entirely to the floor, there being no decoration on the walls of any sort, no shelves or bookcases, and no furniture, apart from the TV, the sofa, and a legless couch that might well have been a bed, when his eye was caught by a partially buried head, a bald head, over which was combed a shiny, black strip of hair reminiscent of a warped phonograph record. His heart leapt. Hasty excavation uncovered a studio portrait in a black plastic frame. Two words were moulded into the frame in a florid script: "Best Friend."

"So he is your best friend, Mr. Hyatt? The Chrisco Kidd?"

"Eh? Who? Oh that. That's just, I mean I had to put the picture in something didn't I and that was the only frame I could find, I don't remember who gave it to me originally, it had a picture of a giraffe in it." The high points of his cheeks and the rims of his ears had become quite red. "Give it here." PF handed the picture to Mr. Hyatt, who opened the back and slid out the photo of the Reverend Christopher Kidd, which he let fall negligently to the floor. He reclosed the frame and handed it back to Paul-François. It now contained a close-up of a giraffe with gracefully curved eyelashes and a facial expression suggesting the giraffe had been feeding on acacia leaves marinated in the best barbiturates.

"Watch your golf, Paul-François," said Mr. Hyatt with a vague, muted surliness that indicated this was not what he wanted at all.

"No, no," said PF, unsettled by the choir director's moodiness, by his blatant need to be entertained coupled with his unwillingness to allow himself to be so. PF had never before been with Mr. Hyatt in a context entirely removed from that of the choir. He was unnerved, a little desperate, his face was hot, he adopted a reckless, almost goofy tone, as though Mr. Hyatt were barely older than he was. "Stokey Leggatt is weird," he said. "He tol' me Reverend Kidd is not wearing *no*thing under his cassock."

The words exploded inside the head of *inspecteur-chef* PF. He sat bolt upright in his blue LeSabre and was astonished to discover that the car was no longer advancing along the Eastern Townships Auto-route, not moving at all. The impossibility of this filled him with a fear so concentrated and scalding that for the briefest instant he could only believe that he had died. Until he realized that the car was in fact parked on the shoulder beside the highway. He slumped with relief against the steering wheel.

He did recall pulling over. Certainly he did. But on another trip surely, under different circumstances, when the weather had been less glorious.

Not in years had he thought about Daniel Hyatt.

Not in years, and yet his memories were strikingly, overwhelmingly vivid. It was not so much that he had remembered saying, "Reverend Kidd is not wearing nothing under his cassock," as he had said it again for the first time, his English still poor, Frank Beard and Dan Sikes still on the course at the New Orleans Country Club, Stokey Leggatt still salacious, and Daniel Hyatt, although technically younger than PF now, still exuding a haze of adult cologne.

Not in years.

Rarely, probably never in his lifetime, had he said anything so stupid.

To be fair: at the time, that is to say when he was . . . twelve? thirteen? he had assumed, had gotten it into his head, that girls, like boys, peed forward, and therefore — Stokey's drawings notwithstanding — that the vagina was located more or less in front of the thighs rather than between them. He thought that this should have obviated the need for the legs to be spread during "innercourse," as he then apprehended the word. Nevertheless, a not inconsiderable amount of obscenity, French and English, had seemed to insist on just this requirement, that the legs be spread.

To be fair, given the nature of his education and the tenor of the times, and given that he wasn't as yet completely clear even on how the sex act was performed with a girl, PF had been far, far from capable of assimilating, or even conceiving of, such a notion as homosexuality.

But why, why, when all he wanted to do was get back to Montreal as quickly as possible and be with Sandra, why was he assailed by this onslaught of memory?

He watched with an unformed envy the steady procession of cars streaming by along the autoroute, as though he were a rejected item from a production line. He remembered again Sandra's stringy, leek-white thighs closing and opening according to the musical requirements of her feet, breathtaking shadows appearing under her puffy grey underwear. And again, as though for the first time, he was invaded by a stifling admiration, a sense of austere privilege. It occurred to him then that his conniving memory's true intention was not to torment him with his own distant past but, in an oblique way, to soothe him with the recollection of Sandra's cancer. Because she was fine, after all, she was. It was more than twenty years now since the operation to amputate her foot, more than twenty years during which their daughter Josée had managed to get born, grow up, travel to Adolescentland and back, and end up a perfectly autonomous adult. The operation had been completely successful. Although the heel had not been saved. But Sandra, being Sandra, had rejected all thought of a prosthesis, had proclaimed herself fiercely an anticripple, had become a virtuoso in the art of using crutches, and had learned to cross her legs with intoxicating nonchalance so that her long, wraparound skirt fell open and her interlocutor, man or woman, was faced with her stern, unabashed knee, and the fragile defiance of her elegantly tapered stump.

He could feel Mont Rougemont staring at his back, but resisted the temptation to turn around. He would be soothed then, if that was what his memory wanted. He sat up, gripped the key in the ignition, looked back over his left shoulder to check the oncoming traffic.

Never, he thought, definitely, never, had he ever said *any*thing. So stupid.

The choir was practising William Byrd's canon. PF's voice, airworthy, windtight, was gliding under the rehearsal room ceiling, ". . . *Domine, non nobis, sed nomini* . . .," and was about to soar up to ". . . *tuo da* . . .," when it crumpled, as though shot in the wing, and fell to the floor where it did not flutter. No, it hissed and coiled, before slithering away.

Generous, vengeful laughter.

The voice was changing, mutating, learning to crawl.

By Easter PF was out of the choir.

Once she had her son back, his relieved mother could vaunt the benefits of his choir experience to all her friends.

She was not, however, the only one who was relieved. The truth was that PF had had enough of the choir, despite, or perhaps because of, his initial infatuation.

Certainly he was glad to be out of the clutches of Stokey Legatt.

And something had changed after the Sunday afternoon he had spent watching golf on television in Mr. Hyatt's apartment. The choir director had become distant, his enthusiasm had flagged. Rehearsals started late, finished early, and were devoted as much to nattering as to singing. PF found the endless English conversation impenetrable, exhausting. He was tormented with the idea that Mr. Hyatt did not really like him anymore.

And although she still played the organ on Sunday, Sandra Beck no longer came to rehearsals. She was busy, and there was not the same need as during the Christmas season. PF, who had repeated out loud in front of the mirror dozens of times, "I just wanted to say that when you play the organ it's the most georgeousest thing I've ever heard," never got the chance even to have to find the courage to actually say it.

So that it was easier to side-step his disappointment by simply dropping out.

Which did not prevent him, after school or on Saturday afternoon, from taking the *rue Wellington sud* bus out to Lennoxville, getting off near Saint Peter's Church, and exploring on foot.

The streets looked very different without snow, the trees in leaf. PF was never completely certain which house was Sandra's.

Sometimes he sat in the cemetery behind the church and ate the May West he had bought at the bus depot. The fir trees were very dark, very still and superb, each one trying to pretend the others didn't exist.

There were some very old gravestones in the cemetery. None bearing the name Beck. The Hyatt family, on the other hand, had their own weathered monument, a hundred years old, overseen by a painted wooden statue of Jesus on the cross. On his left side, under his ribs, Jesus had a vertical mouth with a pair of thin, grey lips, drooling drops of blood. His eyes were gloomy and bloodshot. He was so close to being life-sized that he looked like a short, sinewy pirate, a castaway, no taller than a cabin boy.

In time, however, PF gave up on these trips as well.

October, Friday, late in the afternoon. PF's shadow was so long that its head watched him from the other side of the street as he stood waiting for his bus. The May West he had bought was in the pocket of his windbreaker. Why after so many months he had decided suddenly to go out to Lennoxville he did not know. He hadn't eaten a May West in ages.

When he arrived he was startled to discover that a fire truck was parked outside Saint Peter's Church. The red light on top of the cab was flashing with desperate, almost frenzied insistence. And yet the firemen themselves, grey-haired, pot-bellied, were leaning nonchalantly against the fenders or sitting on the running boards, their black-and-yellow coats undone, their boots sagging.

A knot of people had gathered. One or two were sitting in folding chairs. They had the look of early arrivals at a high school track meet.

Spotlights were being installed on the church lawn. The instant they were turned on, the church burst into flame, orange and cold. The fire truck's red light flashed more frantically still, the firemen remained unconcerned.

A sudden flight of pigeons from the church roof drew PF's attention upward. He gasped. There was a man on the roof, squatting on the ridge. A man he almost thought he recognized.

"Excuse me," he said to one of the onlookers, "who is he, that guy up there?"

"That," answered the man very soberly, "is Reverend Kidd."

"Why he's up there?"

The man paused for a considerable moment before answering, more soberly still, "He seems to have gone . . . a little mad."

"A little mad at who?"

The man smiled imperceptibly.

"At God."

The flock of pigeons described a long arc against the deepening eastern sky and settled on the other end of the church. Reverend

Kidd scrabbled back along the ridge of the highly pitched roof, howling, gesticulating at the birds.

"I'm terrified," said a woman, "he's going to kill himself."

"Yeah, well his chances are pretty good of doing just that," said the man, the gravity of his manner attenuated by an amiable prosaicness.

Paul-François was horrified to the point of nausea. He was utterly unable to comprehend why, or even how, the Chrisco Kidd had climbed onto the roof, why the firemen were not helping him get down, why the people were not yelling at the firemen to help him get down. He felt as though he were watching a television documentary about the fascinating behaviour of the adult human in its natural habitat. He wished Mr. Hyatt were there watching with him.

A car arrived. A corpulent woman with aluminum hair got out and strode up to the firemen with a determined forward lean that carried considerable authority. A brief caucus was held as the firemen hastily did up their coats. The woman then approached the church, cupped her hands to her mouth, and called up to the Chrisco Kidd. It was darker now and the spotlights, while they illuminated the church until its walls appeared swollen and spongy, actually threw much of the roof into greater obscurity. The Chrisco Kidd was all but invisible as he answered the woman in a voice that was thin, haunting, and unintelligible.

The woman returned. "He wants a hundred balloons," she said. "He'll come down if we bring him a hundred balloons. And string."

Reaction to this ranged from strained incomprehension to hilarious disdain.

"Ask him if he'd like crayons too, and coloured paper."

"Where's Hyatt? Why doesn't Hyatt talk to him?"

"Hyatt is why he's up there."

"Yes I realize that, but . . ."

"Can somebody get a portable spotlight so we can see him properly?"

". . . can't Hyatt at least talk to him?"

"Listen. Hyatt has gone, left him, disappeared, miles away. *That* is why he's up there."

"Yes but . . . Christ, queers, eh? Queers. Just because you're a queer doesn't mean you don't know how to live, does it?"

Inspecteur-chef PF's left arm was draped over the steering wheel of his blue LeSabre so that he could, with his fingers, pull the gearshift lever up slightly, this being necessary in order for the key to turn in the ignition. His right hand was holding the key in the slot.

Not in years had he thought about Daniel Hyatt and Christopher Kidd. He was seized by the soothing vividness of his memories, was reliving them with such new intensity that he was not even aware how the story they were telling him ended. He dared not move for fear of interrupting the flow of reminiscence, of returning to his present life where the outcome of events was known ahead of time.

Reverend Kidd could still be seen on the ridge of the church roof, squatting in a puddle of white light, blowing up his balloons. The puddle, which was fed by the beam of a six-volt Rayovac flashlight, slid erratically over the church roof as the flashlight was passed from one spectator to another.

An undeniably festive atmosphere reigned. The froth of conversation rose and subsided. The corpulent, authoritative woman had given a short speech in which she'd said that Reverend Kidd had been a help to any number of Lennoxville citizens and that now it was their turn to help him. Period. They were to make him feel welcome — welcome — when he came down. Consequently, a communal generosity had gripped the townspeople, an altruism that was of necessity fervid and celebratory, in that it was founded in their muffled repugnance for the reverend's homosexuality. There was folk singing, hand clapping. New arrivals brought food, sandwiches, eggs, and potato salad. PF was offered, and accepted, beer. The taste in his throat was loud and daring.

Silence, suddenly. The reverend was straightening. He was upright, on his knees, massaging his lower back, surrounded by his balloons.

The spectators were fascinated, utterly still. The maraschino red light of the fire truck streaked rhythmically across the stone wall.

He inched his way forward, the reverend did, bent over, manoeuvring in front of him, with considerable difficulty, an irregular object. He had tied the balloons to this object, which was not small, and which must have been on the roof the entire time. But if it had been seen, as it certainly had, the object had not really been observed, distinguished as being something other than an adjunct to the roof itself. So that a whisper of intrigued curiosity skated among the onlookers.

The reverend struggled to the front of the church where, bracing himself against the lightening rod, he got to his feet. He gathered himself, breathing heavily.

And then he raised the object, held it in his outstretched arms. The applause at first was light, uncertain.

The object in question was the wooden statue of Jesus, sawed from the cross of the Hyatt family monument in the cemetery. The balloons had been tied with long pieces of string around the waist and upper body, making Jesus look, without the cross behind him, like a short, sinewy paratrooper on a holiday jump, wearing an outdated, baggy swimsuit.

The applause, while it would have liked to bolster the morale of the disconsolate minister, was not sure it could condone the defacing of an historically valuable cemetery monument. It remained sparse, hesitant, while the statue, from its position of ascendancy, regarded the townspeople with impenetrable calm. And then, revealing its innate sense of the moment, the statue acknowledged the timid applause, indicated its appreciation, brightened for an instant, became more radiant. And the applause, having a wide streak of vanity as applause always does, warmed in response, fed on its own enthusiasm until it was completely won over, confident and loud. It surged with anticipation when the Chrisco Kidd drew the statue in close to his chest, and thundered its approval when he launched the statue into the air.

Paul-François watched the statue lurch and bob before steadying itself, suspended in the flashlight beam under the barely visible canopy of balloons. He did not applaud. It was late, cold, dark, the beer was eating into the lining of his stomach, his bladder was full. He should have gotten on a bus back to Sherbrooke ages ago. He felt an impulse to cry. He was in no danger of doing so, but he would have liked to. To cry. His exaggerated admiration for the Chrisco Kidd had evaporated. Not because he felt that it had been misplaced. He simply realized that the Reverend Kidd lived in a universe he knew nothing about. Nothing. Any more than, despite having called himself the Chrisco Kidd's henchman, he actually knew what a henchman was. Or despite having been watching now for several hours, he really knew what was going on. He knew nothing. His admiration was meaningless, juvenile, empty.

And yet, if he could not tear himself away, it was because he still felt bound to the reverend by a mysterious apprehension, a nameless uneasiness that scurried up his spine and set him on edge. He had the strange and exasperating impression that the townspeople, in their adult way, were just as awkward and unaware of what was happening as he was. Of course there was nothing he could say. He would not be listened to for one and, for two, there was no possibility, none, of his being able to find the words.

And so he watched the statue as it dropped earthward. Its descent was graceful, brief. But even before the statue touched down, the companion applause began to disintegrate, not of its own accord, but because it was being undermined, infiltrated by a second sound. This second sound grew with terrifying rapidness until it was all that could be heard. It was little more than a murmur, a distant hiss, little more than silence itself, and yet its impression on the ears was so intense as to be almost painful. So intense it made PF's temples pound. He wanted to scream, was even on the point of doing so, he would have, certainly, had not an adult beat him to it.

"Call an ambulance!" screamed the adult. "Somebody! Christ oh Christ, call a fucking ambulance!"

Inspecteur-chef PF's arm was draped over the steering wheel. He gripped the key in the ignition slot. He was crying.

Paul-François was shivering, crying. He was standing in exactly the same place as he had been, although the entire gallery of spectators had left him now to form a compact mass at the front of the church. The siren of a distant ambulance could be heard. The siren would grow louder. He thought how strange it was that so many people along the way would wonder who the ambulance was for, where it was going, and that he knew and could have told them. Thirteen he was now, and a quarter. He was convinced that he had known the Chrisco Kidd was going to jump. From the very first moment he had seen the reverend on the church roof, he had known. He should have said something to the adults. If only he had. If only. But there had been no possibility, none, of his finding the words. Not even to tell himself.

He realized suddenly that he was not alone. There was a presence close to him. This presence he resented the instant he became aware of it. He refused to look.

And yet the presence loomed, dark, breathing, and tentacular. It was impossible not to look, impossible. His head whipped around.

Sandra Beck, too, was crying. A clear drop of mucus clung to the bottom of her red nose. She was not ten feet away, not looking at PF. She was observing the maraschino red light streak across the church wall. PF did not know how long she had been there, but he was sure from her manner that she had been standing close to him, watching him, almost from the outset. He wanted to be snide, sarcastic. It set his nerves on edge that she refused to look at him now that she had let herself be discovered, that she still did not say anything, that she was crying harder than he was, that she had so many projects, that her un-enormous chest seemed to contain so much life.

She cupped her hand over her mouth.

But he had no idea how to be snide and sarcastic with girls. What was more, he hadn't spoken English in months. He squirmed under the incontrovertible necessity of being the first to say something, of finding words that were foreign and artificial.

No, he would not be the first to speak. He would just keep his mouth shut.

He was deciding this even as the words themselves were searing their way up his throat and erupting through the vent of his mouth.

"Fuck off," he hissed, without the trace of an accent.

Sandra ducked as if she had been startled by an insect flying close to her ear. And then she ran.

"And that, Pauline," said *inspecteur-chef* PF, addressing the ignition key which he was holding but still had not turned, "is how Sandra and I first met."

He sat back in his seat, wiped his eyes with the pads of his fingers, ran his hands through the corrugated side panels of his hair.

Not in years had he thought about that October evening. He had almost succeeded in convincing himself he had forgotten.

But did he not, to this day, when he ate a cheeseburger, pull it apart to check the machined disk of raw onion, whether there was one or not?

Lax he felt, indolent, inclined to sleep. Proud. Proud of his memory.

You don't forget, he thought. Nothing is lost. There are all kinds of things you don't remember. Some of which you're a lot better off not remembering. But you don't, you can't forget.

His memory had been protecting him, that was all. Overprotecting perhaps.

Proud he was. Of himself. To be able to review with relative level-headedness the events of that October evening gave him an impression of having progressed in life, grown. Not unlike, he imagined, the feeling that Sandra talked about when she discovered that a piece of music she had not played in a long time, and that had always been a struggle to get through, had suddenly become perfectly playable for her. Chopin, say, a Ballade.

Certainly he was no stranger now to homosexuality; in that area he had definitely progressed. He had even interviewed Montreal's first openly gay police officer on *C'est la loi/It's the Law*. The first one willing to be interviewed, in any case. There were tons of gays on the force now. Well, not tons. He couldn't remember the officer's name. His memory was overprotecting him again. It had been an

unsettling interview. First, because Leblanc had startled him by
— Leblanc, yeah, that was the guy's name, Valmont Leblanc, see?
nothing is lost — by saying that he thought it was not necessarily
appropriate for him, as a gay officer, to work in the gay community.
"Oh no?" a surprised PF had said. "I would have thought you'd
have a greater understanding of how gays might respond to police
authority." Yes, but there was the danger of his overcompensating,
of his being overzealous, the danger of his being influenced, despite
himself, by his emotions. PF, far from convinced, had adopted a tone
of sly sarcasm: "So it wouldn't be appropriate — necessarily — for
*hetero*sexuals to work in the *straight* community, I suppose?" Leblanc,
impervious to the sarcasm, had answered that he thought that that
was exactly right. "*Ohh!* Which, taken to its logical conclusion,
would mean that homosexuals, according to you, would, society
taken as a whole, actually make better cops. *Bet*ter cops? Is that
what you're saying?" And Leblanc: "Quite possibly, more caring, less
headstrong." And second, because Leblanc had been in such perfect
command of himself, had talked about his homosexuality with such
directness and even humour, had, in short, been so completely at
ease in PF's company that PF had been forced to accept that he,
Leblanc, had not found him, PF, even mildly attractive. Sexually,
sexually attractive. Despite PF's having already been voted to the
list of *"les dix hommes plus 'hots' de la télé québequoise"* in a poll
conducted by *TV Hebdo*.

"You realize, Officer Leblanc," said *inspecteur-chef* PF, addressing
the ignition key, "that you were talking to one of the ten sexiest men
on Quebec TV?"

"Maybe I'm the kind," answered the key, "who protects himself
by hiding his sexual curiosity behind a screen of chatty, unassailable
bonhomie. Did you ever think of that?"

"Oh. So you mean, you did find me, you know, attractive. Sexually."

"No."

Yes. He had progressed in life. The proof being that while all he wanted was to get home, to be with Sandra, to drive steadily and as fast as possible, to lurch up the driveway, slam the shifter into park, and burst into the house like a glob of mustard dropped into a crystal goblet of immaculate ice water, his memory was slowing him down, presenting him with new points of view on the events of his life, suggesting he pull over and consider.

Marriages by and large, his memory was saying, are not big on surprises. At least not surprises that are unexpected. Marriages don't feel it's necessary, by and large, for you to arrive ahead of the time you've said you will arrive at. And when exactly *did* you say you would arrive?

PF wasn't sure. He didn't think he'd specified a time.

Ah, his memory was saying. How much do you think you know then about what's been going on lately in your wife's life, when you've not been around? What did you say her name was again?

"Sandra," said *inspecteur-chef* PF, turning the key in the ignition, "Sandra Beck. I'm ass-hauling, Sandra," hearing the motor catch, "m'awn my way, kid. I'll be there'n less'n'n hour." He checked the outside mirror, which must have gotten itself out of adjustment because what it reflected was uniformly greyish-green and had silver buttons. He was lowering his window, in fact, to adjust the mirror when a voice said:

"Inspecteur Bastarache? C'est bien vous?"

PF twisted around to discover a uniformed member of the Sûreté du Québec bending to look into his car like a congenial Irish setter looking into the hideout of a downed waterbird.

"Yes," he answered in French, "it's me."

"Everything all right?"

"Sure. Fine."

As the host of the popular television program *C'est la loi/It's the Law*, *inspecteur-chef* PF was not unaccustomed to being recognized. He had, in fact, no sooner set foot on the tarmac in Florida once when a workman driving a baggage train had called out his name and waved. So that he found nothing surprising in the officer's knowing who he was. At first. It occurred to him, however, that the officer had approached from behind and could not possibly have seen his face. A flash of alarm lit up his brain and subsided immediately. He turned off the engine.

"How the fuck did you know it was me? Have you been on my tail ever since I left Sherbrooke?"

"No, no, no. Not at all. The LeSabre, your car. I was going the other way, heading out to my cottage in Cowansville, when I saw what looked like your car pulled over and I wondered if you might, assuming it really was you I mean, if you might be . . . I mean, you don't see too many of these on the road anymore. *Mint* condition. Vinyl roof. What year is it? Eighty-two, eighty-three? You used to drive up in it at the start of *It's the Law*, and drive off at the end."

PF was willing to admit that his suspiciousness might have been exaggerated. Nevertheless he did not like the look of this officer. Despite his admiration for the LeSabre.

"That's right, I did. They don't let me do that anymore. We're not even supposed to show police cars so you can recognize the make." He looked up and down the officer's silver buttons. "So when you're in the provincial police you get a uniform for going to the cottage in. Nice. You get a golf uniform too?"

"This *is* the golf uniform." The officer grinned. Briefly. "Actually, I was just in a hurry to get out there and didn't take the time . . ."

Pause.

"So everything's fine then?"

. Pause.

"The thing is, my father collects antique cars. You remember Rambler? American Motors? He's fixing up a '66 Ambassador, and he's told me a hundred times about how, before I was old enough to remember even, he had the exact, the *exact* same LeSabre as Inspector PF and it was his all-time favourite car, mostly because he drove it into a lake and almost drowned himself in it and he'd *love*, really, I mean if you're at *all* interested in selling, he's told me a hundred times . . ."

The officer broke off, having, as he did, the impression that his proposition was simply evaporating the instant it left his lips.

"Have you ever used crutches?" asked *inspecteur-chef* PF. "Did you know there's such a thing as a Canadian crutch?"

"A Canadian crutch. Really. No, I don't think I did."

"A Canadian crutch is the kind that's relatively short, made out of metal and you slide your forearm into. My wife has one, several actually, different colours to go with different outfits. But she likes her ancient, wooden, crutches best. Signed by me of course, most of her other lovers too I imagine, along with every single member of the Montreal Symphony Orchestra. On a good, flat surface, she can walk faster with crutches than you or I can without."

"Can she? She must have been using them," said the officer, who, being in the process of lowering himself until he was almost sitting on his heels, had not heard everything the inspector had said, "for quite some time then."

"Oh yeah," said PF, "what, twenty years? More than that even."

The officer made as if to rest his forearms on the car door, reconsidered, stuffed his hands instead between his knees, staggering slightly to maintain his balance. "What did she . . . ?" he said, letting his voice tail off negligently, allowing PF to ignore the question if he so desired.

"What did she what?" said PF pointedly. "Have for breakfast?" He grinned at the ham-handed humour of his remark. "What she *had* was, she had osteosarcoma." He pronounced the word with exaggerated precision. "Know what that is?"

"Sarcoma sounds to me like cancer."

"Hey, give the man a prize. Osteo—? No? Bone, having to do with bone. So she had bone cancer. In her foot."

"Fuck. She was awfully young, wasn't she, to be having cancer?"

"Not bone cancer. She was relatively old, in fact. Young people whose bones are still growing are the ones who generally get bone cancer, unfortunately. Not usually in the foot, mind you. You've got a bunch of little bones in your foot, twenty-six in all I think it is. The largest one is the heel bone, the calinous."

PF abruptly opened the door of his blue LeSabre, requiring the provincial police officer to straighten quickly and move out of the way. "You've got two bumps on either side of your ankle, right?" He placed his left foot on the door tread, pulled up his dress uniform pant leg, and lowered his thin black sock. "These bumps here?"

"Yeah," said the officer who, having circumvented the door, bent down to observe PF's bare ankle, as white as boiled chicken.

"They're caused by the knobs at the ends of your leg bones, the tibia on the inside, the fibula on the outside. Between those two bones and the calinous, you've got another small bone called the talus. That's where she had the sarcoma."

"Shit. So, did she have to have, like, chemo?"

"She did, she did indeed. By the truck-fucking-load. After they'd amputated her foot. There was some talk of saving the heel but that was just wishful thinking. Today they might be able to, they've made progress."

"Fuck."

"Yeah, fuck."

"Couldn't she get, you know, an artificial something?"

"She could, yes. I think she will, in fact, one day. She's beginning to be less, what's the word, headstrong? But she likes the crutches, she can get around fine on them. She can drive with just one foot. Automatic, obviously."

Pause.

"The day they amputated her foot, that was one strange fucking day."

Pause.

"One fucking strange fucking day. I was still in homicide at the time. I got the fuck out of there. Strange day. I had to interrogate a whale."

"A what?" The officer snorted inwardy.

Inspecteur-chef PF did not immediately answer. He was disconcerted by the confidentiality of his manner and the laxness of his language. Why was he speaking so openly to this individual, if he didn't think much of him?

Precisely, he thought, *because* I don't like him, I suppose. What do I care what the jerk-off gets to hear about me? God knows in the provincial police you're allowed five unmotivated absences a week if you can furnish proof of ownership of a cottage in Cowansville. He snorted inwardly. How often, I wonder, do we pick as friends, as confidants, people for whom, basically, we have no great respect?

Nevertheless, he did regret the word "whale." Certainly the woman he had interrogated the day of Sandra's operation had been, if not obese, at least very fat. No, obese. And had he not been disconcertingly confidential during the course of that strange day as well? Yes, he had. And did that indicate a lack of respect on his part for the woman? No, he didn't think so. No, he thought that "whale" had been meant for the officer's ears only, to put him off the scent, yes, definitely, because confidentiality was one thing but under no circumstances did he want to hear himself telling the truth, not to this or any other officer for that matter, the truth being that even now the memory of the obese woman's voice was making his mouth dry and causing his sleeping testicles to wake and shift position.

"That's right," said the officer, "you *were* in homicide." He seemed to want to keep PF talking, hoping they might still get around to the LeSabre, "There's a story . . ."

"Story?" said PF. He knew perfectly well to which story the officer was referring. But he was mildly aroused now, more than mildly, his imagination was stirring the lapping, hypnotic murmur of the obese woman's voice into the intoxicating scent of Sandra's stump which, despite the potent, floral perfumes of any number of staggeringly expensive hydrating creams, still managed to smell of itself: dry, sullen, wanting to be touched, resenting its own desire to be touched. He was running the inside of his index finger over the almost invisible lip of flesh at the base of the stump, thinking it resembled the slim, belligerent mouth of an eyeless snout. His gaze was moving along the stump, over Sandra's knee and up to where her leg disappeared at last behind the sober and strapless formal gown that gave her the form of a white mermaid. She was dancing to the fluent stylings of the Marty Payne Orchestra, barely moving, anchored to her white, Canadian crutches. But dancing nonetheless, moving her shoulders with an undeniable rhythmic flair, her eyelids heavy, her lips pursed into an absorbed expression, as though she herself were part of the orchestra. The Saint Patrick

Society Ball. Sandra qualified for membership in the society thanks to her great-great-Irish-grandmother. Interestingly, PF as well had a great-great-grandmother who had been Irish, a fact he had never bothered to mention. He was not, however, the one dancing with Sandra. There were three men in her immediate vicinity, dancing, if attempting to wiggle out of a barely flexible, invisible tube can be said to be dancing. Their three female counterparts were also in the vicinity, true, but the overall impression was that the men were trying to be with Sandra, and the women with themselves.

PF felt his body expand to fill the tuxedo he had rented for the occasion from A. Gold & Sons. He was in a state of advanced elation, at his best when wearing a uniform of some kind. He knew this, and he knew why: because only then did he feel he had a clear idea of how he was perceived by others. Still, the tuxedo was only a small part of his elation. As was the fact that he knew what no one else knew, namely that Sandra herself had made the gown she was wearing, that its realization had been the source not only of considerable howling and bad language, but also of silent tears and desperation, that the finished product had clung to her body briefly, courageously, before losing its meagre grip and dropping stiffly around her feet . . . foot. That if she was barely moving now as she danced, it was not so much due to her being anchored to the crutches as it was to the danger of putting too much strain on the long, disguised seam of straight pins — inserted at the last minute by the Hungarian cleaning lady — that assured the gown's perfect fit.

He hitched up his right eyebrow like a hussar on leave and sauntered handsomely over to the temporary bar.

"Whisky."

"Scotch?"

He straightened with surprise. "Aren't they the same thing?"

"Yeess, but there are other kinds of whisky. Irish whisky, Canadian whisky, American, usually called bourbon, . . ."

"There's such a thing as Canadian whisky? Really. I don't think I knew that."

In such a good mood he was, it was almost a pleasure to be shown up by a temporary bartender unable to hide the sparkle of English condescension in his eye.

He accepted a glass of rye, found it excellent, basked in the golden estrangement of the elated.

"Sergeant Bastarachay."

"Yeah."

"My name is George Gonzalez."

"Good to meet you, George." They shook hands. "Tell me, what part of Ireland do the Gonzalezes come from?"

"Ireland? Why? I am from Venezuela."

"Right." In such a mood, it was a distinct pleasure to have a clever remark fall harmlessly on its face. "How'd you know it was me, George?"

"I have seen you before. At the Montreal General. I was the anaesthetist at your wife's operation."

"Oh, well, thank you, thank you. Great job, great. This is kind of her coming out, her first public appearance. *Public*, public appearance. To be honest, I'm kind of happy myself, kind of floating in thin air, if you really want to know. I wasn't sure we'd ever get here."

"I knew you would be here. Sandra told me."

"Sandra told you." PF wouldn't have thought that anaesthetists would keep in touch with their clients necessarily, assuming "clients" was the right word. However, the earnestness of Gonzalez's manner ruled out, theoretically, any hint of suspicion as lacking in generosity. "Why don't you go over and say hello?" he said. "Dance with her. If you can find some room."

"I have come here to talk to you."

"To me."

Gonzalez stood utterly still for a long moment, watching, apparently, the core of the universe as it grew more distant. PF observed the show-rodent quality of his stiff and short black hair, the smoothness of his cheeks, almost without beard and the colour of buttered cloves. He knew that this was a man that Sandra could find irresistibly attractive.

"I did not," said Gonzalez at last, softly, distinctly, "as you say, do a great job." He was forcing himself to look at PF, staring at a point just beside the inspector's nose. "During the operation, your wife's heart stopped pumping blood. It was twitching, trembling, instead of beating regularly. This is a very dangerous situation. In minutes, she would die."

PF stepped back. He had taken a paramedic course in California several years before, had even saved the life of a rubber dummy in a state of cardiac arrhythmia by using an unplugged defibrillator.

"I got scared," went on Gonzalez. "I passed out."

The core of the universe stopped abruptly, turned, and listened in.

"Fortunately her heart was what we call defibrillated successfully. It started beating steadily again. And I was given an injection of adrenaline. Everything went fine after that."

The core of the universe, disappointed perhaps, resumed its course.

"I let myself be influenced by my emotions."

"Emotions," repeated PF. He had the impression of hearing a recording of his voice.

"Yes. The thought of this woman, so young still, so . . . , losing a foot . . ."

They were silent.

"Worse things can happen," said PF at last, his voice dry, sandy, barely audible.

"Yes, yes, clearly, certainly. I appreciate that, yes, and I appreciate that you listen. It is very important to me that you listen. That I tell you. *You*, Sergeant Bastara*chay*, the man she loves. You are my patron now. You will always be watching me. Not you personally. But you. Do you understand? It must never happen again."

Again they were silent.

"It won't happen again," said PF, surprised somewhat by his own charitableness. The tuxedo, no doubt. "I'm glad you told me, George."

Gonzalez pursed his lips in gratitude. And then he took his leave progressively, backing up a short distance, almost bowing, turning, striding off, his confidence reasserting itself with each step.

PF still felt very much as though he were floating in thin air. His elation, however, had disappeared utterly. He turned his back to the ballroom, closed his eyes to steady himself. He had no impression whatsoever of falling, and yet he could see a surface far below rising to meet him, not quickly, but steadily, and seeming to gain speed. He opened his eyes, intrigued, waited a moment, and closed them again. Already the surface was much closer. But how much closer? He opened his eyes. His scalp tingled with curiosity and misgiving. The surface was entirely without distinguishing features, a sea of flat, dense cloud. And yet he had the distinct impression of having seen it before. Somewhere. Again he closed his eyes. The surface was huge, everywhere, screaming upwards at tremendous speed, breaking over him in the same terrifying instant he forced his lids open.

His breathless heart fluttered in his chest like a pinned moth. A new apprehension seized him. He looked down at his feet, not knowing whether it was the left or the right. But no, it was Sandra it had happened to. Sandra. His relief was immeasurable, it broke over him like a sea of flat, dense cloud.

He realized then that the temporary bartender was looking at him, holding his hands clasped in front of his genitals in an attitude of majestic servility.

The door of his blue LeSabre was wide open. He could see the officer's mouth moving, but he could not hear what he was saying. It was as though he, the officer, were talking inside a barely flexible, invisible tube.

"I talked to George, tonight," said PF. "Or he talked to me."

"George?"

"Your anaesthetist."

"Oh. Hor-hay, you mean. He's from Venezuela. He pronounces his name Hor-hay."

"He introduced himself to me as George."

"That may be. But his name is Hor-hay. J, o, r, j, e."

"Georgeay."

"*Hor*-hay."

He remembered the show-rodent quality of Gonzalez's stiff and short black hair, the smoothness of his cheeks, almost without beard and the colour of buttered cloves.

"He said his name was George, so I suppose I should call him George."

"Call him what you like. But his name is Hor-hay. His colleagues all call him Hor-hay. *I* call him Hor-hay."

"And he calls you Sandra."

"Which happens to be my name."

He let his voice drop to a murmur of capitulation. "I guess I could always call him Horses-hassay."

He shifted his weight in the familiar velour seat of his blue

LeSabre. "Sorry," he said, the loudness of his voice startling him, "what did you say?"

"I said there's a story about you when you were in homicide."

"That much I got. What did you say after that?"

"Nothing," said the officer defensively, giving the impression that he *had* been thinking, thinking perhaps that *inspecteur-chef* Bastarache was the police version of the minimally talented pro athlete who manages to make it big as a mouthy TV commentator.

"No," said PF, "I don't know what story you could mean, really."

He wasn't jealous of George the anaesthetist. Or if he was, that jealousy at least was understandable, admissible, Georgeay having been present, after all, when the surgeon had entered the very flesh and bone, the blood vessels and nerve fibres of Sandra Beck. PF couldn't match that. But what man would not bow his head and drop to one knee as his wife and her surgeon, arm in arm, strode past him into the theatre of amputations, she wearing nothing much under her sky blue hospitalwear, he wearing nothing but Yves Saint-Laurent under his. And when the wife emerged at last, bruised, maimed, fucked forever by the bistoury, what man would not still shake the surgeon's hand, knowing he had at least given generously for the pound, the pounds, of flesh he had excised? Given in time. A lifetime, perhaps.

"Do you know what's strange?" he said, more to himself than to the officer. "Even after all these years, if you were to ask me if it was the left foot or the right that my wife had amputated, I would be hard put to give you an answer."

"You're kidding."

"No, I'm not."

Yes, and what was the surgeon's name again? McGillicuddy the Knife was it? Jacques Couteau? You see? It wasn't the surgeon's name that popped up in the conversation, it was Horhay the anaesthetist's. Why? Because Horhay screwed up. And that, PF could match. He and Horhay were rivals in ineptness, in the need to apologize and be forgiven, unqualities right up Sandra's windmill.

"So everything's fine then," said the officer.

Horhay's ineptness, however, had almost cost Sandra her life, winning him a place in her heart forever.

"I'll let you get on your way. Great car."

PF watched the officer in his rear-view mirror as he got into his vehicle, watched him drive past and continue a short distance down the autoroute before lurching to his left and cutting over the wide median strip, bouncing and bucking his way to the other side.

He threw his door open suddenly and tumbled out in time to see the policeman come roaring back on his way to his cottage in Cowansville.

"Hey," he yelled, "I thought you wanted me to tell you the story!" He was running, chasing after the disappearing car. "The story!" he barked. "Don't you want to hear the fucking story? It all started with the fucking photographer . . ."

. . . the photographer, on what was a day, yes, I remember, a day dominated by sky, perfect sky. Perfectly distant, perfectly close, the very colour blue made manifest. Inviting, impenetrable. One of the simplest and most grandiose works of nature, no? A sky impossible not to admire, ignored only by those for whom it seemed especially intended. Children, I mean. I could hear them, although I couldn't see them. There must have been a school nearby, it must have been recess. And there I was, thirty-one? -two? with my little Cégep de Sherbrooke diploma in *techniques policières*, my B.Sc. in criminology from the Université d'Ottawa, my fifty or so months as a member of the Montreal Urban Community police force including my two twelve-week *stages* in California, internships I think they called them there, *Agent* Bastarache, Paul-François, working my first homicide, not my first first maybe, but my first juicy. Posted I was on the porch outside the door of the residence, a sexplex? six apartments in any case, two on each level, rue Alma, secteur Petite-Patrie, the sexplex on the floor of the third floor of which the victim was lying. No one, for the moment, was to go up or anywhere near. Which was my job. I was not in uniform. There were no flashing lights or marked vehicles anywhere. Nothing to kindle the *frayeur*, the anxiety, the terror perhaps, of the local residents. I had not seen the victim, nor would I ever see her, except in the pictures the police photographer was now in the process of taking, pictures I would stare at for hours, hours. I was naming to myself the makes of the cars parked along the street, thinking idly that if they had had tails they might have been able to brush off the yellow leaves irritating their windshields. No, I cannot say I was unpleased with the progression of my life, and I was, as I say, admiring the sparkling and cloudless, the late September sky, the sound of children's voices percolating into my ears, when the photographer opened the door and came outside.

A galoot he was, as Sandra would have said, a big galoot wearing a white shirt that had come partly untucked and clung like a loosely wrapped sail to the capacious waistband of his pants. The sleeves were rolled up to the elbows, revealing thick, pig-pink forearms covered with white curls. He looked as though he would have had little difficulty lifting an entire tavern and dumping its unruly contents out onto the street. The long blade of his wide tie lay against his shirt like the giant minute-hand of a cardboard clock meant to teach children how to tell time. It pointed directly at six, at his genitals in other words, which, I could only presume, were nestled in there somewhere. His camera with its impressive lens looked like a toy, perched against his breastplate, just below his powerful head, which was certainly made of the same meaty material as his forearms. His eyes were closed and he was holding a cloth handkerchief over his mouth.

"Salut," I said, *"ça va bien?"* It was the sunlight, I think, that made me want to talk. "Hey, I wouldn't mind having your job," I said in French. "Tell me, are you a cop who turned into a photographer or a photographer who turned into a cop?" His only answer was to open his eyes, lower his head slightly, step down off the porch and stride through the leaves to the sidewalk. Only then did he remove the handkerchief from his mouth and stuff it into his pocket. He set off down the street, looking everywhere at once, like a Japanese tourist in old Montreal.

I wasn't miffed. I was thinking of the incontrovertibility of photographic evidence, not only with respect to serious but equally with respect to less consequential crime. That it was the endless administration of innumerable, almost trivial offences that drained the energy and sense of purpose of the agents of social shepherdship, as I think they used to call policemen in California. That, to take only one example, if motor vehicles could be fitted with properly adapted photographic equipment — a great deal of technical work would have to be done of course, but still, supposing — how much more efficiently and equitably traffic enforcement and collision reporting issues could be resolved. And I was thinking that this might be an area in which I might like to involve myself at some future date, that I should cultivate the photographer as an individual from whom I might be able to learn something. I remember not being able to keep myself from smiling when he came into view again, looking like Louis Cyr strapped to a pop-gun camera, his billowy shirt appearing in the sunlight to be itself a source of low-voltage illumination. He walked back through the leaves and up the porch steps. "Hey, I wouldn't mind having your job," he said, mimicking my intonation. "Have you seen what's upstairs yet? I didn't think so. I thought I was going to puke."

I would become all too familiar with this photographer's pictures. I would have enlargements tacked to my corkboard. For months.

"Yeah, so to answer your question, I was an officer for sixteen years in Montmagny." I guessed from his accent he was from Gaspésie, or New Brunswick maybe. "The woman I was with decided I wasn't fat enough for her so she left me for a guy even fatter. The last time she ever spoke to me was to ask me for her Pentax K1000. 'What Pentax K1000?' I said. I was being honest. I didn't even know the thing existed. I let her look, but she couldn't find it. I did though, one day. Hidden under the towels in the bathroom cupboard over the toilet. I thought my fingers would turn to stone when I touched it. I got the film developed at Pharmaprix. 'What gives?' I said, 'there's only four pictures here.' The girl looked at me, with her gloss lipstick, her shimmering earrings and her white, semi-transparent drugstore dress, right at me, not a trace of embarrassment, and said, 'This is not the place to have erotic photographs developed, sir. You have to take these to a professional.' Yeah. No need though. For the pro, I mean. The four that had been developed were enough to give me the general idea. So anyway, to make a short story long, I was spending half my life looking around to make sure she wasn't wherever it was I was, and the other half driving around in my car hoping to catch a glimpse of her. I had to get out of Montmagny. So I learned how to use the camera properly, took a couple of courses, and landed myself in Montreal. This is my Pentax LX. Fabulous camera, incredible light meter, overkill for police work, but I use it for my own stuff as well. I left the Vivitar upstairs. I use it a lot. You like taking pictures? It's dead easy, as long as you keep your shots in sharp focus. I use a tripod whenever I can. Strictly front lighting unless I want shadows to indicate the shapes of objects. I should have brought more black-and-white film, though. I didn't realize this was going to be . . ." He stopped, swallowed deliberately, and raked his throat loudly before resuming. "Colour is good for banged-up cars, but when it comes to mangled flesh, judges generally want black-and-white shots. Colour carries too much emotion. It can influence a jury's objectivity."

Did that mean, I wondered, that the September sky, in dead perfect focus but saturated with blue, would not have been admitted as evidence in a court of law? Likely not. My body, inside its firm outer shell, was as though shrinking, closing in on itself, developing its own heat. My lungs could only manage short, shallow breaths. I did not know why this was, exactly. I simply knew I did not want the photographer to go back inside. I wanted him to drown me in the technical details of his work, about which I knew nothing, and certainly not what a Vivitar was. Enthusiasm, the enthusiasm of others, has a drifting, nonsensical quality, like a full head of beer floating on thin air. Not that the photographer seemed to want to go back inside. He rattled on about colour-coded depths of field, about thyristors and hot feet, not particularly concerned if I was paying attention. Although I was. And then he just stopped, gazed straight ahead for a time, turned, and went back into the sexplex. The surrounding air rushed to fill the vacuum left by the departure of his substantial presence, making breathing that much more difficult. The school children must have gone back inside as well, I couldn't hear their voices any more. I was steeped in heat, alone, restless. I wanted rain and high wind now but the street was deserted, bright, stiflingly silent.

No. No, I was not alone. That was where I was wrong. I had been alone, and perfectly happy to be so, before the photographer came out. But I wasn't alone now. I had her with me. I couldn't see her but I could feel her behind me, moving to her left if I tried to peek around to the right, to her right if I went to the left. She was holding something, a picture. For the approval of the court, she was saying, I submit this black-and-white photograph of myself, duly labelled "Mangled Flesh." The temptation to wheel around and catch her before she had time to move was as overpowering as it was ridiculous. I wanted to race upstairs to the third floor, to see with my own eyes what it was the galoot was photographing, to observe Le Chien murmuring orders in his understated, methodical way. But she was there, behind me, barring my way. And still the sky, inviting, impenetrable, admired itself as though in its own mirror, far above my head, while beside me, a second human presence, dense and smelling of alcohol, simply appeared, coalesced in the autumn air, catching me unaware, so that I was reminded I had a job to do.

"*Vous voulez quelque chose?*" I said, with a gruffness meant principally to revive my own alertness. I realized then it was only the concierge who lived in one of the ground level apartments, a European immigrant, somewhere between the ages of forty and ninety. He didn't speak a recognizable version of French. "Can I help you with something?" I said in English, my tone a good deal more accommodating. And although he did smell of alcohol, he did not convey the impression of having been drinking. If anything he seemed overly sober. I could see his eyes flit and twitch, not in a quick, observant way, but as though they were unable to tolerate the brightness of any surface whatsoever. He said he couldn't stay in his apartment. He had been told to. But he couldn't. I had to strain to decipher his English, which was heavily accented and hardly better than his French. I said that was fine, he could stay on the porch as long as I was there, although he'd have to go back inside if I was called away. He wanted to know how long the victim had been dead. I said I didn't know. Hours? Days? I didn't know. It was, he said, impossible to live in a building where a person had been killed. Yes, I could understand that. He said he was old, they might come for him next, he could die at any time. He might lie dead for weeks. No, no, I said, you're young, young! I asked him which country in Europe he was from so he would think about something else. Poland. And when did he come to Canada? He shook his head vaguely. During the war. He elaborated somewhat, but I couldn't make out much of what he said. I asked him if he'd been back to Poland. No, never. Did he have Polish friends? No, no. Was there somewhere he could go where people spoke Polish? Churches or community centres? I had to repeat myself. No, he said, once he understood, he had no desire to speak Polish, hadn't done so in thirty years, had forgotten how. "I'm good only in English now." This remark, despite, or perhaps because of, the pride with which it was spoken, caused me to shudder in the warm sun. After that, I couldn't say anything. It seemed unfair, impolite to do so, to speak to a man who spoke no languages. The silence wrapped itself around us like bark, growing a new ring every second. My heart was racing. It was surely just as impolite not to speak. But then the concierge, of his own accord, opened the door to go back in, pausing briefly to ask, as a matter of courtesy, knowing I would refuse, if I wanted a drink.

I felt like I had failed a spot-check in human conduct, one in the unending series of such tests set me by the course of events. Wasn't the porch I was standing on gleaming? It was. Freshly painted with grey enamel? Yes, and closed at one end with a trellis over which climbed what must have been, in July, an impressive *clématite*. Why had I not had the presence of mind to compliment the concierge on how well he kept the building maintained?

I felt thwarted, uneasy. I was fairly sure I would have to sit there and rot all day long seeing as Le Chien, Lucien that is, Taillon, *Lieutenant-détective* Lucien Taillon, was, if not a quiet revolutionary, at least a silent *patriote*, who didn't think much of the fact that I could speak English better than he could, which wasn't saying very much, and even less of the fact that I had an English-speaking girlfriend. If there was a joe-job to be done, he gave it unfailingly to me.

Nor could I rid myself of the impression that the victim's eyes were on me, just her eyes, watching me. They were cold, almost empty eyes, suggestive, nevertheless, of a lurid, a humiliating sexuality. They and the warm September sun infiltrated my pants, felt me up, pleased with themselves and my eager response.

I pressed my fingertips into my closed eyelids and thought of Sandra, Sandra Beck, with whom I was living, of her lifeless, colourless skin, riveted to her frame by means of innumerable rubbery, mud-black moles and *nevi*. I was convinced that these growths were the source of the starchy, tuberous odour that permeated the sheets as she slept and woke me in a state of breathless, anxious arousal. I thought of her liquid musculature, of how she might, at this very moment, be sitting at her Knabe piano, eliciting from it a detonating radiance totally incommensurate with her slender form. Her face would be a mask of impassive concentration. Only her lips would be tensing subtly, rhythmically, monitoring the intensity of her effort. I saw myself huddled under the piano bench, which was made of glass, intent on observing the lips of her sex to see if they too, as she played, tensed subtly, rhythmically. She did not see me when she entered the room and sat down at the piano, pushing out behind her the tail of the bathrobe under which, miraculously, she was wearing nothing at all. And yet the bench, while still perfectly transparent, was cloudy, milky, impossible to see through. It was softening like warm plaster, shrinking around me, stifling me.

I shuddered, removed my hands from my eyes, the September light flooded my brain with tonic clarity.

I opened the front door of the sexplex then. The vestibule was narrow and led back to the stairs with their chocolate-brown rubber treads. The walls were lined with wood panelling, inexpensive but so painstakingly varnished as to seem worthy of a ski resort chalet. The concierge's door was close enough that I could knock without actually stepping inside.

I waited. He didn't answer. I waited. And then I closed the front door again, soundlessly.

I had only just glanced at the stairs. But even so, it was impossible not to imagine the victim climbing, for the last time, the steps she had used so often, staggering no doubt, giggling perhaps, having been encouraged by the individual accompanying her, who should not have been accompanying her, to ingest an eggless nog of toxic substances, her dishevelled deportment contrasting strangely with the fastidious immaculateness of the vestibule, the concierge close by, dreaming dreams filled with words in his thick, alcoholic sleep. It struck me then, as it has struck me since, that we attribute a number to every one of the seconds of our lives, a number between one and sixty preceded by other numbers representing minutes, hours, days, and years, every number equivalent to every other. And yet, while most seconds may, indeed, drop onto the discard pile of forgetfulness, from which they can be retrieved, yes, but only in random clumps doctored by nostalgia, one, one second in several thousand million, perhaps, explodes with a terrifying intensity that scorches our memories forever.

If, that is, we survive.

I thought of Sandra's lifeless, colourless skin, her *fesses* — never have I been able to grasp what the words "ass" and "buttocks" really mean or who is meant to use them — her *fesses* that, when she was standing without her clothes on, sagged as though they were made of canvas and holding rainwater, but that when she was on all fours, rounded into a whitish planet with a long, central fault and a subtly varied, if barren, surface topography. I thought of her anus, not gigglyish, not raunchy, not a stink-hole or a sinkhole either, but fascinatingly commonplace, anatomically correct, and the source of her intoxicating, alluvial odour. I did not dream, and never have, of inserting anything but an admiring, breathless fingertip into her anus. A mistake, perhaps.

Sandra. The physical attraction she held for me then was as daunting as it was uplifting. I'd had, I don't know, five or six sexual relationships, perhaps, of varying lengths, the perfectly functional sex taking place in designated areas for defined time periods outside of which nothing was going to happen, and so my desire simply slept, twitching its tail occasionally as it dreamed. But it was as though I had fallen into a vat of Sandra's pollen, I was dredged with her, penetrated by her. I desired her as though she belonged to another man. My body could barely keep up. Hours later, after we made love, the particles of my brain would still be reassembling themselves, I would still be having difficulty following a line of thought. My eyes would be as though on standby, while my other senses would be so alive that ballpoint pens would be heavy with odour, and the coolness of water would be an exhilaratingly complex flavour in my mouth.

Not that we made love often. No, I was busy all day being the police officer, and Sandra was working at night at the Wolfred

Nelson Pub, on de la Montagne — where I met her, actually. Sort of. On occasion, I was fairly certain she took advantage of me when she got in, at four in the morning, because at six-thirty, when I winched myself up from a dreamless abyss of sleep, I could smell the gin and smoke on my skin, I had an eerie recollection of having had sex although not at all of having ejaculated, and I was in such a state of sensorial prickliness that my pyjamas felt like they were made of dried leaves, and every one of my teeth had a separate existence.

So that my thoughts were exploring Sandra's anus, with its purplish and pleated border so strikingly reminiscent of the perimeter of a sunspot, when the front door of the sexplex banged open, Le Chien rushed out, all but ran down to his unmarked, blue-grey Pontiac Bonneville, and disappeared inside.

He strode back purposefully some time later. I knew he was aware that my face was still burning from the embarrassment of my insubordination in thought because he avoided looking at me directly. He did pause in front of the entranceway long enough to say, to the door handle, that the coroner would be coming, although not right away, that a serologist would be arriving shortly, and that someone from the Pharmaprix would be delivering a hundred rolls of black-and-white film. He did not seem to realize that he had a smear of blood on his cheek.

So there I stood, on the porch, under the relentlessly perfect September sky, having served myself with a formal injunction against the thinking of any thought whatsoever related even obliquely to sex, with not even the concierge to not talk to, and nothing really to do but execute an endless chain of drills in self-distraction — adjust the collar of my shirt, for example, or comb my hair with my fingers, or scratch, rub, scrape my cheek where I was convinced that I, too, had a smear of blood.

It was well on into the afternoon. A taxi pulled up in front of the building. A man got out, yanked his suitcase out of the trunk, and scuffed his way through the leaves towards the porch.

"Excusez-moi, monsieur," I said, placing myself in front of the door, my heart pounding after so much inactivity, *"Je suis agent Bastarache du Service de police de la communauté urbaine de Montréal."* I showed him my identification. *"Une enquête policière se déroule en ce moment à l'intérieur. Personne ne peut entrer."* The one and only time during this entire day that I would pronounce these words.

The man was clearly taken aback, not to say shaken. He was young, by which I mean he was close to my own age, wearing a tan suede coat with a sheepskin collar, bell-bottoms, and Wellingtons. His hair was rich, almost flowing, and his long sideburns were shaped the way children draw the trunks of trees. His face was uncluttered, affable, openly intelligent.

"I, I'm sorry," he said, in French.

"You don't have to apologize," I said, doing my best to de-dramatize the atmosphere, seeing as it was clear he was not going to be difficult or insist on entering.

"I mean, I couldn't have known. I've been out of town. In Sherbrooke. What happened? What's going on?"

"Sherbrooke," I said, the name uncapping, with a perfectly audible hiss, my bottled-up instinct for conversation, "That's my town."

"Is it." Intelligent he was, openly affable, his manner inviting.

"Yeah, my father worked his whole life, practically, in the rubber factory. Do you have family there?"

"No, no. Business." He handed me a card. "We make educational furniture. Sherbrooke University buys a lot from us."

I said then, moved by a desire to be helpful, which is, I believe, or should be, a meritorious quality in a police officer, especially one who has been standing all day, alone, baking in the sun, trying to not think about sex, even obliquely, "Out of curiosity, where do you stay when you're in Sherbrooke?"

He told me, and so I suggested some places in the neighbouring town of Lennoxville that might interest him, being less expensive and actually closer to the university. He seemed to appreciate my comments. He naturally asked about the investigation. I said I wasn't authorized to speak about it but that being a resident of the building he could expect to be interviewed by the police, that we would probably be leaving the premises shortly, and that, in the unlikely case of his not being able to use his apartment that night, he should keep receipts for any expenses incurred. He would be reimbursed.

"What if I stay at a friend's?"

"Friends can write receipts." I may have smiled when I said this.

"Okay. Is it all right if I leave my bag here?"

"Certainly, if you're sure you're not going to need it."

He knelt down and opened the suitcase. I looked away immediately, but he took out an open bottle of Johnnie Walker Red Label and handed it up to me, requiring me to observe his crumpled pyjamas lying on top of the jumble of his clothes.

"I'm worried this is going to leak," he said. He then stuffed a few things into the deep pockets of his suede coat and reclosed the bag.

If I report this conversation in some detail, it is because it would cost me, a good many months later, considerable sleep, anger, and embarrassment. It would cost me tears. Le Chien would not choose to dress me down out in the open but would instead call me into his office and glare at me until the silence infiltrated my skull and reverberated against my temples. He would eventually drop his eyes and mutter the only two English words he could pronounce without an accent like the federal Member of Parliament for Abitibi-Témiscamingue, "fucking" being one, and "asshole" being the other. And although the words would immediately bring the blood to my cheeks, their force would be attenuated by the realization that they were not directed exclusively at me. They would be meant for others as well. Including Le Chien himself.

He would then say more clearly, in his mother tongue naturally, "Is it true what I hear about Sandra?"

"Depends on what you hear," I would answer, strangely eased by my own humiliation.

"I hear she's getting married."

"Oh yeah, that. That's true."

It may seem strange, but I'm not sure I really remember how I first met Sandra Beck.

The Wolfred Nelson Pub in Montreal, you see, was famous for its shandygaff, a mix of beer and ginger beer principally. After sweating at the downtown Y for a couple of hours, you and your badminton partner would head over to the Wolfred Nelson where the spicy, supercooled shandygaff would be so astonishingly thirst-quenching that after downing no more than a pitcherful in less than a minute, you would be all set for more badminton. Only you would be finding it difficult to stand up.

So I was sitting, with my racket across my knees, in the Wolfred Nelson. I may have been looking at the walls, which were covered with poorly executed drawings of overlapping men firing muskets in front of a large stone house, a *maison canadienne*. Every man had exactly the same face and every musket had exactly the same puff of smoke plugging the end of its barrel. A woman about my age, or maybe slightly older, sat down in the chair beside me and asked me in French that sounded as though it had been freshly pressed with an English steam iron, how I was, what I was up to, and so on, tacking on at the end, "Paul-Frawnswa." My shandygaffed brain took some time to reach the conclusion that she knew me and that I, in all probability, knew her. She was sitting so close that her knee was in contact with mine, so that I had to lean back slightly in order to see her face.

"Too ne te rappell paw de mwa?" she said. No, I didn't. I didn't remember her at all.

"Pawnse," she said, inviting me to think. But I was thinking. That I should ask her how she managed to breathe in enough air through such a minuscule nose.

After a time she stood, squeezed my shoulder, said, "You haven't changed, Paul-François. Not too much, I mean," and moved on.

Shandygaff or not, there was not a cell in my body, not one, that warmed to the memory of this woman. I simply did not know her. And yet.

And yet, when the waiter, wearing a *ceinture fléchée* and a shirt that was more like a blouse, arrived not long afterwards and deposited still another pitcher of shandygaff on the table, which pitcher I immediately pushed over to my badminton partner who was, in fact, no longer there, and when the waiter said, "This comes compliments of the extremely attractive lady standing over there at the bar. Her name is . . . ," it surged up from the glowing magma of my subducted memory without the cold rock of my brain having the slightest idea of what was happening. It seared its way up my throat and erupted through the vent of my mouth, exploded, annihilating the waiter before he even had time to say:

"*Sandra Beck!*" The pub fell silent. "I didn't think you spoke French."

And generally speaking, when it comes up, which is not often, I say that Sandra and I met at the Wolfred Nelson. Which is not, of course, strictly true.

We met, sort of, when we were thirteen — she's older than I am, her birthday's in February, mine's in August. The fact is, I had a not half-bad singing voice when I was a boy. I even sang in a church choir for a while. No girls. On the other hand, there was one boy who knew more about sex than I do now or ever will. What was his name? Stoagy? No, I don't think so.

Sandra Beck was the organist. Imagine. I could not believe that her wormy little thirteen-year-old fingers could produce so much sound. But really beautiful sound. I was entranced whenever she played. I could have listened for hours. She could even make it up as she went along. Imagine. Thirteen.

The word Stoagy, that not being his name, used to describe Sandra was "scrag." I don't think I've ever heard the word since. A "dippy scrag," he said she was, and Stoagy, at least in the time I knew him, was never wrong. She was certainly scrawny, her excuse of a nose was always dripping, and she had brown moles on her face that made me queasy. I should add that she had no use for me whatsoever and never talked to me except once to say she couldn't speak French.

I can't say I remember a great deal about my time in the choir. My voice broke only a few months after I joined, putting an abrupt end to my brief career. But what I do remember, or re-remember, now, with absolute clarity, is the moment I saw Sandra for the first time. It was the night of my first rehearsal and raining very hard. She arrived late, soaking wet. The instant I laid my eyes on her, I was certain I'd seen her before, somewhere, I didn't know where. But I was absolutely certain, and equally sure she would recognize me.

Which, under the circumstances, was the last thing in the world I wanted. To be singled out, to be asked questions, me, a French kid and a Catholic.

But she didn't recognize me.

I never did remember where it was I'd seen her. And I never have. Which only serves to reinforce my conviction that we did meet sometime, somewhere, when we were both very young. Some school activity, some sporting event, a dentist's office maybe. Somewhere.

So no, I'm not sure when or how I first met Sandra Beck, although it was even before she turned into a dippy scrag. But I have known her, off and on, for most of my life.

It was after six o'clock by now, the colour of the sky over the row houses on the opposite side of the street seemed to have been artificially enhanced. It was an impossibly deep shade of blue, like the middle depths of the Indian Ocean. The streetlights had already come on and were eerily yellow and pale. From the porch, which by now was completely in shadow, I watched the local residents returning home with restrained eagerness, of a kind that suggested they likely needed the john, and I thought that I would have been perfectly happy to live on this street.

The photographer came out with his gear packed into a leather shoulder bag the size of a cat kennel. "You still here?" he said. He breathed in deeply through his mouth.

Still there, yes, my face to the early magic of a September evening in Montreal, my back to the nameless horrors. And where was that then?

"Did you," I said, "use up all those rolls of black-and-white film you got them to bring you from the drugstore?"

"I might have a couple left. The serologist worked me pretty hard. She's right in her element up there." He snorted softly. "Her elements."

A forensic serologist's elements are blood, excrement, urine, semen, and tears.

"I'm getting the fuck out of here," he said. And yet he continued to stand there, unmoving, almost as if he wanted to go back and take more pictures. As if he were afraid that releasing himself from the objective, frozen brutality of photographs would expose him to the liquid flow of images concocted by his own imagination, contorted, grotesque, obsessive.

And he was still there when the serologist came out, an imposingly staunch and tall woman, her face centred around her mouth and her jaw, which was noticeably wider than her forehead. It was a dominatingly capable face, itself dominated by a thick corona of blue-black curls, as though the mass of her hair, in reaction to some trauma, had boiled over and never returned to its former state.

This woman I would remember principally eating vending machine snacks in the corridor of the courthouse, recklessly stuffing red licorice into her mouth with fingers that were long, arousing, and perfectly manicured. I would remember her sitting in the witness stand, under the parallel rows of fluorescent lights, the utterly bored Quebec flag hanging limply behind her, describing, with stainless professionalism and remarkable powers of deduction, what, in her view, had taken place in the third-floor apartment of the sexplex, citing, for example, the delicate spray of blood droplets on the toaster as indicating that it had been within so many inches to the left or right that the perpetrator had snapped off the victim's little finger, or deducing from the nature of the fecal matter found in every room, along with small bits of the lining of the colon, that the victim had eaten little more than an orange during the course of the day, that forceful expulsions had continued well after the victim's bowel had been entirely empty, and that the perpetrator, in his childlike delirium, had mixed his own fecal matter with that of the victim and spread it throughout the apartment.

She would go on. And on.

None of her analysis, however, brilliant though it was, would succeed in inculcating a perpetrator. Much to her anguish. Inculpating a perpetrator, I meant to say.

She thanked the photographer with formal politeness. She seemed to feel that shaking his hand was also called for, but discovered that her own hands were occupied holding equipment. She hesitated, the indecision causing her a degree of embarrassment strangely out of keeping with her competent self-possession. She settled for repeating her thanks word-for-word, which made the photographer grin and deepened her embarrassment still further. She attempted to thank him again, more generously this time. And yet again, before she finally managed to hurry off.

"You seem to have an unsettling effect on the woman," I said.

"She's just tired," he said. "So am I."

I remember the officers coming out, lugging battered suitcases chock full of carefully wrapped pieces of evidence, plaster casts, plastic bags containing samples of skin, hair, and various serological elements. I remember them walking discreetly down to their van.

And then it was the coroner's turn. I don't think he could have been upstairs for more than forty-five minutes.

The coroner was in his early forties, I'd say. He had a ten-gallon walking style, his legs wide apart, as though he had square testicles as large as the dice that hung from his car mirror. He was wearing a pink shirt and a blue-green necktie under his trench coat, which was expensive and came complete with gun flaps and a knotted belt. His slick hair was combed into two fenders over the wheels of his ears.

The photographer asked him what his impressions were. He answered with gum-chewing sententiousness, "When it's white and comes in a bottle, you've got to figure it's milk." I had no idea what he meant by this, but he was the coroner and he had decided he was going to express himself. "This is bullshit," he said. "It's bullshit, just fucking bullshit. Tomorrow we're going to let this out, right, and it's going to be fucking everywhere. Papers, TV, everywhere. Bullshit. There's going to be a crowd from here to Jarry fucking Park. Nobody'll buy a house on this street for eighty-eight fucking years. It's bullshit, bullshit, it's just . . ."

It was Le Chien who put an end to the tirade, stepping out onto the porch and gripping the coroner's shoulder, not with any apparent insistence, and yet the coroner was immediately silent, and my own shoulder tingled.

"The coroner's had a long day," said Le Chien softly. "He had another job this morning, which is why he was late getting here." Late being quite the understatement. He paused before adding, "A crib death." The coroner decided to interpret this as an invitation to elaborate, which it likely was. "Crib death," he said, "remains unexplained, which is why the coroner's office has to investigate every case. The parents weren't too happy to have me there in their house today, I can tell you that. The father, I think, would have liked to even up the score by assassinating me. The mother would have settled for cutting my eyes out. I had a long questionnaire for them. They were really up for long questionnaires." He broke off here to give Le Chien a chance to rescind his invitation. Le Chien remained silent. "The current thinking," continued the coroner, with disconcerting enthusiasm, forced, and yet genuine, as though he had suddenly turned into the host of a kids' TV science show, "is that the baby forgets it's not still a fetus. A fetus breathes, right, pumps its lungs, not to get oxygen, but just to practise, to get the lungs ready for real breathing. When, for whatever reason, a fetus lacks oxygen, it stops breathing because it has to use oxygen to power its lung muscles. Right? It is thought that a very young infant, if it's sleeping and finds itself short of oxygen — it might be congested, it might have its face stuffed into the pillow — might unconsciously revert to the fetal strategy and stop breathing altogether, which obviously is fatal. What's this?"

These last two words I did not in fact hear. I was thinking that Sandra would really be very interested in the coroner's crib death theory, and so I was wording it to myself even as the coroner spoke, in order not to forget.

"What's what?" said Le Chien, I did not know why.

"This," said the coroner, indicating the suitcase that belonged to the man wearing the tan suede coat with the sheepskin collar.

"Good question," said Le Chien. "Whose suitcase is this?" His voice was quiet, peremptory. "And why is there a bottle of scotch beside it?"

And so I told them about the sexplex resident who had arrived in a taxi, having just got back from Sherbrooke where he had been staying for several days, who was waiting for the police to leave so he could get back into his apartment, and who had, in the meantime, entrusted me with his suitcase, which I had set against the wall along with the open bottle of Johnnie Walker Red.

There followed a strange silence, like a hole in time through which the seconds simply drained, without actually occurring. Out of this hole of silence emanated a warmth so unexpected it made me shiver and almost want to smile. On the other side of the warmth stood the coroner, smiling himself, observing me.

"So he is going to come and get the suitcase," he said. "You think."

There was an ironic twist in his voice that I could not fathom. Of course the man was going to come and get his suitcase. He might arrive at any moment.

"What did you say his name was?" The irony had become heavy-handed, menacing. The coroner knew perfectly well I hadn't said the man's name. I didn't know what the man's name was. The warmth, instead of dissipating as it logically should have now that the hole in time had closed, grew more intense. "You didn't ask," said the coroner, a statement that might have been preceded by the words, "you have shit for a brain therefore . . ." And yet the man's name was no secret. He lived in the sexplex. There was very likely a name tag attached to his suitcase. The warmth was stifling, my lungs were heavy and stiff and pulled down on my voice.

"I have his business card here," I managed to mutter, not at all sure that my voice was loud enough to be audible.

"You do," said the coroner. The threat subsided, the grinning irony remained. "Don't lose it."

Let it be said that the overworked coroner had convinced himself almost from the moment he had entered the third-floor apartment that the woman must have known the perpetrator, known him well, well enough to have placed him in her confidence, and that, there-fore, the perpetrator must almost certainly live in the sexplex. Based on this premise, which was grounded principally in an elemental surge of emotion, he had also let himself be instantly convinced that the man in the suede leather coat could only be the perpetrator, whether he'd been in Sherbrooke or not.

In all of this he was perfectly correct.

And yet the coroner, despite this extraordinary insight, all the more remarkable in that he had never before had to deal with such an atrocious homicide, would not be prevented from remaining as blind as the rest of us to what should have been perfectly obvious.

The victim was born in Montreal. Her parents had returned to their native Yugoslavia when she was in her mid-twenties. Yugoslavia by the way, as I learned at the time, means "land of the south Slavs." She didn't have a camera and she wasn't a person who kept pictures. So that although we would have snapshots of her, a fair number of them, taken at various times by co-workers and acquaintances, we would not have at our disposal a single good photograph with a detailed image of her face. When it was a living face. Which no doubt is why I would not be able to keep from picturing her, putting on her makeup, say, as she was eating breakfast, using the toaster as a mirror, alternating head-bobbing intervals of chewing toast with dead-still intervals of eyebrow-darkening. Or lying on her back on the sofa, her head dangling over the edge, her knees hooked over the back, watching television upside-down. Or standing in front of the open refrigerator, in the middle of a suffocating Montreal night, dressed only in her *bobettes* and her *soutien-gorge*, a bag of frozen vegetables on her head. Often I would hear her walking behind me. Often. Not to say constantly. Her company would grate on my nerves at first. Her insistence on never showing herself and walking exactly in my footsteps would make me wild with exasperation. But gradually I would grow more accustomed to her. And although she would never say anything, I would hear her sniffling almost continuously because of the chronic cold she had. Eventually I wouldn't be able to stop myself from asking her if for once she could just blow her nose. I would realize then that I was actually talking to her. I would be a little alarmed, think wow, now I am starting to lose it.

But, if anything, talking to her would make me feel more at ease, the world wouldn't change, the Canadiens would keep winning, so that I would come to view her presence as little more than a way of thinking. And it would be from the time that I became aware of talking to her that there would start to be periods when she would not be there at all.

Of course, I would also dream about her a great deal. I can never describe my dreams properly, even when I feel I remember them reasonably well. And not only because describing them gives them a daytime logic they don't possess.

The only dream from that time I can say I remember faithfully is this: I'm looking over the various products in the meat section of a grocery store, an IGA, and I come across a package of her eyes, just her eyes, on a little Styrofoam tray, wrapped in plastic film and stuck with a label, weight, price per kilo, selling price, none of which I can actually decipher. It is a pleasant dream. Because the eyes, while being no more than eyes, are at the same time her entire body, crammed onto the Styrofoam tray and wrapped in plastic, all her pieces back together again in a sort of Saran Wrap chrysalis, ready to burst open. She tells me in the dream, frankly and without humour, that she feels embarrassed to be sitting there in the meat section, dressed in just her eyes. The last time I remember seeing the coroner, he placed himself and his square testicles directly in front of *Maître* Brindamour, the perpetrator's lawyer, who was heading towards the giant courthouse doors, and he said with his trademark, gum-chewing sententiousness, "The more human beings I deal with like you," pausing to underscore the heavy-handed sarcasm he was also good at, "the more I think dogs are great."

"You're going to drive me, Bastarache," said Le Chien.

I shrugged as though to say, whatever you say.

"Just hang on a minute." He knocked on the concierge's door. The concierge appeared, looking out at us with the groggy wariness of a zoo panther from inside his personal cage of Geneva gin. Le Chien indicated the suitcase, saying in approximate English that it belonged to the tenant who lived in the other third-storey apartment, across from the victim. The concierge beamed at the mention of this tenant. Le Chien wanted to make sure the suitcase, seeing as it had been entrusted to the police, was taken up to the apartment before he himself left the premises. The concierge beamed more brightly still, grabbed the suitcase proudly and lugged it inside, holding the door open for Le Chien to follow. Le Chien hesitated, it having not been his intention to go back upstairs himself. And then he picked up the bottle of scotch and followed the concierge inside.

He was back only a matter of minutes later. And so at last, after close to twelve hours, I left the porch, in the company of *lieutenant-détective* Lucien Taillon, who walked in silence and with an entirely uncharacteristic slowness, floating and regal, as though he were recovering from an operation to remove his gall bladder. He no longer had a smear of blood on his cheek. Neither, for that matter, did I. He was carrying a black umbrella in order to look less like a policeman, carrying it so naturally, in fact, that I could not help thinking that he might easily have accommodated himself to any number of professions besides that of agent of social shepherdship. It didn't occur to me that I might have as well.

I stopped when I got to my car.

"Do you mind driving mine?" said Le Chien. My car that day was an over-driven, under-maintained, stock Chevrolet. His was a Bonneville, brand new, unmarked, fully loaded. No, I didn't mind.

I goosed the 455 big block V8; 350 horses reared together in the traces.

"Just drive for a while," said Le Chien.

"No problem."

"Your girlfriend's name is Sandra, isn't it?"

I grunted affirmatively, my hands tingling as I ran them over the steering-wheel's finger ridges.

"I had quite a conversation with her the other night at the club where she works. She speaks French perfectly."

French, yes. Perfectly, no.

"Not to mention that she has got to be one of the most stunning waitresses in this entire town. Wow."

Stunning, if you say so. Waitress, definitely not.

"She's not planning on working in a nightclub for the rest of her days, is she?"

No she's not, actually.

"Because she's got far too much going for her for that."

This onslaught of gentility, to my regret, I could no longer resist.

"She has an interview coming up with the Montreal Symphony Orchestra," I said. Although. In fact. She did not.

"You mean she's a musician? On top of everything else?"

She wanted the job so badly she was too terrified even to apply.

"The job isn't playing in the orchestra. It's just go-girl, basically, for the assistant to the assistant-manager's assistant. But she does play the piano. Very well."

"Go-girl? She's too good to be anybody's go-girl."

Yes, but she doesn't think so, or doesn't want to think so. And I, having now mentioned the job to you, have not only broken my promise to her, I've also jostled destiny just enough that the MSO's and Sandra's trajectories will have become irrevocably misaligned, and I will have to say, the next time you ask me if she got the job with the MSO, Job? Which . . . oh, *that*, no, that didn't work out, which is a good thing, because it made her realize you know that she's too good to be anybody's go-girl.

"Although if it's what she wants, I'm sure she'll get it."

When I met, or re-met, Sandra at the Wolfred Nelson Pub, she was paid just to be there, to mingle, to talk up the male clients, to be completely available while being completely unavailable. She never had to say she was not permitted to date clients, which she was not. They knew, they spread the word. That way, they were all free equally to give rein to their sun-drenched, suburban fantasies, without rivalry or embarrassment. She was paid, that is, to breathe life into the two animating forces of the male psyche, longing and irresponsibility. Underpaid, considering how good she was. Ask Le Chien.

She was also trying to add a music degree from McGill to the B.A. she already had from Bishop's.

So that if, after we met, we did start seeing each other occasionally, there was no question, at least not in my mind, of anything actually happening. She was off limits, which was fine, because I was busy taking an administration course or two and being an up-and-coming cop person. I was also playing a little badminton.

We were like two Indonesians, say, who happen to run into each other on the streets of Buenos Aires, two Indonesians working hard to pick up Spanish and fit into Argentinean society. What we had in common was great, sure, but pretty much beside the point. We were breathing-space.

Le Chien fell silent. He sat utterly motionless, leaning into the car door, staring out the window. I had the impression for an instant he might actually be crying. But his voice was perfectly steady when he asked me if I knew where the Église Saint-Édouard was.

"Ah, corner of Saint-Vallier and Beaubien."

"Yeah. Would you mind stopping there? Just briefly."

It happened that one day, one windy day, I received a call to check out the scene of a fatal car accident because, reportedly, the police line tape had blown away. As it turned out, one end had broken free, the thirty-foot length of yellow tape was being whipped and kicked mercilessly by the wind. The oil spills had been filled with sawdust, but there was still considerable debris. A gallery of silent children watched with scientific curiosity as I retied the tape.

I noticed that the piece of chalk that had been used to indicate the position of the fatality had, for no obvious reason, been left lying there on the ground. I picked it up, also for no obvious reason, and put it in my pocket.

That night I waited for Sandra at a twenty-four-hour pancake place, Shitty's, on Metcalfe. I think the real name was Smitty's. It was well after three by the time she got there after her stint at the Wolfred Nelson. She dumped her music books on the table and slid into the booth beside me. I was falling asleep by then and liable to laugh at everything and anything. We both were. I happened to remember the chalk in my pocket, I hauled it out and drew the outline of her hand on the silver-flecked, Arborite tabletop.

"What are you doing with a piece of chalk in your pocket?"

"I've still got my police pants on."

"Oh, well, that explains everything."

This was deemed to be incisively humorous.

"What," she said, containing her smile, "are you doing with chalk in your police pants' pocket? Do they have you visiting schools now?"

This was deemed to be screamingly funny.

"No," I said, still laughing, "I used it to outline a corpse."

"You what?"

"Cops have to do these things. I used it draw a circle around a daaiiid bawdy."

"And that's the chalk you used to draw my hand with?"

"Yeah."

"Well fuck you."

This was deemed to be stratospherically hilarious.

The Église Saint-Édouard is an impressively cavernous church. Built in 1908, by the way. I'm always struck by how the wood in churches smells so old, while the stone smells so young, relatively.

I hadn't been to Mass in fifteen years. The switchboard of my memory was swamped with calls from my childhood.

Le Chien walked down the central aisle using the umbrella as a cane, as though his gall bladder operation were causing him considerable discomfort. He slid into the first pew and knelt. Something in the stillness of his manner suggested to me that he was inwardly tossing and turning, unable to pray.

So we left Shitty's, Sandra and I did, and ended up in the little park between the Sun Life building and the CIBC tower. It was still windy, but the wind was high and invisible, we could hear it more than feel it. I'd had such success with the dead body chalk that I hauled it out again, got down on my hands and knees, and outlined Sandra's feet on the asphalt path as she walked. She squealed appropriately, while I received a surreptitious erotic charge so inconsequential I felt sure I was still well within limits. I was drunk on sleepiness, enjoying myself, not paying much attention to Sandra, really. So that when she took the chalk out of my hand, ordered me to lie down, and traced my perimeter, I simply played along, laughing. And even when she gave the chalk back to me and lay down herself, expecting me to reciprocate, I still, incredibly, did not see.

No, it was only when, as I was drawing her outline, she pulled up her elegant, black sweater, oh, barely an inch or two, and I felt the rapidness of her breath on my lips, that I finally, finally . . .

Here? I thought. Now? And the limits?

The limits had broken free and were being kicked by the invisible wind.

This moment, to which my initial reaction was one of terror, seeing as one, my career in the *forces policières* would come to an abrupt end were I to be discovered doing what I was being urged to do and two, and infinitely more importantly, it was very late, I was extremely tired, *extremely,* tired, I was not Mr. Randy by a long shot, and not just terror but terror tinged with resentment seeing as I had, safe within the limits, been enjoying myself immensely and now was not, this moment, in which I realized that Sandra Beck wanted to have sex with me, with *me*, has become the central moment of my existence, my true birth in many ways. The thought of it still turns the blood in my veins to ash.

And so as the Sun Life building and the CIBC tower looked on sedately, discreetly, caressing themselves, I have no doubt, we made love, there in the park, at four in the morning, inside the dead body chalk circle. And if for me it was not, from a purely sexual point of view, the most intense experience I have known, it had nothing to do with my being terrified or tired, no, it was because I was touched, overwhelmed, humbled even, by the capacity for passion of Sandra Beck's body, whose spindly legs, which had once had to strain to reach the organ pedals, linked themselves behind my back, and squeezed me half to death.

We strode back to the car, Le Chien and I.

"I'll drive," he said.

He raced the engine brutally, and then just sat there, drumming his fingers against his knee, struggling to contain his tense agitation. He dug into his pocket and pulled out a crumpled Kleenex. With blood on it.

"I found this in his room."

"*His* room? You mean the guy with the scotch and the suitcase?"

"Yes. Him. So tell me, what did he look like exactly, this *guy*?"

"And what," *Maître* Brindamour would say, several months later, "was he wearing?" His voice would be mechanical, as though he were reading from a list of standard questions. He would be sitting behind his table, his black-robed torso appearing extraordinarily wide, as though his body was filled with warm sand and spread when he sat down. He would not be looking at me, or even appearing to listen to me for that matter, but would be busy studying the various papers spread out in front of him, so that there would frequently be a long moment of silence between the end of my answer and the posing of the next question. I would be in uniform, standing in front of the utterly bored Quebec flag, standing erect, trying to see myself in the convex mirror at the opposite end of the room, swaying ever so slightly, hoping to glimpse the movement in the mirror.

"Go on," he would say, eventually.

And I would say, "But that's all. He got back in the taxi then and the taxi drove off."

And he, still not looking up, "Fine, then. Thank you."

And I would step down, thinking it would be over.

Ah, but I can still quote you the memorandum signed by Le Chien and taped over the enlargement of the victim's bloodied nipple which by then had been tacked to my corkboard for weeks:

Plusieurs motifs ont servi à l'avocat de la défense, Maître Claude Brindamour, pour faire exclure certains éléments de preuve. En faveur de son client, il a ainsi pu invoquer les faits suivants :

Il a été interrogé sans avoir l'occasion de consulter un avocat.

Translation: *Maître* Claude Brindamour is a king dickhead capable of attempting to have the evidence against his monstrosity of a client disqualified because it had supposedly been collected through improper police methods.

However.

I did not interrogate his client without his client's having a chance to consult a lawyer. I did not interrogate his client at all. I was making conversation for fuck's sake. Conversation.

Les policiers ont fouillé ses effets personels sans mandat.

Les policiers ont pénétré chez lui, également sans mandat, et sans y avoir été invités. Ils ont usé de subterfuges pour fouiller sa résidence.

I hope you speak French, or I hope you don't, because I'm not going to lower myself to translate. I did not search the client's personal effects without a warrant. He opened his suitcase in front of me of his own accord. I was trying not to look. I did not seize the bottle of Scotch, he gave it to me. Le Chien did not enter the client's apartment, the concierge did. I think. And if he, Le Chien, picked up a piece of Kleenex in the apartment, that does not constitute searching. You don't need a warrant to pick up a piece of bloody Kleenex. Or at least you shouldn't.

It was after seven by the time Le Chien and I got back to the police station. I hadn't eaten since lunch. Le Chien might not have eaten since the morning. Having spent the day tramping through the swamp of the vilest human conduct imaginable, he was in an over-extended state of brittle nervousness which neither gentility nor prayer had managed to appease. It would be fair to say I think that he was daunted by the oppressive moral requirement of convicting the perpetrator, as well as by the realization that doing so would necessitate tramping through the swamp for quite some time to come.

In any case, I don't know how else to explain why, when he discovered he had left his umbrella in the church, he went more than slightly apeshit. He stormed and ranted and finished by all but yelling at me, "Bastarache, go get my fucking umbrella. Christ, you couldn't see I didn't have it? A police officer is supposed to pay attention!"

I was not happy with this outburst, but I didn't say anything. I simply looked at him, which was apparently the right answer.

"Bastarache," he started over, "go back to the church and see if my umbrella is still there."

I continued to look at him.

"Take it," he said, "take it. Take the Bonneville. You can drive it into a streetlight for all I care."

The police reaction to *Maître* Brindamour's courtroom tactics would be noisy and outraged. However, the intensity of the reaction would, in my view, now, looking back, be a measure of our uneasiness, an attempt to distract ourselves from the fact that our case against the perpetrator was not at all strong. It should also be pointed out that the tactics would not ultimately be successful. Although he would, among other things, manage to delay proceedings, *Maître* Brindamour's attempt to have his client acquitted without trial would fail.

But as I say, our case was not strong. Despite the hundreds of expertly taken black-and-white photographs. Despite the serologist's brilliant analysis. Despite any number of pieces of evidence that proved what never required proving: that what had taken place in the sexplex had been utterly inhuman.

Inhuman. Although no animal certainly, other than a human one, would be capable of such . . .

The inhuman in question had, in his exalted frenzy, bitten off the victim's left nipple. Completely. Cleanly. The teeth marks were recognizably clear. A plaster cast had been successfully made of the wound. This cast would be thought of as being our best chance.

I can still see the predatorial glow in Le Chien's eyes when he received the package containing the orthodontist's certified mould of the perpetrator's teeth. I can still see him, with all the stiff ceremony of a wise man in an elementary school Christmas pageant, carry the package back to his desk and place it beside the skim-milk-white cast of the mutilated breast in its deep nest of newspaper. I can see him telephone the coroner, his eyes never leaving the package. And with the coroner, in his best rodeo pose, now looking on, I can see Le Chien at last open the package, take the orthodontist's mould in one hand, the plaster cast in the other, and regally, reverentially, place the two together. Once, only once. And I can see him put them back down on the table side by side, observe them for an instant and quickly, without a word, leave the room.

They did not fit together.

I was dumbfounded. It was not possible. But I had seen with my own eyes.

They did not fit together. They simply did not.

After that, I found one of the photographer's meticulously focused shots of the fleshy lesion where the victim's nipple had been, and I had an enlargement made. I tacked the enlargement to the corkboard over my desk and left it there, convinced it would reveal its secret to me eventually. I left it there so long, it became distorted with familiarity, the wound no longer appeared to be in flesh but in rock, the breast like a raggedy meteoroid in a junkyard nebula.

By the time I stopped the Bonneville at the first red light, I had decided I was never going to drive a Bonneville again. Something was rattling somewhere, I pounded on the dashboard to try to get it to stop. The heat was rising from my lungs and collecting in the back of my throat, nauseating me. I could not believe that I, with my little Cégep de Sherbrooke diploma in *techniques policières*, my B.Sc. in criminology from the Université d'Ottawa, my fifty or so months as a member of the Montreal Urban Community police force including my two twelve-week *stages* in California, internships I think they called them there, that I, *agent* Bastarache, Paul-François, was chasing after an umbrella.

By the time I got to the second light, I realized that what was demeaning was not that I was being treated like a go-boy, but that I was perfectly happy being treated like one. Perfectly happy having the next little section of my life laid out for me. I was the man for the joe-job.

By the time I got to the third light, I realized that the rattle was not coming from the dashboard, but from somewhere behind me. That it wasn't a rattle exactly, and maybe not a rattle at all. It was more like the sound of someone, a woman, with a cold, sniffling.

By the time I got to the fourth light, the temptation to drive the Bonneville into a streetlight was suffocating me.

Contrary to legend, the enlargement never would reveal its secret to me. The months would go by, *Maître* Brindamour would do his job, the *procureur* would do his, at least as far as I knew he would, the police certainly would do theirs. Life would continue. With a hum. Like the hum of my parents' old Viking television, which seemed to grow louder during the silences between ads and all but disappear during the ads themselves, but which in fact was constant and invariable. The hum in this case being the thought, acknowledged only occasionally but always, always present, that we would not be able to convict the perpetrator.

With Sandra, you've got to do the work. You've got to keep after her and after her until she gets her *curriculum vitae* up to date, the job application form filled in, and her letter written. You have to put the brown envelope into the mail after having addressed it to the managing director of the Montreal Symphony Orchestra. On the day of the interview, you have to get her out of bed, dressed and fed, have to pour her into the car and drive her there yourself. And when, a short time later, she tells you that her candidature was so strong she was offered the job before the interview was even over, you must not so much as congratulate her without first allowing her to object to such a flagrantly unethical lack of fairness to the other applicants. And you must, but absolutely must not remind her, when she says that she is not sure she can accept the job under the circumstances, that it is the one job in ten thousand she would like to have.

Not if you want, and you want, the embrace of her spindly legs to stay you as you re-enter the vehemently honest atmosphere of her sexuality.

Le Chien, you see, would assume that the perpetrator had bitten off the victim's nipple during intercourse. Not for an instant would I question, or feel like questioning, this assumption. Nor would anyone. Gradually, however, gradually, the acids of my brain would eat away at the assumption's protective coating, exposing it for what it was: a possibility, nothing more.

The perpetrator could have done the biting at any moment. From any position relative to the victim. Obviously.

Obviously.

When this would dawn on me, or rather when I would at last admit to myself that it had dawned on me, I would feel as though I had committed an offence myself, the heat would rise from my lungs, collecting in the back of my throat, nauseating me. No, I wouldn't run up to Le Chien with my little find, wouldn't knock on his door and say, Hey, are we assholes or what?

I mean eventually, yes, I would.

I would be convinced that, even though he might thank me later on, Le Chien would resent my showing him what an idiot he'd been. But I would be wrong. His eyes would catch fire, he would clamp me triumphantly on both shoulders and shake me like a doll.

It was so simple, a question of turning the two moulds until the right angle was found. That was all. As it turned out, the perpetrator had been standing, when he did the biting, at the victim's head.

I no sooner entered the twilit sobriety of the church, the Église Saint-Édouard, than I saw the umbrella. It was at the other end of the nave, open, floating in the air as though on the surface of a transparent pond. The weight I was carrying split open with a crack and slid off my back, my legs buckled under the sudden lightness of my body.

The handle of the umbrella was being held by a woman. I approached little by little, when her back was turned. She was a robust woman, with hair that might have been styled by an engraver at the Canadian Mint. The upper surface of her breasts formed a broad and gently sloping plain below the imposing, rocky belvedere of her head. This undulating plain was draped in a glimmering, sea-green garment so ample and long, and that fell with such Niagaran verticality, that it resembled a curtain far more than a dress. Under this curtain there may have been an incongruously slender body. It was not impossible. What was certain was that the woman, as she held high the umbrella, was dancing, gliding, soft-shoeing, with a grace and lightness rarely associated with the corpulent.

I slid into a pew silently, hiding as much of myself as I could. There was not another soul in the church. I watched enthralled as the woman danced in her suavely syncopated way, singing softly under her breath.

When suddenly there rang out such a thunderous burst of organ music that my startled brain leapt out of its skull like a partridge, thrashing its frantic wings.

Sandra, I thought, trying to squeeze the partridge back in, Sandra, take it easy for the love of, what are you trying to do to me?

Not until I reached the end of this thought did I become aware of its absurdity. It was not Sandra playing the organ. Obviously.

Obviously.

And yet, having evoked her name, I realized that Sandra was present in the church, more so than if she had actually been there, in which case her presence would have been contained within the limits of her body.

The music stopped. A moment later, the organist strode out, grinning broadly, his music under his arm. He kissed the air beside the woman's cheeks. They talked in eager undertones, every consonant as though chiselled in the air, every word perfectly audible and sparkling with admirative flattery.

The woman spun away. "It has been," she said, "a wonderful, a miraculous day. I've found an umbrella. Do you like it? I've lost so many over the years, hundreds, oh yes believe me, hundreds, and today, finally, I've found one, one, I've got my revenge, all the revenge I require in any case. We shall be inseparable now, I promise, my black umbrella and I." She pirouetted once more. "Shall we?"

"We shall," said the organist, striding back to his post. And so they rehearsed. I listened, listened intently, not simply because of the music, but because Sandra was there. I could feel her bristle at the singer's skating up to the high notes, could feel her lean into me, saying, "Get a load of the umbrella. She thinks she's Keen Jelly. Sorry, Gene Kelly." She was everywhere, perfectly close, perfectly distant, inviting, impenetrable. It was her genius playing the organ through the hands of a stranger, her intelligence singing in the sea-green dress, skating up to the high notes.

It was her spirit that inhabited the ghost sitting in the pew behind me, with a cold, sniffling.

Inspecteur-chef Paul-François Bastarache had no idea, none, why it was that he was standing in the weeds and gravel on the shoulder of the Eastern Townships Autoroute, staring eastward, in the general direction of Cowansville. He swung around to face the west, and was surprised to see his blue LeSabre at a considerable distance, parked beside the highway. A thrill of panic scurried up his windpipe, his hand slid itself warily into the pocket of his dress uniform pants. His keys, as the hand had suspected, were not there. *Inspecteur* PF checked his other pockets rapidly, clutching at them hard, as though searching for his body as much as for his keys. I must, he thought, have left them in the ignition. He swore succinctly and started running back to the car, thanking his stars it hadn't been stolen. And then he stopped, panting heavily, and asked himself what, really, were the chances that anyone barrelling down the highway would slow down, pull over, back up, and make off with a parked car while driving their own car at the same time. Not great. And if it hadn't happened so far, it wasn't going to in the time it would take him to walk back to the vehicle at a relaxed pace.

He took a long breath to steady his breathing, adjusted his coat on his shoulders, and set out at a purposeful amble, his eyes never leaving the blue LeSabre. The memory of the provincial police officer now returned to him with such naturalness and immediacy that he was no longer aware of ever having forgotten him.

He had been suspicious of the officer from the first moment, had known, without realizing he had known, that the officer was only interested in buying his car, so that when he, the officer, had asked if it were for sale, pretending to be asking on the part of someone else, his father, mmn, a transparent tactic if ever there was one, PF had already known the question was coming. Again, without knowing he had known. But he had, which was why he had been able simply to ignore the question as if it hadn't been asked.

"I do know what's going on, you know," he said, "a lot of the time." And then, facing the clatter of traffic hurtling down the autoroute, he shouted at the top of his lungs, "I just get distracted by all the fucking noise!"

The distraction in this case being no, not the emotional-organizational rigmarole of getting married, not at all, although he was supposed to be, according to various colleagues and friends who chose to express themselves on the subject, leery of seeing his bachelor's autonomy evaporate, not to say britting shicks about it. He was standing in Room RC-146, if he remembered correctly, of the Palais de Justice de Montréal, the room designated for civil marriages, which room contained yet another bored Quebec flag, an electric organ not much larger than a big dog, and a mini-grandstand where a number of wedding guests were sitting, black as topsoil all of them, wrapped in brightly coloured sheets, wearing matching pill-box hats, and murmuring among themselves in a throaty language. They were there not for PF and Sandra's wedding, but for the one scheduled to take place twenty minutes later. Certainly the black-robed officiant, an energetic woman with a face that seemed to have been squeezed, vertically, her forehead overhanging her eyes, her wide mouth taking up all the short space between her projecting nose and shining chin, had suggested to the Africans that they wait outside, to which they had answered with resonant magnanimity that they had no objection whatsoever to the marriage taking place while they were in the room, and that they would be honoured if PF and Sandra would stay for their wedding as well, so that the officiant had glanced at *sergent* PF, her eyes dancing, had shrugged, and let the matter drop. He was somewhat nervous, yes, preoccupied, yes, but not because he was about to lose, supposedly, his bachelor's autonomy. If he had learned anything at all in his six or seven years in the police, it was that autonomy is like a knotted cord tied around the skull of every human, which gets tighter, ever so slightly, every day, tighter, tighter, until it drives ordinary people to do unordinary things of an inspiring nature, yes, no doubt, at times, but far more often, at least from a policeman's point of view, of a desperate and malignant nature; that what distinguishes the human from the other animals is his, or her, inability to live harmoniously with her, or his, intrinsic autonomy, into which a change in marital status puts hardly a kink. So that if he was uneasy and distracted, as he stood between *agent* Dominic Charles, his current badminton partner and witness who, interestingly enough, was also black, and the officiant reading over the text she must surely know by now upside-down and backwards, waiting, along with the murmuring, celebratory Africans, for Sandra to enter, it had more to do with time, oceans of time, with the heady challenge of finding an endless stream of projects to fill so much upcoming married time, combined with the knowledge that he did not have one single such project in mind, not one, even the obvious ones, like buying a house, being unable to formulate themselves clearly in his mind, so complex they seemed and yet so trivial compared to the vast amount of time they were required to fill. The proof that he was preoccupied, if proof were needed, was that he did not even notice Sandra's friend, Adrian Something, slip in and sit down at the organ. He remembered he was thinking about a television show, a documentary of some sort he had seen, that showed a ship's captain talking to an invisible interviewer, smiling and saying that, Oh, yes, they had definitely entered the Amazon River now, although, as the camera panned the horizon on all sides, there was not so much as the shadow of land to be seen anywhere. He knew he was thinking this because it was at this very moment that Adrian Something startled him by playing the familiar opening bars of *Wachet auf* on the congested, canine organ, the door at the back of the room opened, and Sandra entered on the arm of her father. She had decided that if, seeing as she was marrying a Catholic, or rather a non-denominational individual with a Catholic background, she was not going to be able to walk down the aisle, she was at least going to walk across the room. And he was distracted, he must have been, because he did not notice, or at least did not notice that he noticed, because his idea of love, you see, vague and unformed though it certainly was, had to do with intimacy, with sex obviously — what didn't? — but with the intimacy of sex more than with the sex itself, with ruffled sheets that were never more than half-heartedly straightened because they would just be ruffled again, with a concert of unsuspected odours that floated across the body's surface, odours that might almost have been unpleasant had they not been, again, intimate, genuine, with the sound of urinating in a bathroom whose door was left open, the *whrr* of the paper being unrolled, with the idea of nakedness generally applied to the face and hands extended to the entire body, with an intimacy that altered the rate at which time flowed, so that when you stepped out of it into the non-intimate world, you were unfailingly surprised when you looked at your watch and saw what time it actually was, an intimacy he had discovered with, and only with, Sandra Beck, that was true, only Sandra, definitely, but marriage, marriage was a public affair that had, he felt sure, far more to do with the management of non-intimate time than of intimate non-time, and this did preoccupy him, even as Adrian Something finished off the last bars of Johnny Bach's very nice piece and Sandra stationed herself beside him in front of the black-robed officiant, getting married, he was thinking, when he should have been concentrating on what he was doing, although that was what he was doing, getting married was not a little like being told you have definitely entered the Amazon River when you have not a single shred of visual evidence to corroborate the fact. And it was only later — when he parked in front of the sort of lodge place on Lac Ouimet where they were to spend the seventeen hours allotted to their honeymoon, and they started walking up the hill to the entrance — that he noticed. Or rather became aware that he had already noticed during the ceremony when Sandra had walked across the room but had been too distracted to actually observe, the retroactiveness of his reaction giving the observation an exaggerated significance, perhaps. But he noticed. It was as if the air in his lungs became for an instant scalding cold, an inexplicable dread seized him, and he said with an almost accusatory intensity, "You're limping."

The blue LeSabre by now had approached to the point where it was bobbing up and down in concert with the inspector's strides.

He must be on the third hole, said PF to himself, still thinking about Officer Cowansville, dressed in his Sûreté du Québec golf uniform. What am I saying? That would mean that he took off over an hour ago. It can't have been that long, surely. What time is it getting to be anyway?

"It's these shoes I bought to get married in," said Sandra. "I knew they were too small when I tried them on."

PF looked at the shoes, which were as red as Danilo Milic's red MGA. Although, although, when he and Sandra had married, Danilo hadn't been on the scene yet. Or had he? Sandra had started with the MSO by then, of course. When exactly did Milic join the clarinet section? In any case, he still wouldn't have had his red MG. He had been a member of the orchestra for at least a couple of years before he bought the car. So PF looked at the high-heeled shoes, which were as sloped as the high slides in playgrounds and as red and gleaming as Danilo Milic's MGA-to-be.

"Why have you still got them on, then? Take them off if they hurt."

"But I love them. I got them especially for today. Once I take them off, I can't ever wear them again."

His fingers were hooked under the door handle of the blue LeSabre, although he had not yet pulled up on it. He did so now, the door swung open, drawing with it a draft of air from the car's interior, a draft whose automotive, musty odour, heated by the sun, was so richly familiar and conciliatory that PF could not resist a thrill of victory. For had he not, for the first time in a very long time, just thought about Danilo Milic? He had.

Yes, and was there not, *inspecteur-chef* Bastarache, a time when you drove, at every available opportunity, past the townhouse in Mount Royal that you and Sandra could barely afford, in order to see if Danilo Milic's red MG were parked outside?

There was.

And was not the said vehicle parked there with considerable frequency?

It was, yes. Considerable.

And would you say that, at the time, the sight of the red MG unfailingly injected a stiffening agent directly into your heart so that each beat became a painful and thudding jolt? Each and every heartbeat?

Yes, I would.

And were you willing, then, to admit that the aforementioned Danilo Milic and your wife Sandra were engaged in an affair of the heart?

Ah . . . no, maybe not. I think, you know, I tried to convince myself . . . All right. Consider carefully now, *inspecteur-chef* Bastarache, before answering. What, exactly, was your reaction just now, at the mention of Danilo Milic's name?

Nothing in particular, nothing too much at all.

You did not, and do not still, feel, raining down on you, the slings and arrows of outrageous jealousy?

I did, and do, not.

And is, therefore, in your opinion, the red arrow out there, hanging over your head?

It is. It definitely is.

He was beaming with triumph.

And are you willing, now, to admit what surely was obvious to us all, that Mr. Milic and your wife Sandra were indeed having an affair?

Yes. Yes I am, and you do well to ask because who, after all, who could have been better suited to afford Sandra spiritual and physical succour and support after her ordeal — not in the weeks after, I mean, but in the years, when she had to come to terms with the inescapable and implacable fact that she would be stumped forever, until the very end — who better — I mean not me, not me — than Danilo Milic, a man branded for life with a flame-red birthmark that completely covered his cheek, part of his lower lip, and even the lids of his eye?

A hideous thing.

I don't know about hideous. Not gorgeous though. Fascinating in a way. But difficult to look at. The temptation to drop your eyes was overwhelming.

And who better to understand Danilo than Sandra?

Sure. Absolutely. Absolutely. No clue what Milic is up to now. He was playing jazz in Sweden the last I heard. I mean the guy could play anything. Fabulous clarinettist. He could make the thing sound like a horse.

Uncle Danilo.

Uncle Danilo, yeah. My daughter Josée called him that, didn't she. I'd forgotten.

A longing surged through the inspector's chest, a longing for the sense of wholeness, of complementarity, that he could achieve with, and only with, Sandra Beck, a longing more vibrant even than the delight of actually being with her. He installed himself in the driver's seat, jammed home the seatbelt, turned the key in the ignition, raced the engine unnecessarily, checked his mirrors, and pulled away.

The dashboard gauges looked at each other, more than a little impressed by the inspector's clear-headedness.

The blue LeSabre reassumed its course down the Eastern Townships Autoroute. To the south, Mont Saint-Grégoire, an isolated, conical hill, was revolving slowly, propelling the car forward, having connected itself to it by means of an atmospheric, irresistible cable.

Inspecteur-chef Paul-François Bastarache was singing to himself a clarinet solo in a nameless Dixieland tune, one he might have heard as, dog-tired, he opened the front door of his house and discovered an after-midnight, post-concert musical debriefing underway in his living room. He was ebullient, enthusiastic, not only because he could feel the point of the red arrow kissing the exact middle of the top of his head, but also because, seeing as he had stopped for some time and was now driving at moderate speed, he could not possibly be in danger of being accused of arriving unexpectedly early and was entitled, therefore, to admit freely to the exhilarating, anticipatory pleasure of knowing he would soon find himself in the company of Sandra Beck, whom he had known, off and on, for most of his life.

Although, he reminded himself, it is never a good idea to make too much of a show of being happy to see people. Not Sandra anyway. Either she resents having to keep up with your good mood, or else she wonders what you've been doing that you're trying to cover up.

"At times," he said, "when I'm talking to Sandra," looking into the rear-view mirror to establish eye contact with the non-existent passenger in the back seat, "or rather when she's talking to me, my eardrums go dead, I lose the signal. Sometimes it's just a question of banging my headbox, jiggling my ears, and the signal kicks in again. Usually, though, I don't realize I've lost it until I've lost it for long enough that, even if I were to find it again, I'd be listening across a dislocation in time. I'd be on cenozoic mean time, say, while Sandra'd be on neozoic daylight savings somewhere.

"Sometimes I wonder if I'm listening in the same language she's talking in. Or if the molecules in the intervening air are faithfully transmitting every detail of her English. If English it is. How do I know they're not playing games, the molecules I mean, changing what leaves her mouth as 'hassle,' into what enters my ears as 'asshole.'

"Because we love each other.

"When you love someone, you often understand perfectly what they're going to say even before they say it. It's when they say it that you find yourself struggling to grasp what they're attempting to tell you.

"You get used to it.

"Sometimes, when she's talking with a bunch of her music people, I hear their voices clacking together, *k'thwak*, *b'dang*, *b'ding*, like city hall flags, their leading edges frayed into ribbons, and then I notice that Sandra's voice is just hanging limp. Which, meteorologically, does not seem possible. I don't say anything, I rock on the back legs of my chair, I wonder if the other flags are not secretly just as aware as I am that Sandra is not clacking intelligibly. I give it time, I wait for the wind. And then I ask her if she wouldn't mind backing up and repeating herself because what she was trying to say, if she was trying, wasn't at all clear, at least not to me. Because we love each other. Nothing happens. The flags keep clacking as if I hadn't said anything at all. Only the lights go dim around me, just me. I'm out. Eliminated. Thanks for playing.

"You get used to it. Love dimming the lights.

"Who was it? Some friend of Sandra's with I don't know how many children to play house with who said to me she didn't know what it was to be lonely, didn't have time to be lonely, hadn't even been alone, physically, in exteen number of years. She almost made me wish I'd never been in love either.

"You never know when it's going to happen.

"I might be drying my hands under the blower in the men's room. I might be rubbing out my name with my thumb, having just written it in ballpoint on the top of my modular desk. And suddenly, around me, the lights go dim.

"I might be in the TV studio, on the set of *C'est la loi/It's the Law*, in December 1989, say, the studio spots trained on me like my own private interrogation lights. I might be very warm and quite nervous because I have decided to recite from memory, out of respect, without the benefit of cue cards or cheat-sheets, the names of the fourteen young women assassinated two days earlier, on the sixth of December, as I say, 1989, at the École Polytechnique de Montréal. It is an unprofessional decision perhaps. Granted, I have repeated the names perfectly any number of times in front of the tall mirror in the bedroom, but that is a very different thing from saying them while standing alone in front of a camera, with all of Montreal watching. And all of Montreal will be watching. I start in, a quaver in my voice that, as I will discover subsequently, the microphones do not faithfully record. 'Geneviève Bergeron, Hélène Colgan,' the names, except for one, are in alphabetic order, which makes it easier, 'Nathalie Croteau, Barbara Daigneault, Anne-Marie Edward, Maud Haviernick,' they are not names, really, but chains of syllables, rolling out of my mouth, 'Maryse Laganière, Anne-Marie Lemay, Sonia Pelletier, Michèle Richard,' the two Annies-in-a-row, 'Annie St-Arneault, Annie Turcotte,' and the difficult, which also makes it easier, 'Barbara Klucznik-Widajewicz.' Thirteen names, one to go, it is almost over. I am enormously relieved and even slightly light-headed. I now say that shortly after the tragedy, a police officer was standing outside the Polytechnique briefing reporters. I pay a very brief tribute to this officer who, like me, is involved with public relations, is even the Director of Public Relations for the Montreal Urban Community police force. I do not, of course, say that this officer dislikes me intensely, that he considers my puddle of celebrity as host of a local police-related TV show to be not only undeserved, but a personal affront, or that he would can the show, and me, in the wink of a bat's ass were it not for the show's considerable not-unpopularity. I go on to say that this officer, after he had finished briefing reporters, entered the Polytechnique and himself discovered the fourteenth victim, who had been stabbed to death after having been wounded by a bullet. And who was — incredibly, although this I do not, of course, say — who was . . . his own daughter. The sombreness of the moment suffocates me, I am alone in front of a non-existent audience that, being imaginary, is everywhere, in the very dust and air I am breathing. At the same time, I am somewhat giddy, as though drifting upwards through the spotlight beams, because I have said all the names correctly, except the fourteenth, which I know perfectly well. And it is at this moment that the lights go dim around me, just me, I stop, congeal, my brain empties. And although the impression I convey of being overcome by the emotion of having to pronounce the name of the officer's daughter is so convincing that I receive many, many letters and even a terse but personally signed memo of recognition from the Director of Public Relations who nevertheless dislikes me intensely, I have simply fallen in love, into the loneliness of love that is, *je bande, oui, je bande,* I want to have sex with Sandra, who is alive, only Sandra, every cell of my body has a hard-on on, I want to have sex with her ribs and phalanges, her liver and kidneys, her gall bladder, aorta, and trigeminal nerves. I want to be intimate, on intimate terms, with Sandra, preferably with some discretion, with lightness, preferably without clothing, but not necessarily, intimate, intimate necessarily, in silence, and intimate, and anywhere.

"Sandra, however, is not anywhere. She is somewhere quite specific. As am I, of course. I am on the set of *C'est la loi/It's the Law* trying desperately to say, 'Maryse Leclair.'

"Naturally, being human, I wonder if the lights go dim around Sandra from time to time. At the same time as me, perhaps, but in her specific time zone. Although when it comes to love, even contiguous time zones do not necessarily touch.

"Oh, she comes equipped. She can talk on the phone, write perfectly legible notes very quickly, smoke Cameos, check her eyes in her chrome desk lamp. All at the same time. She can stare into the fridge as though it contained the horizon. She can drive automatic with her one foot to the floor while chatterboxing with her passengers. She can transmit pure information, rehearsal schedules, travel dates, hotel arrangements, without confusion or misunderstanding. She can persuade, coax, cajole. She can convince her musicians that what's really bothering them is something other than that they're not getting paid enough. Or that the best thing to loosen up their blazing tendinitis is to continue rehearsing Sibelius's fourth three hours a day.

"She, Sandra, is, quite obviously, a communicator. Therefore the problem is with me. I take her perfectly plain language and turn it into code. Any number of unspoken meanings and veiled intentions then emerge to exercise my brain seeing as it has decided not to sleep anyway. I admit that it took me a while to get used to it, but I accept now that it's a problem I have.

"A problem I have with Sandra, just Sandra.

"I love her."

The irresistible atmospheric cable thrown out by Mont Saint-Grégoire detached itself from the blue LeSabre and swung loosely across the Eastern Townships Autoroute, releasing the car from the protecting influence of the Monteregian Hills. Mont Saint-Hilaire and Mont Bruno were too far to the north now, Mont Royal was not yet in range. As if to signal the fact, a sudden, premonitory rush of wind threw a spray of raindrops across the windshield, startling the inspector, who inadvertently snapped on the wipers at full tilt. The rubber blades slapped frenetically across the windshield. What sounded like a human name leapt out: *dee-cee-lan-dree-dee-cee-lan-dree-dee-cee-lan-dree.*

PF set the wipers on a slower speed and listened: Dee-cie Lan-dry, Dee-cie Lan-dry.

Fascinated, he turned the wipers off.

He had no idea what aleatory force could have summoned the name of Deecie Landry, whom he had not seen or had any news of in well over a decade. He remembered her with her new boyfriend, the one she had first discovered under the physiotherapy tent of the Montreal marathon. Barely bigger than a fourteen-year-old, he was, barely bigger than her daughters in other words, half the size of Deecie herself, black as night, buoyant and loose-headed when he was not running, which was not often. He could run for hours and hours faster than PF could run period. He ran as a Dutch national, Deecie ended up moving to the Netherlands with him.

The inspector was interrupted here by the rattling and bouncing of the car as it crossed the uneven bridge over the Richelieu River.

Once on the other side, the LeSabre found itself inside the vortex created by the noisy, spinning star of the Island of Montreal. It was soon surrounded by every make and model of vehicle, all bearing down intently on the Champlain Bridge. It was somewhat intimidated, not being as young as it had been. It looked for an opening in the safe centre lane, and found a spot behind a turquoise Jetta with a worn licence plate.

Inspecteur-chef Bastarache's mind, assailed now by the clatter and rush of traffic on all sides, was unwilling to consider any but the most immediate aspects of the inspector's existence. It cancelled the name of Deecie Landry, and reminded PF that he was a Montreal policeman, an experienced one, that he should concentrate on driving in order to arrive home in one piece, and that he also had work to do. He had to prepare himself for the next meeting of the MUC Police Integrated Policies Committee, Monday morning, in fact.

Paul-François understood that he would not necessarily be expected to attend this meeting, or any other meeting of the committee for that matter, but a policy he was proposing was to be on the agenda, and he wanted to be present in order to argue his case. He considered that it should be official policy that urban community police not engage in high-speed chases of motorcyclists who were not wearing helmets. He knew what the first challenge would be and where it would come from: Gélinas, a squat, pompous individual with a moustache that looked like it should spin very quickly and be used to clean the teeth of zoo animals. Gélinas would say that the policy was *complètement ridicule* because if the bikers found out about it, they'd just take off their helmets and ride at any speed they liked. To which PF would respond that the objection was *complètement ridicule* because no biker anywhere had the faintest idea about official police policy, and how would they find out? Unless Gélinas told them. Another likely objection would be that the policy was unnecessary, seeing as every self-respecting biker considered his helmet to be the identifying piece of his gear, and never rode without it. To which PF would say that he had in mind the young individual rider, the hot-dogging adolescent. If such a rider were to suffer a serious head injury as the result of a high-speed chase, the police force might find itself being sued for a great deal of money. The city might be required to pay an indemnity large enough to destabilize its finances, and thereby the police's, for years to come.

The Champlain Bridge was in view now. PF continued to follow the turquoise Jetta. He was aware of the jockeying for position going on around him, but he was content to stay where he was.

Also, he had to tape an interview for *C'est la loi/It's the Law* sometime during the week with an individual who had gone to the media because, he claimed, he had to pay the outrageous amount of $500 for feeding peanuts to the squirrels in Lafontaine Park. PF was looking forward to this interview. For behind the apparent absurdity of the item lay an opportunity to inform the public, and informing the public was, he felt, the main intent of his television show. Obviously the man had not actually been fined $500. He had been fined $70. Which fine he would have been perfectly justified in challenging by showing up in court and talking to the judge. Which he had not done. He had done nothing at all, in fact, and had, consequently, received a second fine, a stiff one, for failing to appear, which would be due even if the original $70 were ultimately rescinded. Which was unlikely. There was, after all, a reason why you were not supposed to feed the squirrels. They bite, they spread disease.

The truth is, muttered PF to himself, if you go to the trouble of showing up in court . . .

He was interrupted again, this time by the brake lights of the turquoise Jetta ahead of him coming on in a flickering, half-hearted manner. Hoo, *mon ami*, he thought, I ought to pull you over for faulty equipment. Of course, you're driving a Volkswagen. They come off the assembly line with faulty equipment.

All around him the straining vehicles were closing ranks, while ahead loomed the bridge, le pont Champlain. It was a magnificent structure in PF's estimation, and unfailingly reminded him of the boyhood shopping trips to Montreal he had used to make with his family. The crossing of the six-kilometre, steel truss, cantilever bridge had always been a central feature of those trips. The first section was an interminable, steady ascent up to the high span over Nun's Island and the shipping lanes in the Saint Lawrence River, followed by a shorter and more rapid descent to Montreal. It was like a thrilling, elemental roller coaster, enormous and elegant, all the more magnificent in that it was useful.

"Roll down your windows," his father had commanded every time. "You can smell the sea."

He was so close to the turquoise Jetta now that he could see the rust eating through the metal around the chrome lettering on the trunk.

And in fact, PF had often, on humid days especially, been able to detect, apart from the combustive smell of exhaust and oil, a faint odour, cooler and more pungent, which apparently was that of the sea, and which linked, therefore, the Champlain Bridge with a host of powerful associations in his young mind, the landings on the beaches of Normandy, for example, or the stunning, bare-breasted women of Polynesia.

It's the busiest bridge in Canada, he reminded himself with a blush of civic pride, as though the Champlain Bridge at least remained to defend Montreal against its gradual slide into mediocrity. Every day, 160,000 vehicles cross it. On average.

He saw the Jetta in front of him dip, felt the sudden dip himself, followed by the steady, gentle rise that signalled the beginning of the bridge itself. He was now officially on it, one of 160,000 in the close-packed parade of slowly moving vehicles, rising incessantly, heading out over the Saint Lawrence River, under the latticework of steel.

He lowered the electric windows slightly and breathed in deeply.

But his eyes were dead ahead, glued to the worn licence plate of the turquoise Jetta.

He was rising. Rising.

Carolyn her name was. Landry. A French name that she insisted was pronounced "Lawndry," and did so with such eight-year-old, aristocratic airiness that everyone simply sniggered and jumped at such a wide open invitation to invent nicknames. The fact was, she was as mediocre in French as she was in every other subject, and she lived in Lennoxville, right across the street from Sandra Beck who did not like her and whose nicknames for her alternated between "Lawnding-gear" and "Landromat." Other names that enjoyed long-standing currency were "Washerwoman" and "Dirty Clothes," especially in their abbreviated forms, "Weewee" and, to a lesser extent, "Deecie." Despite its relatively slow start, it was the second of these that would, in time, become an inextricable part of her identity, her veritable name in fact, "Carolyn" being retained only by her driver's licence and health care card, so that even her own daughters, years later, called her "Deecie" instead of "Mum."

Deecie Landry. Not fat, no, but formless, without a chin or a waist, without clearly definable breasts, buttocks, elbows, or knees. Animated by a monolithic personality composed entirely of generosity, but a generosity that could be shrill, demandingly verbose, and that even at its most placid and dewy-eyed insisted on being taken advantage of with a devoted importunateness. According to legend, her grandfather had been in love with the grandmother of Sandra Beck, had proposed to her and been turned down, and then had almost immediately married Deecie's grandmother. Sandra could not conceive of how any member of her family could interest themselves in any member of Deecie's family even to the point of turning them down. But for Deecie, there existed between the two girls a kindred bond more occult and mysterious than that between true sisters. A bond that gave her rights. Sandra's inventiveness was hard-pressed to find enough reasons not to go over to Deecie's house, or not to have Deecie come over to hers. And then, when Deecie got her driver's licence at sixteen, principally in order to become Sandra's private chauffeur, not even Sandra could resist what was not only an undeniable convenience, but also a prestigious access to adulthood. With increasing regularity, she found herself sitting in the passenger seat, squeezing herself against the door, trying to pretend that she was not being drawn in by Deecie's unending chatter. They both went to Champlain College after finishing high school. Deecie pleaded with Sandra to help her improve her marks so she could get into pre-med at McGill, and Sandra, who was planning to go to Bishop's, let herself be coaxed only because she saw a chance to rid herself of Deecie for ever and good. The two girls worked hard together, and the plan paid off. Deecie got into McGill, and Sandra went to Bishop's, feeling as though she had lost forty pounds of formless flesh, and marvelling how easy it was to forget someone despite having spent countless hours in their company.

Almost a decade later, Sandra was living in Montreal and working as an assistant manager for the Montreal Symphony Orchestra. When she accepted the job, which she did with joyous trepidation, it being the one job in ten thousand she would have liked to have, she had no idea she was becoming the orchestra's medical officer. Being an accomplished pianist herself and never having experienced the slightest discomfort, she was astonished to discover that at any given moment, a third of the orchestra's musicians might be either playing with pain or unable to play at all, that she would be expected to maintain a roster of stand-by musicians and keep careful track of their hours and considerable fees, that she would have to familiarize herself with a host of afflictions, carpal tunnel syndrome, tendinitis, bursitis, tenosynovitis, de Quervain's syndrome, tendinosis, thoracic outlet syndrome, laryngoceles, retinal hemorrhage, myofascial pain syndrome, cubital tunnel syndrome, trigger finger, focal dystonia, and maintain a register of health care professionals to suit every taste and condition, physiotherapists, neurologists, osteopaths, chiropractors, myotherapists, acupuncturists, magnetotherapists, biofeedback specialists, masseurs, Feldenkrais therapists, hypnosis therapists, Hoshino therapists, and practitioners of shiatsu, of tai chi and yoga. Nor was she aware that she would have to be able to decipher the needs equally of those whose response to any injury was simply to play and play, and those who bounced from treatment to treatment, convinced beforehand they would not see any improvement. Many musicians sought out their own care and only came to Sandra if they couldn't find what they were looking for. One such was a flautist who found her ability to play rapid passages diminishing inexplicably. Having heard about a new treatment called the Alexander technique, she asked Sandra if she might be able to find a practitioner for her, in Toronto or New York perhaps. Sandra spent an afternoon on the phone, without much success. The word spread quickly, though, because the next day she received a call from a therapist who said she knew the Alexander technique.

"Excellent," said Sandra, "When can you come to Montreal?"

"But I am in Montreal. I live here."

"Ahhh! Well. Would you be willing to meet at my place, say, so I can sit in on the first session? Or somewhere else if you prefer."

"No, your place will be fine."

The flautist had already arrived when the doorbell rang a second time. Sandra opened the door to a pair of white sunglasses as big and round as lollipops stuck onto the head of a neckless but recognizably human form.

"Sandra!" said the form, "It is you! I told myself that it couldn't be, but that it had to be. You haven't changed one iota. Still as skinny as two rakes and as gorgeous as gorgeous. I, on the other hand, yes, I know I've changed. I don't blame you for not recognizing me. I'm Deecie."

Sandra, who had recognized Deecie instantly, was marvelling how easy it was to remember someone despite not having seen or even thought about them in years. It was almost as if the intervening time had evaporated, she was in Cégep again, heavier by forty pounds of formless flesh.

"Carolyn Landry," she said limply. "It's been a while."

"I'll say. Donkey's decades. I never did do pre-med, you know. I lied to you about that. I'll explain after." Deecie unravelled the pet scarf coiled around the upper portion of her body.

After? thought Sandra.

"So where's my flute player?"

"This way."

Deecie the therapist was a very different person from Deecie the simili-sister. She was patient, restrained, and spoke no more than necessary. She asked the flautist to play some slower passages and then some rapid ones, after which she told her to put her instrument away and lie down on the floor.

"Imagine," she said, "that you're lying on a board, and that the board is getting narrower and narrower. And also shorter."

Eventually, the flautist was lying on an imaginary board four inches wide and too short to support either her head or her feet. She was lifting her limbs in various combinations and trying to maintain her balance on the board. The flautist's concentration was striking, as was the deliberateness with which she carried out the movements. She stopped often in mid-movement, adjusted her balance, trembled, trying to stabilize her position on the board, as if such a board really existed.

"What would you most like to fall into," said Deecie, "if you do fall?"

"Sand. Warm sand."

"What would you most like not to fall into?"

"The Atlantic Ocean."

"So what do you think is under you?"

"The sand. I'm sure it's the sand."

"A beach, say? Beside the Atlantic?"

"Mmn. I just might fall off on purpose."

"Go ahead."

The session was over. The flautist took up her instrument again.

"Don't use just your fingers," said Deecie. "Play from your back. Your back controls your shoulders, which control your arms, which control your hands, which control your fingers. Try it."

The flautist played through the rapid passages several times, her instrument emitting a froth of sparks. She lowered her head for a moment. When she raised it, there were tears in her eyes.

"Thank you so much," she said.

Sandra, who could not honestly say she had heard much variation in the perfection of the flautist's playing, could nevertheless feel an imaginary board rubbing against her spine.

"I never applied even to pre-med," said Deecie, bravely, after Sandra had seen the flautist to the door. "I was only trying to get into physiotherapy. Pre-med was just an idea I had to get you to work with me. The strange thing was, you made me work so hard, I maybe could almost have gotten into pre-med. I never knew how to get good marks until you showed me."

Sandra did not require this explanation. She thought Deecie might have at least made a show of leaving so that she, Sandra, might have at least had the opportunity of inviting her to stay. She was impressed and even a little intimidated by this new, competent Deecie whom she had never seen before. Also, she had work to do. And she was eager to sit down at the piano and try playing from her back.

"Are you hungry, Deecie? Coffee? Tea?"

"Oh, a cup of coffee, I'd love that. It's amazing that the Alexander technique is what's brought us together. It's a good technique, I learned it to help a patient of mine, a kid whose right hand tightened up into a fist every time he used his fingers for fine movements, like writing or painting. Just the right hand, the left was okay. I work with kids. I'm connected with the CLSC in Parc-Ex. I received a message there to call you.

"I used to watch you practise the piano, you know, through your living room window. There was a painting behind the piano, in a gold frame. Every time I was in your house I tried to find some new detail in the painting, because I knew the detail would still be there when I watched you through the window. It was of a stream running through the woods, with the snow melting. And it was signed 'Maclarren.' I remember so much. I remember how your father used to slam the bar of Mackintosh's toffee onto the floor to break it into pieces, and how your mother used to cross her legs when she talked on the telephone and say, 'Hell.' 'Hell, Joanna, why don't we just go anyway?' I remember her saying that. I remember wondering who Joanna was."

Her mother did say "hell" when, and only when, she talked on the telephone. Now that Deecie pointed it out to her, Sandra realized this was true.

"I remember your grandfather wearing his maroon V-neck sweater and his indoor-outdoor slippers. When he was in charge of doing the potatoes, he scraped them with a knife instead of peeling them, because, he said, they were new potatoes. I thought he meant they were a new kind of potato that didn't need peeling."

But these, thought Sandra, these are *my* memories.

"Remember when he had his stroke? He tried to get up from his chair in the garden and couldn't? He fell back and the chair toppled over. We were so scared. I ran in and told your mother."

Yes, and my frantic mother heaped redundant thanks on you, while I stood there frozen, unable to touch my grandfather, my heart breaking.

"Deecie, do you remember my mother's grilled-cheese sandwiches?"

"Oh, Sandra, can you?"

"I can come pretty close."

This manoeuvre of Sandra's succeeded at least in distracting Deecie from further appropriating her memories. However, it also, as Sandra dug out her non-stick frying pan, launched Deecie on another, potentially more oppressive topic. Deecie herself.

"I love my work, Sandra. I have two lovely twin daughters now. I'm with a good man. I'm very happy." Uttered with inspired fervour. So that Sandra could not help wondering if it was she Deecie was trying to convince, or Deecie herself.

"Twin girls. Yikes. How old are they? Are they walking yet?"

"They walk to school, Sandra. They're eight years old."

"Ah."

Eight. Sandra pressed down ferociously on the grilled-cheese sandwiches with the plastic flipper, this being her mother's technique. Eight. Deecie therefore, who was, naturally, of the non-contraceptive persuasion, had had the girls while she was in her first or second year at McGill. And still she had managed to graduate, find work, develop a practice, learn the Alexander technique. The complexity of such an existence seemed so overwhelming to Sandra that she felt her shoulders slump, her chest tighten.

"I spoil them unmercifully," said Deecie with a thin smile. "Whatever they want I let them have. I don't care if they love me. I need them to like me. It's terrible of me, I know."

The sandwiches were ready, very hot and flattened to the point that cheese had oozed out and was cooked onto the outside. Deecie took hers with eager gluttony, bit into it with the tips of her teeth, chewed rapidly while fanning cool air into her mouth, swallowed.

After which, she wept.

She dug out of her handbag then what appeared to be a man's handkerchief and, with the help of a pocket mirror that she set up on the microwave, daubed at her mascara. She took out a plastic freezer bag containing her Maybelline cosmetics and relined her eyes with practised skill using short, rapid strokes of the black pencil. She put away her meagre equipment, crossed her arms in front of herself, holding her elbows, and looked squarely at Sandra with an expression that was equally joyous and forlorn.

"Look at you," she said. "Just look. Managing the Montreal Symphony Orchestra. And you're not even thirty years old yet."

That, thought Sandra, is the problem with Deecie.

"Deecie. Eat."

Admiration. In the first place, she was not managing the orchestra, she was an assistant. For now. In the second place, she would never have mustered the courage even to apply for the job had it not been for Paul-François' constant harassment. Sandra, for Deecie, was a golden girl with the self-assurance of a Carnival Queen-elect. But Sandra, for Sandra, was an anonymously attractive drudge, a worker, whose only true talent was the knack for making applied effort give an impression of true talent.

Example: why the pint-sized, home-town school of Bishop's, where yes, she had, in fact, been the Winter Carnival Queen, instead of a more respected institution, a real university, like McGill? Why? To keep the admiration coming, right? To be high honcha on the low totem, to live up to Deecie's, and the people like Deecie's, but principally Deecie-bloody-Deecie's, image of her.

Deecie, by now, was into her handbag again. She took out a pair of photographs and handed them to Sandra. They might have been copies of the same Grade Two school picture, each one having the same atrocious purple curtain as backdrop for the same young girl gazing at the camera with the same capricious self-possession, assessing, apparently, the proficiency of the photographer, the festive island of her face connected to the tranquil mainland of her shoulders by the isthmus of a perfect neck, except that in the white margin at the bottom of one was written Janet, and of the other, Samantha.

"Those are last year's pictures. They're seven there."

"They're . . . just . . . ," said Sandra lamely. "Which one's older?"

"Sam I guess. She was taken out first. I had a C-section."

The image of a scalpel sliding through buttery flesh clouded Sandra's imagination and set her nerves on edge. She was thinking how easy it was for Deecie to infiltrate her existence, while she remained firmly on the perimeter of Deecie's. She did not seem to realize, Deecie didn't, that her relentless admiration amounted to so much added weight for Sandra to lug around. Only when she had escaped Deecie's influence had she got her ass in gear, got the music degree from McGill she should have taken in the first place, got a job that was not simply a job. Started building in other words, and found someone to build with.

The truth, plain and simple, was that Deecie Landry was not good for her.

Having thought this and firmly established her distance, Sandra felt strong enough to ask Deecie to leave. Soon. Not right away. In the meantime, she could afford to make amends. "Deece," she said, "want the grand tour?"

"Do I!" said Deecie, stuffing her pictures back in her handbag.

It was a townhouse of recent construction. Sandra and the man she was married to, *sergent* Bastarache, Paul-François, of the Montreal Urban Community police force, had lived in it for less than a year. It was still largely undecorated. Even the curtains, despite being of expensive material, were only pinned in place, and could not be opened and closed properly. Still, Deecie managed to find some detail to praise in every room, reaffirming thereby her faith in Sandra's innate sense of decorative style.

They came to a small room that had a single, tall window covered hastily with a broken Venetian blind. The room was completely empty.

"This," said Sandra, "is going to be my office. Eventually." She could almost hear Deecie's brain working, trying desperately to find something to praise. She decided to help her out. "The light switches are quite attractive, don't you think?"

"Very," said Deecie, smiling, thinking Sandra's remark was

directed at herself, that she was chiding herself for not having done anything to the room.

Sandra closed the door. "Well, that's about it for the tour, Deece. What time is it getting to be?"

It was well after eleven by the time *sergent* PF arrived home. He sauntered into the kitchen wearily.

"*Salut,*" said Sandra.

"*Salut.*"

"This is Deecie Landry. She used to live across the street from me in Lennoxville. Beer?"

"Hi," to Deecie. "Sure," to Sandra.

The two women were sitting across from each other at the kitchen table. Between them, there was a half-full ashtray that was closer to Sandra, as well as a small grove of empty beer bottles.

"On second thoughts," said PF, "I think I'll just head upstairs. It's been a long one."

The instant he was gone, the women broke into silent peals of laughter, laughter not of mockery, although PF would likely have thought so had he re-entered the kitchen at that moment, but of understanding, community.

The ashtray and the grove of bottles were still on the table the next morning when Sandra re-entered the kitchen. There was also a note of thanks from Deecie, who had ended up sleeping in the living room.

Sandra's throat felt as though it had gone to seed. She was not sure if this had been caused by the beer, the cigarettes, or the endless, endless conversation. She had a great deal of work to do, especially seeing as she had done so little the previous day. Also, she had a dull, nagging pain in her heel, a not unfamiliar pain. And not entirely disagreeable either, seeing as she had become aware of it for the first time on the very day of her marriage.

Deecie Lawnding-gear. Being nothing if not tenacious, Deecie would be calling again sometime within the next twenty-four hours. She had talked expansively about every single aspect of her life, from the spiritual, including her belief in God, to the soporific, including her belief in God. Every aspect of her life, that is, but one: the man in it. A good man he may well have been, but if his paternity seemed certifiable, his personality and even his presence remained as vague as his contribution to the household finances. Sandra, as she slumped at the table, gazing at the bottles, luxuriating in the temptation to sleep there and then for ten more minutes, could not help being lulled by a sense of competitive ascendancy. The man she was with was hard at it already, uniformed, out the door. And not to be back, either, until eleven or later.

Deecie was resilient, yes, courageous. Although, much of the time, it was her lack of selectivity that required her to be so.

Hmn, thought Sandra wryly, that lack of selectivity didn't extend to her, did it?

In any case, Deecie had been, and was still, a good friend.

Sandra knew that this early morning largesse was underwritten by the sense of ascendancy, which tended towards the complacent, but she would make it up to Deecie. When Deecie called, Sandra would be all ears. She too would be a friend. In deed, if not in need.

But Deecie did not call.

After a time, Sandra wrote a memo to the members of the orchestra stating that she had found an Alexander technique practitioner in Montreal whose work with the first flautist had given excellent results, and that she could set up an appointment in her home at any convenient time. But no one seemed interested.

After a longer time, she found herself walking by the Estée Lauder counter in Eaton's. She was reminded of Deecie, re-doing her eyes, her pocket mirror perched on the microwave, and she was remembering Deecie's explanation for why she used so much eyeliner: when she was pregnant she had taken to crying at any moment for no obvious reason, and after the twins were born, she had continued to be a walking sob story until she noticed that, when she had eyeliner on, it started to tingle just before the tearburst, so that now she did her eyes almost as soon as she got out of bed. That way, if the eyeliner started to tingle, she at least had time to get hold of herself.

This gave Sandra an idea.

When she got home, she dialled Deecie's number.

"Hello," said a young girl's voice.

"Hello," said Sandra, "are you Janet or Sam?"

"Hello-o!"

"What, you can't hear me? I'd like to speak to your mum!"

"One *mo*ment!"

Sandra heard, distantly but distinctly, the young girl holler, "Deecie!" Deecie, eventually, came to the phone.

"I got a little something for you," said Sandra, "just a small-little something. When can I drop it off?"

"You don't need to find excuses, Sandra, to come and visit, you know."

". . . I know. But I saw this little cosmetics kit and I thought of you with your makeup in a plastic freezer bag and I thought, you know . . ."

"I *like* my plastic freezer bag. But come, come."

And so Deecie germinated again in Sandra's life, sprouted, sent out roots, like a weed so intertwined with other plants as to be impossible to dislodge. Not an obtrusive weed, not even an unattractive one, but still, a weed.

Whenever she spent time with Deecie, Sandra returned to the business of her life irked, exasperated. Deecie's apartment was a cluttered playground overflowing with furniture, every piece of which had belonged to someone else before belonging to Deecie. Mementos and memorabilia — "keepsakes" in Deecie's vocabulary, "why-do-you-keep-them-for-heaven's-sakes?" in Sandra's — occupied every available surface. The walls were covered with the twins' childish drawings.

And the twins. They were indistinguishable, conjugated sweethearts with pixilated, cellophane eyes. Until confronted with even mild resistance to receiving whatever it was they wanted, in which case they instantly turned into pixilated, screeching demons, only to become, instantly, sweethearts again when they had their way.

But what set Sandra's nerves on edge the most was Deecie's relentless solicitousness, both medical and spiritual, her insistent, dizzying dietary recommendations, her evangelical enthusiasm for exercise programs, unvigorous and vigorous, in which she did not participate herself, her relentless, handicrafted, Christian propaganda. Sandra could not see how anyone with a university education could, in the second half of the twentieth century, believe in God. But Deecie did, and she was not alone, as Sandra realized on the rare occasions when she let Deecie convince her to go to church. Sandra had played the organ in the Anglican church when she was a teenager, and she was still enthralled by the decorative aspects of the liturgy, the music, and ceremony.

Nor could she help being touched and even moved by Deecie's inexorable devotion to others. All others. She took them under one of her seven or eight wings, pampered, domineered, cajoled, coddled, coerced. Not only her minikin, artful daughters and her thick-set and -headed husband who, generally speaking, was "on the road," but also her friends, her friends' friends, her patients, their parents, siblings, blood and social relations, not to mention all the unsuccessful, unlucky, undernourished, the underdogged and underloved who roamed the galaxy of Montreal. She was constantly occupied, searching the city for therapeutic aids and techniques for her patients, her kids as she called them, doing errands for people she barely knew, buying groceries for ill or elderly people she had met by chance. She was always tired and always late, and still she took time, when necessary, to reapply her eyeliner, using the mirror taped to the sun visor of her car.

Not surprisingly, she was, on occasion, ill. Often enough she pushed on despite being sick, but there were times when she simply was unable to. Her daughters could not understand why their feverish lump of a mother did not get up and prepare their orange juice, iron the busy pleats of their school uniforms, and brush their hair. Even less could they comprehend how she seemed to expect them to carry out these tasks themselves, never having shown them how. Both of them shirked all responsibility, found perfectly logical arguments in favour of the other's doing everything, and fought tirelessly at full, brain-piercing volume.

Sandra made an effort, during these periods of illness, to overcome her reluctance and visit Deecie more often. Especially as it now seemed that Deecie's man had gone on the road once more often than he had returned home. She arrived with a lasagna or a giant salad, did Deecie's groceries and paid for them herself. Sometimes she met some of Deecie's other friends, discovering, somewhat surprised at her own surprise, that she was not the only person to help Deecie out. Occasionally she cleaned up the kitchen after the twins, in a moment of bipartisan inspiration, had used every available bowl, utensil, and measuring device to make a rough approximation of banana bread.

"Have a piece," said Deecie. "It's really excellent."

"It is not. It's way overdone, baked to within an inch of its life. But they still think they deserve a standing ovation."

"Oh Sandra. It's my fault. You've seen how I spoil them. What do you expect?"

But Sandra again would forget about Deecie. And everything else.

The nagging pain in her heel became more persistent, bothersome. It no longer reminded her of anything but itself. She told her doctor finally. X-rays were taken.

Sergent Paul-François Bastarache, *Enquêtes, Région sud,* lay in bed, sleepless, breathless, his heart racing. The stillness in the bedroom suggested it might be snowing outside. He could hear the ticking of the baseboard heater as it warmed. Beside him, Sandra Beck lay on her side, her back to him, sleeping the sleep of the carefree, breathing with mechanical regularity.

And yet, he thought, she's the one who's got the cancer, not me.

He rubbed his eyes, opened them as wide as possible, but did not succeed in eliminating the fantasmic clouds scurrying through the darkness. He was convinced that if he did not sleep, they would grow in intensity, surround him, invade him.

She was to have her foot amputated, Sandra was. Within the month — the date was already set. The hulking health care bureaucracy, so bearish with the everyday ill, roared with concern when she walked through the door, and went straightaway to work for her.

He could not prevent himself from imagining the surgeon in his blood-stained smock, tapping the shin of Sandra Beck with the stainless steel cleaver to mark the spot, and then raising it gleefully high above his head.

His own life was being amputated, as it seemed to him. Amputated of its future.

He had used to fall asleep, when he was young and falling asleep was easy, thinking of the things he would invent when he was grown, of a jet fighter, for example, whose cockpit spun inside the fuselage, remaining upright no matter how much the jet dipped and turned so that, during dogfights, an ultra-sophisticated automatic pilot, guided by any number of superior sensors, could set the plane on a hallucinatory zigzag course, rendering it untouchable — while the floating pilot, PF in other words, simply rode the fight out.

He fell asleep, when he was young, and still did, dreaming about what he might, one way or another, eventually do. Or wish to.

But now, when he tried to imagine his future, all he could see were fantasmic clouds scurrying through the darkness. Sandra Beck, whom he had known, off and on, for most of his life and had married what, a little more than three years ago, barely forty months, Sandra Beck might now die. She might, although the doctors were saying that oh, no, no, no, that was very, really very unlikely. She would be cured. But cured only after the foot had been lopped off. And who would Sandra be then?

Who was she now? A silent, unattainable stranger, determined, unafraid, already practising walking with a new pair of wooden crutches.

"Since the day we got married and you told me to take off my shoes if my foot was sore, remember? and I said I didn't want to because I'd bought the shoes to get married in? I've known there was something wrong, that something serious was wrong with me, but I made light of it to myself. Because I was afraid. Now, at last, I know what I'm up against. And I'm going to get through it. It's intimidating, yes, but at least I don't have to be afraid."

Oh, come on, thought PF, that's just so much . . .

"But you, you don't know what you're up against, do you? You didn't plan on having to live with a peg-leg. You don't have to, you know, if you don't want to."

He lay in bed, assailed by, and as though entangled in, Sandra's opalescent, lucid detachment, prey to a ferocious, squirming, sexual desire. He slid off his pyjamas stealthily, concentrating on Sandra's breathing to be sure it continued uninterrupted. He took hold of his sex roughly. But if his spirit was on fire, his body was not. His sex was more concerned about Sandra, apparently, than it was excited about him.

Fuck me, he thought. The only thing I know for sure is, whatever happens, I'm getting the fuck out of homicide.

He saw the blood-stained cleaver rise again, rising against a blue, a perfect sky.

Fuck me, he thought, pulling up his pyjamas quickly and rolling onto his side. Fuck me.

He arrived at the hospital later than he had planned, but it did not matter. He was wet, having had to walk up from the Champ-de-Mars metro station in the dark through the invisible January rain. Sandra had not yet recovered from the effects of the anaesthetic. She was grey-looking, unresponsive, not fully conscious.

He pulled the green leatherette armchair up to the head of the bed. It made a startling, uncivil, windy sound when he sat down in it. It was comfortable. He was tired, having had to conduct a lengthy interrogation that day. He had not eaten.

For a long time he examined Sandra's face, so expressionless as to be almost unfamiliar. She had a brown mole under her eye.

Finally he turned his head to one side, casually, as though simply to look elsewhere, having looked in the same direction for some time, and observed the contours of the thin blanket. It had once been yellowish but now, after a thousand washings, it was almost white, the colour of pudding. Its matted surface was stippled with tiny balls of fluff.

He did not look away. His gaze observed how the blanket followed the form of Sandra's body, faithfully but discreetly, making her appear somewhat more substantial than she really was. His gaze skied over the hills of her legs and came to a stop at the base of the sugarloaf of her foot. Her right foot.

He had been living this moment, one way or another, for weeks, perhaps, but weeks that seemed like most of his life.

He did not look away. There was something deeply touching about the one, solitary sugarloaf. And yet, something humorous as well, something cartoonish. He felt a wave of tenderness, of compassion, so unrestrained as to be almost nauseating, he could feel the tension drain from his body and drip onto the floor.

He was fascinated, prey to a delicious curiosity. He was tempted to slide his hands under the pudding-coloured blanket, to pull up the hospital smock stealthily and feel the fleshy pad just above the knee, the pad that he imagined was, among discriminating cannibals, considered a highly prized delicacy, to feel the knee itself, the endless shin, and the sudden, bulky bandage. He wanted to see the wound, to pick at the edges of the bandage. His fingertips burned with the need to touch the stump, he had to wedge his hands between his knees.

He looked again at Sandra's neutral, empty face, and let his head drop onto the mattress beside hers.

He could see himself carrying her up the gangway of an enormous passenger liner. She was holding on to her crutches now, there were streamers in the air, the whistle sounded deafeningly, the cheers were overwhelming, and yet utterly silent. He was carrying Sandra up the surface of the silent cheers. Or he might have been. He was falling asleep too quickly to be sure.

For the first days, when Sandra arrived home, the telephone rang off the hook. PF tried to give each caller an individual answer, but he kept tripping over his tongue, so he gave up and settled for explaining umpteen times in exactly the same words that Sandra, for the moment, was not up to talking and wanted to be left alone.

After which the phone fell extraordinarily silent.

He had not of course said that the conditions of Sandra's not talking and wanting to be alone applied equally to him. Nor was there any need to explain that her inaccessibility seemed to be taking on a strangely permanent quality. That she, who had bravely practised walking with crutches even before the surgery had taken place, now refused to even look at them, but dragged herself listlessly from the bed to the bathroom. Once settled on the toilet, she might stay there for hours, listening to the earth drift through time. She might pull herself back to bed, give up halfway, and just lie on the floor for a distraught PF to find.

"How long have you been like this?" he would say, gathering her up as though she were made of newspaper and she, for all response, would waggle her head vaguely.

He was working reduced hours now and stopped in at the townhouse as often as possible, but it hardly seemed necessary. It sufficed that he left Sandra a lunch of celery sticks and a peanut butter sandwich. His stomach lurched each morning as he spread the childish peanut butter on slices of tasteless bread, but Sandra would eat nothing else.

She returned to life long enough to have the bandages removed, making a game of piloting from her wheelchair: "Oop! Stop, stop, bagup, bagup, right, right some more, straight ahead." But once home, she returned to her muteness with an air of sullen relief.

Not quite a month after the operation, her chemotherapy began. "The poison," she called it, her eyes closed and an eager glint in her voice. The side effects were not dramatic, not as dramatic as Sandra would have liked, perhaps, given her mood. But she did sink deeper into a state of bed-ridden immobility, and barely ate at all.

PF, during this period, made no attempt to understand, plodded on, did not think, did what he was told, did the washing, made something to eat. He got home by seven, spent his evenings trying to find reasons not to go into the bedroom.

And waiting for Deecie Landry to call.

He could not have said when it was exactly that she started calling. She did not ask to speak to Sandra, but only wanted to leave a message for her. PF had met Deecie briefly but was not sure that he would recognize her if he saw her again. She called fairly late every evening and so he took the call in the bedroom as he was stretching the business of getting undressed into as long a procedure as possible. He sat on the edge of the bed, put the phone to his ear, said, "Hello, Deecie," and very little else. He was impressed and even inspired by the triviality of what she said. She could, without recourse to sport teams or political parties, talk about nothing at all, something for which PF had no aptitude whatsoever, and she could inject life into the most routine of occurrences. What's more, although her messages fell into a restricted number of categories — "adventures with my daughters," "adventures with my kid-clients," "culinary discoveries in and around Parc-Ex," "immigration, the changing face of Montreal," "God, as always, gets it right," along with the semi-nightly bonus feature, "birthdays" — she never tripped over her tongue and certainly never repeated herself.

PF, who was not at all aware that Deecie sat at the very top of Sandra's unwanted list, transmitted the messages dutifully, if not faithfully. The best part of Deecie's calls he kept to himself, offering Sandra curt resumés that, in any case, prompted no response.

One evening he hung up, turned to Sandra with the glow of admiration illuminating his cheeks from the inside and said, "Can you believe that? Deecie Landry is physiotherapist to the princes of Europe. I kid you not. She's treating a kid named Charlotte von Habsburg. A *Habsburg* Habsburg. You know, the Habsburgs? Austria, Hungary, the Holy Roman Empire, Anne d'Autriche and all. Right here in Montreal. Her parents had a left-handed marriage."

He looked at the back of Sandra's head and for the first time really had the impression not that she was pretending not to listen, but that she simply was not listening. He was suddenly angry, wanted to shake her, wanted to say, "I don't have to live with a peg-leg if I don't want to, you know." He may well have said it. Not that it mattered. Sandra was not listening.

He turned away, slid off the edge of the bed and sat on the floor. It was his intention to get up and go sleep in the living room where he remembered Deecie had slept once. But he woke up during the night sometime, still on the floor, his brain buzzing in his ears, and he climbed back into the narcotic warmth of the bed.

One evening, just before she hung up, Deecie said, "Oh, and wish her happy birthday for me." She had a staggering knack for remembering birthdays, knew the birthdays of movie stars, hockey players, leading public figures, national and international, as well as all the members of Sandra's family, aunts, uncles, and cousins. She even informed PF when it was his mother's birthday.

"How did you know that," said an astonished PF, "if I didn't even know myself? We should get you working for the police."

"Oh," she said another evening, "and tell her it's my birthday today. Tell her right now while I'm on the line." PF did so. Sandra then, with all the deliberateness of an iceberg breaking off from the coast of Greenland, rolled over, took the phone, and muttered into it, "Happy birthday, Deecie." After which PF heard what, through the receiver, sounded like the passionate remonstrances of a furious bat.

"All right," said Sandra when the tirade, if tirade it was, was over, "but not tonight, Deecie, not tonight. I'll call you, I promise. I will."

"This is nice," said PF, looking around Deecie's apartment and making an attempt at conviviality. "Did it come furnished?"

Sandra threw him a fierce sidelong glance that Deecie, who was trying to push a sofa to the back of the living room, did not see.

"Oh no," said Deecie, "no, the stuff's all mine. The thing is, every time one of my friends moves, they dump the furniture they don't want and can't sell on me, and I don't know how to say no."

It appeared that everything that could be used for sitting on was to be pushed to the back of the living room, to create a small amphitheatre for the twins. It was a Sunday afternoon, PF and Sandra were there in response to a hand-drawn invitation they had received to attend the first-ever performance of the Evening Sisters.

"I'm looking forward to the show," PF went on. He was the only man present, the rest of the audience being composed of a dozen or so avatars of the same ten-year-old girl, all of them friends of the twins. "You must be proud to have such talented daughters."

Sandra stifled a snort.

Deecie straightened, massaged her kidneys with her palms, and looked evenly at PF. "I am, yes. But our impressions of our own children are always distorted by an expectation or an apprehension of some sort."

"So true. Why do they call themselves the Evening Sisters?"

"Oh, you'll find out."

Deecie, however, was not taking into consideration that PF's childhood had been lived almost entirely in French, and that he was not therefore familiar with either knock-knock jokes or the musical comedies of Rodgers and Hammerstein.

The twins regarded *sergent* PF with the same hushed reverence they might have accorded the skeleton of the Tyrannosaurus Rex in the Redpath Museum.

"They saw you on TV," explained Deecie softly.

"Ah. Did you?"

"Of *course*."

"Actually, it' s supposed to be a different investigator each week, the one assigned to, you know, the crime they enact, but they've given me two in a row now, and want me to keep going, I've no idea why. I don't mind. I like it. I think they should make it longer, though, and talk about other aspects of police work besides just break and enters and assaults and whatnot, not that I have any say. Need a hand moving that furniture?"

He glanced over at Sandra, who was eating a large piece of very white cake lathered with even whiter icing. He was under strict orders not to be overly vigilant: "If I fall over you can pick me up off the floor. Otherwise, let me look after myself, okay?"

The show had not been in progress very long before PF wanted it to be over. He was not accustomed to such preteen, bobsy girlishness, found it irresistible, cloyingly so. It did not help that he too by then had eaten a large piece of white cake of almost barbiturate sweetness. Deecie strummed the guitar while the twins danced and sang. PF, however, while he recognized the lyrics as being tantalizingly English, could not decipher the girls' toothy singing diction. Moreover, their voices were so insistently and so penetratingly young that he perceived them not simply through his ears, but over the entire surface of his skull. His temples began to ache from the constant strain of the broad smile that he could no more relax than could a clown in whiteface.

He was, therefore, immensely relieved when the twins announced their last song. "We'd like," they said in reverberant unison, "to dedicate this song to Aunt Sandra. It's called, 'This Boot Is Made for Walking.'"

And then that was over. Everyone clapped.

All that remained was the encore, which was to be special of course and for which Deecie put down her guitar, disappeared into the kitchen, returned almost immediately with an overflowing bouquet of flowers that should, in theory, have been impossible to hide anywhere in the apartment, stationed herself between her two daughters, and led the way. Her mature voice articulated the words with merciful and confident clarity, and the melody, although no more than vaguely familiar to PF, was that of a very famous song from the Rodgers and Hammerstein musical comedy *South Pacific*:

"Sam and Janet Evening . . ."

"Oh Deecie!" interrupted Sandra. "That is *so* old!"

"I know, I know," said Deecie, clearly delighted. She put an arm around each twin then, and they started over:

"Sam and Janet Evening
would like to invite you,
would like to incite you,

to cross the living room.
Aunt Sandra, you know
it's true — and it's just —
that walking on crutches
develops the bust."

Of course, by the end, Deecie was hollering more than she was singing, the dozen or more avatars were standing up and applauding furiously despite never having seen Aunt Sandra before that very day, and Aunt Sandra herself was hitching her crutches under her arms and crossing the living room to accept her flowers.

PF's head by now was not only throbbing from his unremitting smile, but was also assailed by each rapid, percussive whack of his own palms.

And although, like the avatars, he was unable to appreciate all the humour that lay behind the song, he was well aware that Deecie Landry's perseverance and affection, and the vitality that she had transmitted to her twin daughters, had succeeded in resuscitating Sandra Beck, in returning her to the vigorous, gregarious person he had thought he had lost.

Inspecteur-chef Paul-François Bastarache, the visor of his police hat gripped lightly in the fingers of his right hand, the hat itself, like a small, highly strung, broad-billed animal sleeping on his knee, became aware, as he drove, of a shrill, whistling sound, and realized that the electric windows of his blue LeSabre were slightly open. He remembered, as he closed the windows, that he had lowered them on the Champlain Bridge in order to be able to smell the sea.

And yet, he thought, I crossed the bridge ages ago. I'm almost at the end of Décarie now. How did I get here? Who has been driving my car?

He steered off Décarie up the clockwise ramp onto the elevated Metropolitan Boulevard. To his right he could see, in the distance, the last of the Monteregian Hills, Mont Royal, urbane, familiar, graceful, cradling the famous dome of l'Oratoire Saint-Joseph.

He remembered now that he had been thinking about the standing ovation his wife Sandra Beck had received one Sunday afternoon, and about the percussive whacking of his palms that had finished by making his head reel. Sandra had had the excellent idea of organizing a fundraising Sunday matinée concert for the MSO in which accomplished amateur Montreal musicians would be invited to participate. The *chef d'orchestre*, Patrick Bempechat, with whom PF was in fact to spend a part of the Saturday before the event cleaning his blue LeSabre, had agreed to the concert under the unconditional condition that Sandra herself play the second movement of the Ravel Piano Concerto in G, a signal, breathtaking, and terrifying honour in that the MSO was considered at the time to be the foremost interpreter of Ravel in the world.

The performance had been rapturous. The downpour of applause had continued unabated for many minutes. Sandra had steadied herself against the piano with her right hand and executed exactly the same bow so many times, and with such practised elegance, that she gave the impression of being a life-sized marionette controlled by an invisible, convoluted system of pulleys and cords.

After the concert, as a further fundraising activity, an auction had been held. Among the items auctioned off, Sandra's old wooden crutches, tattooed with the signatures of every musician who had played in the orchestra in over a decade, every guest soloist and conductor, and every Montreal police officer who was also a television personality, had been sold to the very first bidder for five hundred dollars.

He was almost. Almost home. The best, the most joyous moment. Containing all the excitement of arriving, without the arrival itself. If only it were possible to reach a final destination without having to stop. Without having to get out, greet, unpack, and generally resume the systematic, chore-filled life of the arrived.

He resisted easily the temptation to swing out of his lane and drive the last kilometre at breakneck speed. The red arrow was out there, he'd had ample proof of that. Now was not the moment for ingratitude.

The dashboard gauges fidgeted with impatience. They could not comprehend why the inspector, who according to all measurements was perfectly apt, alert, and in the very best of moods, insisted on driving at close to octogenarian speed.

He eased down the long, straight ramp off the Metropolitan Boulevard. He was only seconds away now. He only had to continue straight on to Dunkirk and turn right. The townhouse that he and Sandra Beck had barely been able to afford, and that now was paid for, was the third on the right.

He and the blue LeSabre, having performed the manoeuvre together untold thousands of times, knew exactly when to downshift into low so that they could ease gently out to the left, and then swing right into the driveway, coming to a smooth stop just in front of the garage door, without the brakes having been touched except at the very last.

He and the car door knew how to announce their presence by shutting with a certain discreet, suburban loudness.

He and the front door key knew the secret of the worn lock that had needed changing for years and that had confounded any number of house guests.

He stepped inside and closed the door.

It was as though he had entered a dim aquarium filled not with water, but with a thick, almost gelatinous silence, a silence so uniform and tranquil it could not have been disturbed by any human sound in some time. The silence opened before PF as he stepped forward, and closed behind him.

No, Sandra was not home, despite the fact that her wooden crutches, tattooed with the names of dozens of musicians and one Montreal policeman, the crutches that had been bought at auction once for five hundred dollars by *lieutenant-détective* Lucien Taillon, and returned to Sandra in exchange for a new pair bearing her signature only, were leaning in their preferred corner beside the closet door in the front hallway.

PF caught sight of himself in the hallway mirror, and was startled by the realization that his true face must be at least as disappointed as its reflection.

He went upstairs to the bathroom then to wash his face. The late-afternoon sun crashed into the plastic curtain that covered the window, filling the room with a froth of pink light.

He did not wipe his face. Instead, he got into the bathtub without so much as removing his perfectly tailored dress-uniform coat, unscrewed the mushroom-shaped cap over the bathtub drain, and dug out with his fingers a sample of the black sludge that contained a slimy wad of Sandra Beck's hair. He rubbed the wad over his lips.

He knew now that Sandra had been buried that morning in a Lennoxville cemetery. That he had been present, accompanied by his personal assistant, *lieutenant* Donatucci, Carole, an exasperatingly confidential and still more exasperatingly competent woman, who had organized the entire funeral and the following reception, sent out all the invitations, and also managed to stay in touch with his daughter Josée, who was coming, despite being stranded in

Bogotá due to the tropical storm that had closed Miami, who was coming. To be with him. That the funeral had been attended by a large number of musicians, some of them quite young, and that it had poured rain before the ceremony was over, the rain allowing a certain lightheartedness to infiltrate the austerity of the moment, sending, as it did, the elegantly, if sombrely, dressed party scurrying for the parking lot.

He had known Sandra Beck, off and on, for a great many of the nineteen thousand, three hundred, and eighty-six days of her life.

Fifty-three years.

Acknowledgements

PARTS OF THIS BOOK have been previously published, in somewhat different form, in *This Magazine*, online at *Joyland, a hub for short fiction*, and in the print and online versions of *The Puritan*. Many thanks to the editors of these publications: Stuart Ross, David McGimpsey, Spencer Gordon, and Tyler Willis.

Sincere thanks to Sarah MacLachlan at House of Anansi Press. I would very definitely have liked to include the editor, Melanie Little, in these acknowledgements as well. But I don't really see how I can thank her enough.

Thanks also to Michael Holmes of ECW Press.

Thanks to Doctors Sonia Brisson and Frédéric Côté of Gatineau, without whose efforts I would not have finished this book. *Pour moi, la seule différence entre eux et Dieu, c'est que je ne crois pas en Dieu.*

Thanks to Michèle Provost, for proofreading the French, *oui, mais surtout pour son enthousiasme espiègle.*

Thanks to Stuart Ross for his unreasonable backing.

Thanks to the Canada Council for the Arts.

Thanks, in no particular order, to MacDude the fotoboy, Rol the soundman, curryous john the sound-poet, rob the unsound poet, Uncle Grr, Carmelicious, Kid Riddle, Awildmanda (the survivor) and Chuck, the Pearlfriend and Brian, the Guardians of Aidan (Sean and Kira), Peter Abnorman (for not speaking too much French), the Montysaurus, the Maxman, Alex in Wandaland, the Zytguy and the Owl, the Tree people, the Manx cats.

Et puis, un gros merci à Charles-Éric, Madeleine, Coco. Et à Claire.

About the Author

JOHN LAVERY is the author of two acclaimed story collections, *Very Good Butter* and *You, Kwaznievski, You Piss Me Off*. *Very Good Butter* was a finalist for the Hugh MacLennan Prize for Fiction and Lavery has twice been a finalist in the *PRISM International* Fiction Contest. His stories have appeared in *This Magazine, Canadian Forum*, the *Ottawa Citizen*, and the *London Spectator*, as well as in the *Journey Prize Anthology*. John Lavery lives in Gatineau, Quebec.

SANDRA AND PF GO THROUGH CUSTOMS IN LA PAZ

PAUL-FRANÇOIS BASTARACHE, waiting his turn, watched his wife Sandra talking to the customs officer. He was in no hurry, he knew this would take some time, seeing as Sandra, besides being eager to try out her Spanish, could not resist gracing even official encounters with decorative conversation. She was a very attractive woman. Also, because she used crutches, she stood very straight and wore a backpack, both of which factors were drawing the attention of her Bolivian interlocutor to her intelligent and observant breasts. Also, the crutches themselves were not without interest, signed as they were by a large number of musicians, many quite celebrated. If PF was not mistaken, the signature now being shown was that of Vladimir Ashkenazy.

Sandra received her stamped passport, glanced back at PF, and entered the airport proper.

He had been last in line for quite some time. He now was first. There was no one to be seen anywhere: no other passengers, no security guards of any kind. He stepped forward and placed his passport on the counter.

The customs official wore a wrinkled white shirt with sagging epaulettes. He opened the passport, slid the side of his thumb languidly up the inside of the spine.

"Ba-sta-*ra*-chay," he read. He looked up at Paul-François with the air of a disgraced university professor, the heavy pouches under his melancholic eyes filled with jellied tears. "No," he said sombrely "no Basta*ra*-chay."

PF's brain leapt. He was unable to comprehend how the official could fail to recognize him as the person in the passport picture *"Mais oui, mais oui,"* he stammered, "yes Bastarachay, you were just my wife, *sí, sí, sí,* I, *yo*, am Paul-François Bastarache."

"No," repeated the official without modulating the gravity of his tone, *"no bastará el Che. No bastó."*

PF stared. His voice was locked in his throat, making it impossible for him even to ask how large a bribe would be required.

The customs official smiled then, which is to say that his face reconfigured itself entirely until he was beaming with the dissipated joviality of a game show host dispensing prizes worth a good deal less than his salary.

"Do not be nervous," he cackled, "I am making a joke just, on your name, Basta*ra*-chay. In Spanish it's meaning, 'Che will be enough.' But the Che was not enough, he could do nothing to save Boleebia from Boleebia."

PF, who along with Sandra had taken Spanish lessons in preparation for the trip, certainly knew the verb *bastar,* to suffice, to be enough. Conjugating it hastily to himself in the future indicative, *bastará,* he saw that, yes, his name, slightly mispronounced, could be construed as meaning, "he will be enough, Che." The warm syrup of understanding flowed into every fold of his brain, his shoulders slumped with alleviation.

"It is perfect, the passport," said the official, still beaming. He stamped it with vigorous finality, as though there were a chance it might still be breathing, and slid it back.

PF looked at the passport, without picking it up. He felt an absurd gratitude towards the official, an obligation to make at least some attempt at conversation.

"I don't know too much about Che Guevara," he said. "He died in Bolivia did he not?"

The official's face re-reconfigured itself into that of a disgraced professor. He nodded darkly.

"In 1967 was it?"

"Yes, in 1967. The nine of October. Executed. He was captured by the army of Boleebia. But with the guns of America. Prisonered in a small school, in La Higuera. A sergeant, Mario Terán, was ordered to kill him."

The official stood and pushed away his chair before going on.

"He is drinking, the sergeant Terán, because it is his birthday. His army hat sits on his hair like a bird on a nest."

He took up PF's passport again and jammed it into his wiry, ample hair. His eyelids were heavy, he moved with an alcoholic sluggishness, his hands in front of his chest as though holding a machine gun that was poisonous.

"He enters the school, looks at the Che lying on chairs, pale, covered with mud, his feet naked. He can no shoot, he is shaking. '*Serénese,*' says the Che, '*va usted a matar a un hombre, nada más.*' You understand? 'Calm yourself, you're going to kill a man, that's all.'"

The customs official's hands trembled as he aimed his invisible weapon, he turned his head away, closed his eyes. A burst of gunfire hissed from between his teeth and lips.

"He hits the Che only in the legs. The Che bites his arm so he will no scream. Terán closes his eyes again. He fires."

A second burst, the recoil causing the official to stagger backwards this time.

"He hits the Che in the chest, his lungs fill with blood. The Che is dead."

The official dropped the gun with disgust.

"After that, Terán was very afraid. He wore dark glasses no to be recognized. Then he thought dark glasses would make him to be recognized so he threw them away. Then he stay only indoors. Then he stay only outdoors. Then he walk. For two days and two nights he walk, the Che always beside him, always. Then he put a bullet in his head."

PF was spellbound. It occurred to him that technically he had not yet entered Bolivia, and would not do so as long as he remained there talking.

"I'm from Montreal," he said. "1967 was a big year for Montreal."

"*Sí í*, big year, the Exposition."

"Exactly, exactly. Expo 67. I was just a kid. To think that, at the very instant Terán was executing Che Guevara, hundreds of people were standing in line to get into the American pavilion."

The official's face transformed itself again, he laughed the laugh of an aging soccer player with a permanently damaged, aching knee. "And today," he said, disengaging PF's passport from his hair and holding it up triumphantly, "Terán is shooting the Che again, at the very instant you, Señor Bastarache, are standing in line to get into Boleebia!"

PF laughed as well, he did not know why.

"You come to Boleebia with your wife, Señor Bastarache."

"Yes, we're visiting our daughter. She lives in La Paz."

"Yes, your wife tell me this."

"She's in children's theatre."

"In La Paz? There is no children's . . . in a school perhaps?"

"I'm not really certain."

"Ah. And your work is?"

"I'm a police administrator."

"Then you must *stay* in Boleebia! In Boleebia we have many, many police. We also have many, many criminals, fortunately. We need the criminals to bribe the police. Otherwise the police would make no money and become criminals. Many police. But no administrators. Boleebia is such a rich country but it is such a poor country because we have no government, no organization. We need administrators like you, Señor Bastarache."

PF felt warmed by the official's appeal. He found the courage to murmur, in his classroom Spanish:

"Tengo muchas ganas de visitar su país. "

"¡Excelente!" said the soccer player, wincing, transforming himself into a dissipated professor again. He flipped PF's passport over to him.

"Okay," he said. "Welcome to Boleebia, Señor Bastarache."*

---

*Author's note : The story of Mario Terán's suicide was circulated for his own protection. He surfaced in 2007, living under an assumed name in Santa Cruz, Bolivia.